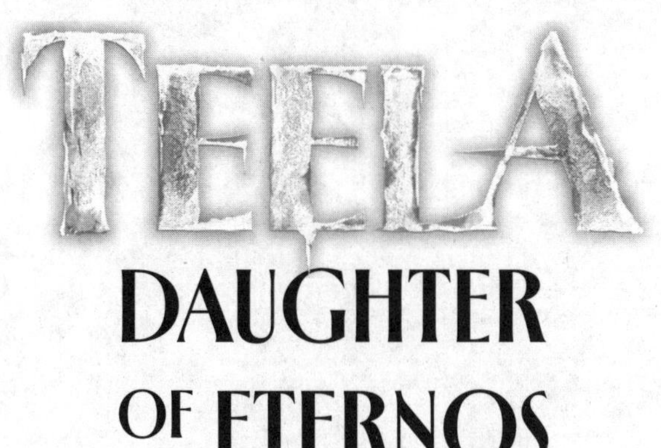

DAUGHTER OF ETERNOS

DAUGHTER OF ETERNOS

MACKENZI LEE

Published by Mattel Press, 333 Continental Boulevard,
El Segundo, CA 90245.

Library of Congress Cataloging-in-Publication Data is available.

9781640366084
10 9 8 7 6 5 4 3 2 1
This edition first printing, June 2026
Printed in the United States of America
Visit us at Mattel.com.

For Molly, Allie, and Ben,
for the many hours of action figures

ONE

P*atience.*

Teela stood, submerged in the river that cut through the Evergreen Forest, her toes barely scraping the sandy bottom and her eyes and nose just above the waterline.

Patience is a virtue of the strongest warriors.

She had braided her long red hair that morning before she left the camp, but the steady current of the river had pulled it out of its plait until it broke free entirely, floating around her head like tentacles. From overhead, it might look like a spill of algae or one of the large lily pads that floated in the slower parts of the river, which Teela reasoned could only add to her camouflaging efforts.

Patience, echoed the voice in her head again, sounding uncannily like her father.

Patience, Teela thought, *is so boring.*

The water had felt shockingly cold when she'd first waded in, but her body had quickly adapted, and now she was feeling pleasantly warm, the numbness in her limbs a result of hours of stillness rather than the temperature. It reminded her of the hours she would spend in the hot springs outside the city of Eternos after long days of training.

Her father, Duncan, the king's man-at-arms and in charge of the schooling of the young recruits for the king's guard, didn't think the young cadets deserved a reward for simply surviving what he thought was the bare minimum asked of a future soldier of Eternos. But occasionally, as a reward after a hard day or a high-scoring exam, he would let the cadets out of their class an hour early, and they would hike together to the hot springs tucked into the hills that surrounded the capital city. There, they would all strip down to their undershirts and jump into the topaz pools, rimmed in white stone that made the water salty and buoyant. Sometimes, Prince Adam tagged along, and he and Teela would always be the last two out of the pools, neither willing to be the first to emerge. One of the many silly, meaningless competitions between her and Adam that had populated her youth.

Teela wondered if Adam—wherever he was now—remembered too . . . the water that felt a different temperature to everyone who swam in it. The smooth rocks at the bottom that looked like dragon eggs. Standing with her under the waterfalls until their skin wrinkled. Had he, like her, thought those days would last forever?

The sky overhead darkened, and Teela was yanked from her memories. The wyverns were beginning to circle, their wings blotting out the sun like clouds. She didn't dare look up—if she moved, she might give herself away, and this morning of waiting for the wyverns to come to drink would be wasted.

She didn't have time to waste. The camp needed food. They were all so hungry, an unexpected frost having decimated the small bed of crops they had managed to grow, and with the rescue party gone to Snake Mountain, their numbers had dwindled, making it hard to do everything that was needed to keep the camp afloat.

Teela had had a vision of her triumphant return to camp, dragging the carcass of a slain wyvern that would feed their small group for at least three meals. They could all eat until they were full. They'd go to bed without empty stomachs. They could all pretend, for one night, they were back in the palace, at a feast King Randor had thrown in celebration of his warriors, and forget it had been four years since the capital had fallen to Skeletor, and Eternia's greatest protectors had been forced on the run.

The Eternian forest was the third site the refugees had settled since escaping the downfall of Eternos. First, they had nestled in the low crags of the Mystic Mountains, before they had eventually been overturned by ogres who had run them out of the area. They'd rebuilt the camp amid the shores of the Harmony Sea, until they were found by Skeletor's henchmen, forcing them to try to shake their tail for over a month before they finally settled among the thick roots of the Evergreen Forest. They had been here almost three seasons, long enough that, aside from the huts and shelters in the clearing, they had built platforms and houses among the trees. It had started to feel, if not like home, like somewhere they lived rather than simply stayed.

One of the wyverns suddenly dipped low, scooping a mouthful of water from the river. Teela struggled not to flinch as the stiletto teeth snapped at the water just beside her head. Another wyvern appeared in front of her, its barbed tail snapping at the waves. Its veined wings beat the air, spraying the surface of the river into Teela's face.

She had to stay still. She had to wait. She had watched the wyverns for days and knew their pattern—the biggest drank first, swooping low and snatching mouthfuls of water, testing to see if the large cats that lurked among the dark trees were waiting to snatch them from the sky or if the toothy fish that swarmed beneath the surface of the water were waiting to jump. The fish venom wasn't poisonous to most beings, but one bite would paralyze a wyvern, leaving them to drop into the river and drown while the fish feasted on their bodies.

Teela had no chance of taking down a full-grown wyvern by herself, but when the bigger ones were finished and had determined it was safe, the smaller ones and the yearlings would come to the water. They'd hover longer, not yet practiced in the art of swooping in for the drink.

Teela tried not to think of her father, currently leading the raiding party to Snake Mountain in hopes of gaining more information about where Skeletor's men were keeping the king and queen prisoner, and maybe snagging some of the essential supplies their refugee camp was lacking. She tried not to think of the four years since they fled Eternos, the constant cycle of hiding, waiting, running, finding the next place to call home, no one sure when or how this cycle would end.

A wyvern swooped suddenly low in front of her. It was smaller than the others, the membrane that webbed its wings so thin she could see the sunlight through it. She could take this one down by herself, she was sure. It was still bigger than her, still probably outweighed her. She should wait for a smaller one, more of a sure thing.

A warrior knows how to wait.

Teela was so tired of waiting. Teela had chosen her spot in the river carefully, one leg under the water on a ledge of rock. She shifted her weight slowly, eyes on the wyvern. Its wings beat at the water like oars as it swooped lower and lower to the water.

She only had one shot at this.

As the wyvern's belly brushed the water, Teela sprang from the river, pushing herself upward out of the water. Before the small wyvern could react, Teela had grabbed it around the neck, wrapping her legs around its torso. It screamed, and together they fell backward into the river.

The water around them turned white from the splash, accompanied by the disruption of all the other wyverns taking flight. The animal thrashed in Teela's arms, twisting its neck in an attempt to catch her in its jaws. Teela clung on, her arms locked. All she had to do was hold her breath longer than the wyvern, and she knew she could. She and Adam used to have competitions of who could stay underwater longer, and she used to practice in the bathtub, determined to not just beat him but decimate him. She always wanted to win.

The wyvern's wings were beating so hard Teela couldn't see anything through the clear water but bubbles. One of the knobby joints on the membrane caught her suddenly in the jaw. Teela opened her mouth in surprise, all the air she had been carefully regulating rushing from her in a torrent. Her grip loosened, and suddenly the wyvern was thrashing free of her grip. She grabbed for it, trying to cling on tight with her feet, but the wyvern's wing caught her again, this time clipping her on the side of her face, and she lost her grip.

By the time Teela surfaced from the river, gasping, the wyvern had taken flight, its gray body disappearing into the canopy above.

She wanted to scream in frustration. She wanted to burst from the water and run, up the slippery banks and through the thick branches of the forest, all the way to the gates of the palace, and find it as it had been in her childhood. She wanted her life back the way it was.

Her ears were ringing, and she dragged herself forward through the river and up onto the mossy bank. She lay for a moment, staring at the sky, trying to catch her breath. It took a moment before she realized—her ears weren't ringing. It was the horn being blown from the refugee camp in short, sharp bursts.

Teela sat up, heart pounding suddenly for a different reason. She listened hard, counting the sharp bursts on the horn and the time between them until she understood the message.

The lookout had spotted the raiding party returning. And something was wrong.

Teela sprang to her feet, snatching her sword up from where she had left it on the riverbank, and took off through the trees, the soft forest dirt turning to mud under her bare, wet feet.

TWO

When Teela arrived back in the clearing where the rebels had built their camp, Sigrid was climbing down from the lookout platform they had built in the crook of one of the largest trees, the hollowed-out stag antler they used as an alarm hung around her neck. Her long white hair was woven into the same elegant arrangement of braids that Teela had seen her wear every day for as long as she could remember. Before the fall of Eternos, it was an elegant complement to her white healer's robes and the small medallion she wore to designate her role as head of the palace medical staff and personal physician to the king's guard. She still took the time each morning to complete the arrangement, though it looked out of place when paired with the ratty, threadbare tunic she now wore.

"Teela!" she called, leaping down the final rung of the ladder.

Teela ground to a halt, grateful for a chance to catch her breath. "You saw the raiding party?"

Sigrid crossed her arms over her chest as she surveyed Teela. "Why are you wet?"

"I was . . . swimming."

"There's a welt on the side of your face."

Teela's hand flew to her cheek. It was throbbing, but she hadn't thought there would be a mark. "I must have—"

"Let me see." Sigrid took Teela's face in her hand, the same firm but gentle grip she had always used to examine the skinned knees and broken bones Teela had accumulated in her youth, both on and off the cadet training grounds. "I have a salve for this. What struck you?"

"Nothing." Sigrid pinned her with her hard gaze, and Teela ducked sheepishly. Aside from her father, no one could pry the truth from her as easily as Sigrid. "A wyvern."

"What were you doing near wyverns?"

"I was trying to hunt."

"You were hunting wyverns? Alone?" Sigrid's mouth puckered. "You can't take down a wyvern alone."

"I almost did!" Teela protested.

Sigrid rolled her eyes. "Ah, the load that *almost* bears."

"I was trying to help," Teela muttered, her pride now smarting as much as the welt on her face.

"I'd rather you were responsible than helpful," Sigrid said. "Never go out alone; you know the rules! You could have been killed!"

"But I wasn't," Teela said, raising her eyebrows, daring Sigrid to argue.

Sigrid sighed, nostrils flaring. "Next time you might not be so lucky. Here." She retrieved her cloak from where she had hung it on a low branch and tossed it to Teela. "Take this."

Teela's fingers were still numb from the river, and it took her several tries to fasten the cloak around her neck. "The raiding party—" she started, but Sigrid interrupted her.

"Half a mile from camp, coming this way. They'll be here soon."

"Did you see my father?" Teela asked.

Sigrid shook her head. "They were too far out for me to see who was among them. But there were . . ." She stopped, and Teela noticed her throat flex as she swallowed hard. "It looked like they were carrying someone."

Teela's stomach dropped. This wasn't the first party the refugees had sent out for supplies or reconnaissance—not even the first time they had sent warriors to Snake Mountain to spy on Skeletor's men and try to determine the location of the king and queen. But each time the party returned more beaten down, more demoralized. Last time, two soldiers had been injured.

The latest raid on Snake Mountain had been Duncan's idea. There had been a rumor spreading among the warriors that Duncan had dedicated their last supply raid to a village outside the tree line just to find liquor and that he had been hoarding it for himself. Teela had heard the rumor and dismissed it—she and her father lived in such close quarters, surely she would know if he was drinking. But when she'd alluded to it, his mood had turned dark, and he had gone off into the forest alone, returning early the next morning having missed his watch shift, announcing that he'd lead another raiding party to Snake Mountain.

The warriors of Eternia were trained to take orders from their man-at-arms without question. So it was a testament to what a bad idea the raid had seemed that several had raised a protest at this, and with good reason: The seasons they'd spent in their camp in the Evergreen Forest had not been a time of bounty. They were all thinner, all hungry more than not, and sunburned and sore from sleeping on the hard-packed earthen floors of the huts they had built. In their previous camps, Duncan had kept the warriors on a training regimen, insisting they needed to be ready for battle at any moment, but when they reached the forest, his training sessions had become less frequent and his enthusiasm waning. Everything about her father had felt as though it was waning lately.

But Duncan had reminded them all in the voice that used to ring across the training fields that he was still their leader and would be followed without question.

The party had been gone only a week—Teela hadn't expected them back for a fortnight. The fact that they were coming back so much earlier than anticipated felt like a bad sign. She could feel a prickle of apprehension running up her spine, growing stronger as she began to hear the approaching heavy tread of the returning warriors cutting a path through the trees. Teela wasn't entirely certain what an early return indicated, but she knew it couldn't be anything good.

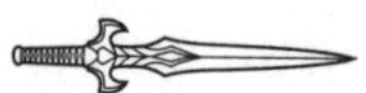

The first thing Teela noticed when the party entered the camp was that her father was not in the lead, like he had been when they left. Like he had been every time they had returned before.

The second thing she noticed was that the king and queen were not among the warriors. Teela pulled Sigrid's cloak tighter around herself, her still-wet clothes suddenly feeling oppressive and freezing against her skin. Her heart sank further when she realized that not only were there no additions to the raiding party, but there appeared to be fewer warriors than had left the camp. The ones who returned were slow moving and splashed with dark blood dried on their tunics.

Her thoughts rebelled at the contradiction of it. Surely Eternia's finest couldn't be defeated by a handful of Skeletor's goons, even if they had spent the last few years always on the run, starving and freezing and evading capture. Fighting for your life was a different kind of fight, Teela had learned quickly. At the head of the party was Malcolm, his ginger hair matted with mud. He looked haggard, with purple bruises on one side of his face and the broadsword that was strapped to his back weighing him down. The cybernetic fingers of his hand were smeared with black, like he had used the gauntlet to put out a fire. Teela started toward him and the rest of the group, but Sigrid put a hand on her arm. "Stay here."

"But my father—"

"Teela," Sigrid interrupted firmly. "Wait here."

Teela wanted to argue, but Sigrid's tone rooted her. She watched as Sigrid hurried forward, meeting Malcolm and exchanging words with heads bent close before she began directing them through the camp. Other refugees were coming forward from their huts, and Sigrid began to rattle off instructions, barking orders to light a fire and attend to the other warriors behind Malcolm.

Behind Malcolm, Dian was holding one arm against her stomach like it had been pulled from its socket. She was supporting Andra, who was limping. Andra had pulled up her dark, curly hair in a scarf, and Teela could see a burn on the back of her neck disappearing under her shirt. All the returning warriors looked in equally bad shape, slow moving as they dragged injured limbs or stumbled beneath the weight of dehydration and hunger. Teela scanned their faces, relieved to see each familiar one, though her heart beat loudly. *Dad. Dad. Dad. Where's my dad?*

Then, at last, she spotted him—toward the back of the group, one arm slung over Locke's shoulder as she supported him. His head lolled onto Locke's shoulder, and Teela's momentary rush of relief was immediately replaced by cold fear. *He's hurt.*

"Dad!" Teela ran toward him, pushing her way through the rescue party. Her wet feet slid on the uneven ground, but she hardly noticed. "Dad!"

Teela was surprised when, upon spotting her, Locke ducked out from beneath Duncan's arm and pushed him forward toward Teela. Duncan stumbled, falling into Teela. She tried to catch him by the elbows, but his deadweight was too much, and he sagged sideways into the dirt. "What are you doing?" Teela demanded, dropping to her knees beside her father and searching for wounds. "He's hurt!"

Locke laughed, one single, cold *hah*. Locke had been a cadet several classes above Teela, about to graduate when the city fell. She was the closest to Teela's age in the camp, both of them younger than the other refugees by at least a decade and the only two members of the camp who hadn't yet been awarded full status in the king's guard when Skeletor invaded. Locke had been at the top of her class, always cold and serious and focused, the first to scold the other cadets for clowning or goofing off. The others used to whisper behind her back that she was just sucking up to Duncan, but Teela had always admired her steely resolve. Teela, sure to be the next man-at-arms when her father retired, had been the top student in her cadet class as well; but where Locke's persona tended to alienate, everyone had treated Teela's single-minded focus as endearing—even now, the other warriors protected her, the youngest among them, like she was precious. Teela had never been sure why the same traits looked so different on Locke.

Until now, when Locke's hard, unforgiving voice buried itself in Teela like an annoying splinter. "He's not hurt," Locke said, her voice dripping with disdain. "He's drunk."

Teela stopped. "What?"

Locke unhooked her sword from her back and jammed it into the ground as she stretched, hands behind her back. "We found a burned-out pub on the road back from Snake Mountain, and he drank from their mead casks until he vomited."

"That's . . ." Teela wanted to argue, but she could smell it on her father now—the honey-sweet alcohol masking the iron tang of blood. She climbed to her feet, staring at her father crumpled on the ground, face streaked with dirt, sick with booze. A defense of him rose automatically in her throat—she would defend Duncan until her last breath, but she was aware of how much more she had been having to rise to his defense lately. She'd defended his decision to lead the party to Snake Mountain. To move the camp to the Evergreen Forest. To stay in their quarters rather than coming out to train with them on the mornings he slept late or didn't get out of bed. And, most recently, his ill-advised attempt to raid Skeletor's lair—again.

"Why are you wet?" Locke asked, wrinkling her nose and interrupting Teela's train of thought.

"I was hunting wyverns."

"In the river? By yourself?" Locke snorted. "So this 'delusions of adequacy' thing is a family trait."

Teela felt anger rising in her. "Don't be cruel."

"Hard not to be when exactly what we warned your father would happen, did."

Teela swallowed, cold fear trickling through her. "The king and queen . . . are they still . . ."

"Who knows?" Locke said. "We were ambushed on the banks of the Blood River. Our lookout was exhausted from lack of food, fell asleep, and Skeletor's men took us by surprise. We never had a chance." There was no satisfaction in Locke's tone, but Teela suddenly remembered the day before the party left on the raid—Locke had not been the one to challenge Duncan's judgment directly, but she had stood behind Zarbone as he had, not a word of defense for the man-at-arms she had once so admired. Locke hadn't had to say she thought it was a bad idea. Just the way she had stood had said it all. "How did they know you were coming?" Teela asked.

Locke shrugged. "Maybe we gave ourselves away. Maybe they have spies that caught our trail. Maybe we're just not the elite force we used to be." The cord that usually held Locke's hair at the back of her head snapped suddenly, and the mass of tangled black hair sagged down the nape of her neck. She looked less bloody than the rest of the warriors, which didn't surprise Teela: She knew Locke was descended from the Rock People of Geolon on her mother's side. The heritage made her skin tougher and harder to pierce with arrows and blades. In the sunlight through the trees, her skin had a crystalline sheen to it.

Teela hadn't realized how hard she had been clinging to the hope of the rescue mission's success until she began to feel it peeling away from her like a tree shedding bark, leaving her vulnerable and unprotected. "Duncan thought we had a chance—"

"Well, your father was wrong," Locke snapped. "He's not the brilliant military strategist he once was."

"Locke." Teela and Locke both turned at the sound of Malcolm's voice. He had come toward them as Locke's voice began to rise. Malcolm stopped behind Locke, glaring hard and with one hand on the pommel of his blade. "Watch your tone."

Locke's scowl deepened. "Why? Our commander is too drunk to hear me."

"Don't be cruel," Malcolm said.

"Or treasonous," Teela muttered under her breath, but Locke still heard her.

"Treason?" Locke laughed. "Why, because I have self-preservation instincts our man-at-arms seems to lack? Because I care about his warriors more than he does?"

"That's enough," Malcolm interrupted. "If you're able, I'm sure Krass could use a hand with the . . ." He trailed off without finishing his thought. Locke glanced over her shoulder, and Teela followed her gaze to where the last of the warriors were emerging from the forest. Krass, his armor tarnished and axe slung low on his belt dragging along the ground, was carrying a wrapped body over one massive shoulder. Behind him, two warriors carried what Teela assumed were more bodies wrapped in sheets.

Teela's heart leaped into her throat, her shock propelling a sick mix of dread and grief along with a horrifying relief that it wasn't her father wrapped in those shrouds. In their previous attempts to breach Snake Mountain, no one had died. In fact, even after all they had been through—famine and cold and fleeing and injuries—no one in their company had died since the fall of Eternos. That was why they stayed together. They helped and took care of one another. They fought for one another.

And now, there were three warriors dead.

THREE

Teela's throat felt thick, and it was hard to speak. "Who . . . ?"

"Moxxu, Zarbone, and Ciza," Locke said before she could even finish.

Tears pricked at Teela's eyes. Moxxu had been the one to teach her how to throw a knife, and she remembered how Ciza used to always carry pouches of sweets concealed in his palace guard uniform. He would slip them to Teela and Adam sometimes, and she suddenly remembered the hard, sweet shape rolling around in her mouth as she and Adam sparred.

Three great warriors, fallen at the hands of Skeletor's men, all for a mission that had come to nothing.

On the ground, Duncan raised his head with a moan. He had lost one of the pieces of armor he usually wore across his forearms, and the helmet he had always worn in the king's service—a helmet he had kept so polished and pristine Teela could remember staring back at her own reflection in it during combat training—was perched on his head like a mismatched lid on a battered pot. His face was spattered with mud and blood, and he hadn't shaved in days. The spray of stubble across his chin was more gray than Teela had expected. His whole face looked older, though she knew he couldn't possibly have changed so much in just a week. It was like she was seeing him anew. He reached out a trembling hand. "Teela . . ."

She dropped to her knees next to him and caught his hand. "I'm here."

"Teela," he said, head falling backward into the mud. "I think I might hurl again."

Teela resisted the urge to pull away from him. Locke laughed again. "If you must, aim for Teela," she called to Duncan. "You've vomited enough on me today."

Malcolm cuffed her on the shoulder, not hard enough to hurt, but the message clear. "There are more useful things to do than stand and pass judgment. Help Sigrid with the wounded."

As Locke stalked away, Malcolm began to dole out orders to the rest of the refugees gathered around the returning party. "Our men need to be fed—we ran out of food two days ago. The wounded should be taken to Sigrid's hut, and the others need rest. Gonso," he called to the soldier who had long ago overseen the construction and maintenance of the capital's memorial to soldiers who died on the battlefield without proper burial, "see to the rites of the dead. We'll have a ceremony tomorrow at dawn."

The company began to break apart. "What can I do?" Teela asked.

Malcolm looked down at her and Duncan and ran his fingers through his hair with a sigh. "Just . . . take care of your father, Teela. He's had a difficult time."

"Right. Okay." Teela stood, taking her father by the hand and trying to pull him to his feet. But Duncan was a deadweight, his legs flopping in the mud as if they were made of jelly, and he did nothing to help her get him upright. "Come on, Dad," Teela said, trying to sound more heartened than she felt.

Malcolm must have heard the desperation she tried to mask from her voice, for he sighed again, then bent down and took Duncan's other arm. "Here we go, Captain. On your feet."

Malcolm hoisted Duncan up, and Teela ducked under her father's other arm, wishing she could do more to help than just stumble alongside them as Malcolm practically carried Duncan back to the downed *Helios* cargo ship they had found crashed in the middle of the Evergreen Forest two seasons ago and had used as the centerpiece around which to build their camp. Teela and Duncan slept there now, amid the camp's meager supplies that needed to be protected from the rain. When they first picked the forest as the location for their new camp, Duncan had been offered the decrepit ship as a lodging and headquarters for his leadership operations, though her father had been horrified by the idea of living in the camp's only covered dwelling while the rest of the refugees slept in the ever-present dew and cold that emanated in white fingers of frost off the trees. Until there were enough shelters constructed that everyone could sleep warmly and somewhat protected, Duncan had slept among the tall, narrow roots of the trees with the others, and though Teela had tried to stay with him, he wasn't the only warrior who had insisted she take the covered shelter of the ship. One night, she was sure she had fallen asleep under a tree, yet had woken tucked into one of the pilot's chairs in the *Helios* cockpit as rain drummed quietly against the windshield.

Now, Teela and Duncan had set up their sleeping quarters on the top level of the *Helios*, the observation deck windows that used to look out at the stars now grimy and webbed with cracks, level with the tops of the shortest trees of the forest. Teela and Malcolm helped Duncan up the steps, then deposited him on his sleeping pallet. Teela looked around in distaste at the clutter and refuse surrounding their mats. Her father would never have tolerated a messy space back in Eternos. He used to conduct so many random checks on the soldiers' barracks that they had started feeling routine. He would run a gloved finger along every surface, checking for dust, and command soldiers to pull their weapons from their sheaths and show him the shine on their blade. A warrior of Eternos, he had told them, was only as strong as he or she was prepared, and preparation could not exist in mess. Strength was meaningless if you were caught off guard without your boots and sword beside your cot.

At first, Duncan had kept their makeshift home here in the downed *Helios* like a soldier's barracks. He had inspired the same organized professionalism in the other refugees, too, never asking they live by his rules, but inspiring them to do so through his actions. But, like so much else, Duncan's high standards of cleanliness seemed to have fallen by the wayside.

Malcolm said something about needing to get back to the others and disappeared onto the *Helios*'s lower deck as Teela pulled her father into a sitting position on his pallet and unbuckled his armor. There was dried blood hardened around the symbol of Eternos etched onto his breastplate, and she noticed a tarnish on the hinges she was certain she had never seen there before. Her father was usually so fastidious about keeping his armor clean, as though at any minute he might be called up again in court to stand by the side of King Randor in the ceremonial raiment of the man-at-arms.

Duncan's eyes fluttered open. "Teela," he muttered.

"I'm here," she said.

"Where am . . ." he started, his eyes unfocused as he looked around the observation deck.

"You're home," Teela said quickly, the word *home* inexact, but it was all she could think of to describe their camp. "Everything's going to be okay."

Duncan's head slumped forward, chin held to his chest, so his words came out through clamped teeth. "Why are you wet?"

Teela almost laughed. "I got bored waiting at home for you and decided to go for a swim," she said, trying to infuse her voice with cheer she didn't feel.

"It's good you didn't come," he mumbled.

"You wouldn't let me, remember? I would have gone if you'd let me."

"You didn't have to see how I let them all down."

Teela's heart twisted in her chest. "It's okay, Dad," she said. "Just rest."

She guided him back down onto the pallet, pulled the thin blanket up to his shoulders, then piled on the coverlet from her own pallet and laid Sigrid's cloak over the top, the lining now damp from her wet clothes. He rolled over, pulling the material tight around him like a protective shell, and Teela waited until she heard his breath even out into sleep before she took the ladder back down to the main deck.

She expected the *Helios* would be deserted, and she jumped when she heard a sound from the cockpit. Teela's gaze tracked forward toward the end of the bridge and up the few short ladder rungs leading to the small pod where a pilot once would have sat, and she saw Locke standing silhouetted against the plexiglass windshield streaked with mud and leaves as she stared down at the control panel of the ship. That morning, in an attempt to clear some of the debris before she'd headed out, Teela had turned on the wipers, and the light beside the switch was still blinking. When Locke flipped it, the wipers bobbed feebly from side to side, smearing mud and foliage across the windshield.

Locke looked up as Teela climbed into the cockpit. "I didn't know this ship still had any power."

"Not much," Teela said. "The solar panels on top sometimes pick up enough power to run things like the wipers or lights, but they barely hold a charge."

Locke seated herself in the pilot's chair, fiddling with the steering mechanism, then flipped one of the escape pod switches. A blue light flashed, then died, but Locke grinned like it was a victory. One of the contingencies Duncan had enforced when he agreed to use the *Helios* for his quarters was that no one was forbidden from coming aboard—the observation deck was theirs, but the ship itself was a space for everyone, not just him and Teela. But Teela found herself suddenly wishing she had grounds to ask Locke to leave.

"Did you need something?" Teela finally asked.

Locke nodded to the pilot's chair, where Teela noticed she had propped Duncan's sword. "I forgot I was carrying it for him. I thought he might want it. Eventually. When he sobers up."

The comment felt unnecessarily barbed, and Teela felt sure Locke was trying to bait her into saying something in defense of her father so she could refute it with evidence, some other devastating anecdote about how he had failed them on this last mission. She bit hard on her back teeth to stop herself from playing into Locke's hand. "Great," she said, taking care to keep her voice even and flat. "Thanks for bringing it back."

"Did your dad ever take you out in the fighters?" Locke asked suddenly.

Teela blinked. "Did he . . . what?"

"You wouldn't have been old enough to go alone," Locke continued. "You would have had to be sixteen to get a pilot's license. But I thought maybe Duncan took you joyriding every once in a while."

"A few times," Teela said warily, not sure where the conversation was leading.

"I love flying," Locke said, sounding almost wistful. "Even before I had my license, I used to loiter around the hangars and hope the pilots would get the hint and offer to take me out."

"I didn't know that," Teela said.

"Why would you?" Locke asked. "It's not like we were friends."

"Yeah, but I thought you were so cool. I really paid attention to what you did."

"*Thought*?" Locke pressed a hand to her heart. "The most devastating use of the past tense I've ever heard."

Teela felt her mouth twitch, but she didn't correct herself.

"Once I had my license, I used to fly a lot. Whenever I could." Locke ran her hand over the control panel. "I miss it."

"I thought you were always too busy studying to have fun."

"I don't know where I got that reputation," Locke said, her tone brimming with pique. "I'm *extremely* fun."

Teela remembered a story that had been passed around the younger cadets about Locke being the only one to show up to class on time the morning after a party the whole class had attended. They had all been sure they would have gotten away with the late start, pleading a bad meal from the night prior, except Locke gave them away. Teela wasn't sure her father would have been fooled so easily, but the story had been passed around as proof of what a square Locke was, a stickler for rules and responsibility. No wonder Duncan had liked her so much. No wonder she felt let down by him now.

But her father hadn't changed, Teela reminded herself. He was just tired. Anyone in his situation would be crumbling under the weight of everything that had happened to them.

Locke put her hands in her pockets and looked up at Teela. "Is he all right? Your dad."

"He's asleep," Teela said. "He'll be fine, though. Thank you for looking out for him."

Locke scrubbed a patch of dried blood on her neck. She looked older than her years, the skin around her mouth beginning to wrinkle, and eyes shadowed with dark bags. The years since the city fell had aged them all, the vibrant heroes of Teela's youth dimmed and tarnished, their shoulders heavy and their weapons weighing them down.

"This is the third time we have tried to liberate the king and queen from Snake Mountain," Locke said suddenly. "On your father's insistence."

"He's their man-at-arms," Teela replied. "He's loyal to them."

"That's what worries me."

Teela crossed her arms. "What's that supposed to mean?"

"Your father serves a god that no longer exists. He cannot accept that the world that created him and the tenets he has built his life around is a world of yesterday. We'll never be able to go back to the way things were. We need a new plan if we want to continue this long term, or else surviving is all we'll ever be doing."

They were interrupted by the piercing sound of a wail from outside the ship, the sharp howls of grief striking Teela in the heart.

"You should talk to him about it," Locke prompted. "He listens to you."

"What exactly do you want me to tell him?" Teela demanded. "That you think we should give up on the king and queen? You think we should leave them to rot in Skeletor's prison because it's too hard for us to rescue them?"

"You want to try again too?"

"We have to!"

"People died, Teela. Warriors died. Because your father pushed us into a raid we weren't strong or prepared enough to fight. All in the name of whatever courtly honor formed the foundation of his personality." Locke pressed her index finger and thumb to one eye. "I'm not saying we leave them to Skeletor. But we're not doing them any favors letting ourselves get picked off in increasingly futile attempts to rescue them."

"So what do you propose we do instead?" Teela asked.

Locke suddenly straightened, shifting her own sword strapped across her back as she pushed back from the pilot's chair. "Never mind. Forget I said anything." She walked past Teela to start back down to the bridge but stopped halfway down the ladder and looked back up at her. "Make sure your father drinks water when he awakes."

"I will," Teela said. Locke started to disappear again, and Teela called after her, feeling suddenly useless and young. "Does Sigrid need a hand? I can help with the wounded. Or with the . . . the funerary rites." The words stuck on her tongue.

"See to Duncan," Locke said. "That's the best thing you can do to help right now." She turned down the bridge and strode away, heels clicking down the gangplank as she disappeared.

Teela sank down into the pilot's seat Locke had occupied, knees pulled up to her chest, watching through the streaked windshield as Locke crossed toward the hut on the edges of the clearing they had designated for medical care. The wispy clouds that had spread across the sky like butter that morning had thickened and turned dark. The cockpit felt suddenly impossibly small, hot, and humid, and Teela could feel the change in the air, like a storm gathering. She just couldn't be sure if it was real or only her imagination.

FOUR

There was no way to give the three members of camp who had died during the raid on Snake Mountain the funerary rites of a true Heroic Warrior of the Eternian Court. The coffins could not be glass, as was the tradition, nor could the bodies be dressed in their ceremonial armor and covered in flowers. They could not lie for two days in the palace rotunda with every available member of the guard taking a shift to march in a circuit around the coffins.

But the refugees did the best they could to make the send-off meaningful. Teela helped fell trees alongside Krass and his heavy axe, which

Malcolm then carved down until he reached the white center of the trees and fashioned the fine alabaster wood into caskets. Teela and several other refugees sat with Malcolm as he worked, passing stories back and forth about Moxxu, Zarbone, and Ciza. Malcolm, who had come up through the ranks of the warriors at the same time as Ciza and Moxxu, with his stories about their wild antics in youth—which ranged from Ciza and Zarbone's terrible cooking giving the entire graduating class food poisoning just before a military parade, to Moxxu's love of poetry and tendency to recite it to people who would rather he didn't—made Teela laugh until her stomach hurt, though afterward, lying on her sleeping pallet in the *Helios*, listening to her father's heavy breathing, she found the shared memories only honed her grief, like a blade grinding against a whetstone. Teela hadn't known any of them particularly well and thought of them mostly as warriors, as Eternians, as refugees like she was. Hearing about their lives—the people they had been, off the battlefield and before Eternos fell—made the loss of each feel distinct, grief separating itself into three unique shapes inside her. She couldn't imagine the pain the others must be feeling—men like Malcolm, who had been friends with them since youth. Or her father.

If he had even sobered up enough to realize they were gone.

Teela shook off the unkind thought that popped unbidden into her brain. It wasn't Duncan's fault, Teela assured herself, staring upward at the shifting branches of the canopy above the observation deck. The leaves looked silver against the moonlit sky. It wasn't anyone's fault.

But they were still gone.

When the coffins were finished, each warrior was laid out with his sword across his chest in the center of the camp for two revolutions of the moon. In Eternos, when a warrior died, the bodies would be draped with enough rich food for a castle feast, fine armor, trophies of their battles, and symbols of their great victories—all their laurels that would see them granted entrance to Preternia to take their place among the heroes of old. Instead, the members of the camp left round stones at the feet of the fallen warriors, along with carved pieces of bark and dried petals from the sparse flowers that bloomed through the dense undergrowth. Someone left a jar of sweet jam made from the berries harvested at their mountain camp, and though Teela knew the warriors needed the sustenance for their journey to the afterlife, her own stomach growled enviously when she saw it.

She hadn't tried again to catch a wyvern, and the long-eared monkeys they had hunted when they'd first encamped seemed to have grown wary of them, for they had stopped showing up around the edges of the clearing in the early hours of dawn, hooting curiously. Sigrid's garden, which had thrived at their previous camps in the mountains and shoreline, was still struggling to recover from the last frost, and the dense undergrowth of the forest made it difficult for most shoots to break through to the sun. Sigrid usually carried buckets of water each day from the river to the camp, though it never seemed enough to make a difference. In the days after the raiding party's return, she had been too busy in the medical hut to make time for it, so Teela had gone in her place, the handles of the buckets cutting grooves into her palms as she wove an increasingly haphazard path back to camp with each successive load.

On the third day of the vigil, the refugees gathered at dawn along the edges of the clearing, where Krass had dug three graves side by side between the tall, buttressing roots of the trees. Teela helped carry Moxxu's wooden coffin alongside Locke, stepping carefully on the uneven forest floor. In the cold dawn, the mud had frozen into hard rivulets, and the leaves were slick with frost. Between the trees, spiderwebs turned silver as the dew caught the morning light. She could see Locke's breath fogging thick and white as they walked through the rows of assembled refugees before reaching the makeshift cemetery and setting the coffin down.

At the head of the group, behind the three graves, Duncan stood, his dark skin polished by the early light. He looked stone-faced, the loss of the three warriors seeming to hang around his neck like an anchor, so heavy he could hardly keep his head up.

He and Teela hadn't spoken much since his return from Snake Mountain. He had spent more time on his pallet on the *Helios* than Teela felt like he should have, given the dire straits of the camp, and didn't take part in any of the funerary preparations other than laying three wreaths he'd woven at the feet of each of the caskets.

A part of Teela wanted to berate him. Not for their failed raid: She knew that even the greatest warriors of Eternia had been taken by surprise and fallen at the hand of a lesser force. Duncan had taught all the cadets that. They could not anticipate everything, nor prepare for every extenuating circumstance. And sometimes, he had told them, his eyes lingering on Adam, life simply dealt you an unfair hand.

No, she wasn't angry at her father for losing a fight. She wasn't even angry about the despair she could feel creeping up on him like floodwater. She was angry at how little he was doing to fight it. He was simply letting the water rise and rise around him, with no intention of swimming.

You cannot give up, she wanted to shout when she had watched him that morning don his armor for the funerals without cleaning the scuff marks from the hinges. *You cannot give up on us! You can't give up on me!*

Duncan drew in a deep breath, then folded his hands before him. Teela bowed her head, waiting with the rest of the camp for Duncan's eulogy. The dawn light filtering through the trees was beginning to shift from purple to pink, and the torches carried by several members of their company flickered golden across the ground. The frost, just beginning to melt, caught firelight, and for a moment, the clearing looked as if it were aflame.

A moment passed. Then two. Teela watched Duncan's fingers flex as he clenched them together. His nails dug into his skin. The camp waited.

The heavy silence grew tenser by the second. Duncan cleared his throat, then pressed his chin to his chest.

But still, he said nothing.

Teela pressed her elbow gently into his side. "Dad." When he didn't react, she said again, "Dad." He jumped, like she'd startled him, and when he looked at her, his eyes were glassy and red-rimmed. For a moment, Teela felt as though he was going to ask her what *he* should do. Like she had any idea—that was his job. The entirety of the responsibilities of the king's man-at-arms could be summarized as *know what to do.*

Teela noticed the assembled warriors beginning to shift nervously, glancing at each other. Locke looked up from where she'd been gazing toward her feet, her eyes meeting Teela's. She raised her eyebrows, then looked down again, long black braid falling over one shoulder.

Teela's chest began to tighten. She had to do something. She had to help.

Before she could think too much about what she was doing, she stepped forward, her toes all the way to the lip of the grave in front of her. A few pebbles tumbled from the ground and landed on the coffin below with a soft patter like rain.

"Forgive my father," Teela said. The eyes of the company all seemed to turn to her as one, and she felt the shift like the wind changing over a fire, blowing smoke into her eyes. She almost stepped straight back to where she had been—farther, even. She wanted to retreat behind her father. Her skin thrummed with anxiety, suddenly overcome with fear she was going to say the wrong thing. How did Duncan always know what to say? Or rather, how had he always known what to say—until now?

Teela swallowed hard, then said, "His voice was stripped by thirst during the journey. He can't speak loudly enough for everyone to hear, and he's asked me to speak for him."

Was it her imagination, or did Locke snort with quiet laughter? Teela ignored her and looked out at the camp, standing in the hollows between the tall, narrow tree roots. These were people she had known her whole life. Who had raised her as much as Duncan had. Who she had seen in their court finery, who had scolded her and Adam not to run down the palace halls, kept her location secret when she and the prince played hide-and-seek. They had been at the feast tables, at the parties, in assembled lines in their dress uniforms in the parades. They had stumbled from the ruins of Eternos, coughing soot from their lungs, and decided together that their world was still worth fighting for. It was worth staying here, in the long shadow of hope that the king and queen could be rescued. The Sorceress would return, and the Power of Grayskull would again be wielded by the worthy. Adam could be found.

Adam. He would have been fourteen now, two years younger than Teela, if he hadn't vanished in the fall of the city. Sometimes she still felt as if the prince were standing just behind her, his voice in her ear, sometimes words of encouragement, sometimes silly teasing, trying to break the stoic warrior face she was trying to get better at keeping fixed. She wished he was here now. He would speak for Duncan. He would speak for her. She had never liked standing in front of a crowd, but Adam had always seemed so at ease with people. He knew how to talk in a way that would make people listen. King Randor had never valued that skill in his son the way he should have. He'd been too hung up on Adam's thin arms and short stature, no matter how much Queen Marlena and Duncan both insisted he would grow, he was still young, give him time. But even if he hadn't—even if he'd been four feet tall and too small to wear armor or heft a broadsword—the way he spoke to his people would have mattered more.

He was a great friend. He would have made a great king.

Teela squared her shoulders and tried to channel Adam as she addressed the assembled camp. "True warriors of Eternia never die," she started, then immediately faltered. "I mean." Her eyes inadvertently flicked down to the graves, and she felt her cheeks color. The first words she spoke, and they were so irrefutably stupid.

Think of Adam.

Earnest, unflappable Adam.

She lifted her chin. "They stand in glory in Preternia with the heroes of old, and today, we honor the journey of three of our fellows as they complete their last great . . ." She couldn't think of a word, so instead finished lamely, "journey."

Another snort. Teela couldn't help but look at Locke this time. Her gaze was turned downward, and she had one hand pressed to her mouth, shoulders shaking. Teela wasn't sure if she was laughing or crying.

Locke must have felt Teela's gaze in the silence, for she looked up, then around at the rest of the assembled crowd looking at her. She held up a hand. "Forgive me," she said, though she sounded in no way penitent. "It just feels so silly to pretend that these great warriors are awaited in Preternia when their numbers are so badly needed here. And when their deaths were so . . ." She wafted a hand through the air as if she were directing smoke. "Needless."

Farther back in the crowd, Teela met Malcolm's eyes. His brow was furrowed, and he started to push forward to Locke, but Teela shook her head. Malcolm stopped, though one hand drifted protectively to his sword.

Teela turned back to Locke. She wasn't sure how many funerals came with hecklers, but she did her best to face hers with dignity. "They died for their king and queen."

"They died for a raid we all knew was futile," Locke said.

Forget dignity—a flare of indignant anger struck in Teela's chest. She looked at Duncan, expecting him to speak up—if not to defend himself, at least to tell Locke to keep her thoughts to herself. This wasn't the time. But Duncan kept his head down. Teela turned back to Locke. If her father wouldn't speak for himself, she would. "Then why did you join?" Teela demanded.

"Because our man-at-arms insisted," Locke said. "And though the world has broken up around us, we are still devoted to the social order we were raised with. No matter how fruitless that world order has become in the face of a new reality so many of us seem unwilling to face."

A ripple went through the assembled refugees. Teela felt her face growing hot. She cursed herself internally for picking a fight and rising to the bait—so much for channeling Adam.

Malcolm pushed forward again, this time reaching through the crowd and clamping his cybernetic hand down hard on Locke's shoulder. "That's enough," he said, firm but gentle. "This is a funeral, not a public forum."

But then, beside Teela, Duncan spoke, lifting his chin slightly. "Let her speak."

Teela looked sideways at her father, hating herself for how much she wished he had kept his mouth shut. Now everyone knew he *could* have spoken, but was frozen—*as if they didn't already*, she thought, and felt her face grow hotter.

Duncan held out a hand to Locke, as though in invitation to keep speaking. He didn't shake, for which Teela was grateful, and his voice was steady. He still had the authority he always had, even if she had doubted him for a moment. "Say your piece, Locke. You do no one any favors by masking your anger and letting it turn to resentment."

Malcolm let his hand fall from Locke's shoulder. Locke suddenly looked cowed, her gaze falling to the ground at her feet, and Teela realized this invitation to speak was far more intimidating than making an uninvited argument.

Locke shook her head. "Forgive me, sir," she said, the old familiar deference for her commanding officer returning to her voice. "Our dead warriors deserve their rites."

"And our living ones deserve your opinion," Duncan said. "Say what you wish to say."

Locke looked around at the assembled refugees, and Teela thought surely she would withdraw. Her father didn't need to raise his voice to put someone in their place. Most of the warriors would salute at the sound, a muscle memory from cadet training and service, same as their drills and parries.

But Locke stepped forward, until she was on the opposite side of the warriors' graves from Teela and Duncan. She turned halfway toward the other refugees, hesitating as though she couldn't decide whether to address the man-at-arms or the assembled people. "I, too, bless their journey," she said, looking down at the caskets. "But if we have come to bury our warriors, we should bury our kingdom alongside them. Eternia as we knew it is gone. Skeletor rules from his iron throne. The king and queen are likely dead. Prince Adam is gone, and the Sorceress has vanished. Grayskull sits abandoned, its magic kept from us. There is nothing left in Eternia, and certainly there is no place in it for us."

"What are you suggesting?" Duncan asked.

"We need to make our home somewhere new," Locke said, "rather than hanging around hoping to return to a world that is long dead."

"We can't leave Eternia," Teela said before she could stop herself. She felt her father's hand on her elbow, but she brushed it off. "The Sorceress will return, and Adam . . ." Her heart ached. "We can't abandon them! They're relying on us. We have to be here if"—she corrected herself quickly—"*when* they come back. We have to be ready."

"No one is relying on us anymore," Locke said. "The world that was served by the warriors of Eternia has died. It's time for us to stop pretending it can be saved."

Teela stared at her, too stunned for a moment to even muster a retort. Teela had suspected Locke had some ulterior motive when they had spoken in the ship after the raiding party returned—all that talk about ships and mechanics and her buoyancy at discovering that parts of the *Helios* still worked. But she hadn't expected this.

She couldn't imagine leaving Eternia. It was their home. Their world. It belonged to them, and they to it. And warriors did not run from a fight. They stood their ground, in the face of insurmountable odds. It was part of what made them who they were. The idea of running—leaving their world to Skeletor—felt like bending a joint in the wrong direction.

When Duncan spoke, his voice was even. Teela wasn't sure how he managed it. Surely he felt the same rage that was coursing through her at Locke's suggestion. "Is that really how you feel?" he asked Locke. "You would leave your home to die?"

Locke's jaw tightened. "If you think we have any other choice, you are deeper in denial than I thought. You all are in denial about the reality of the situation we now find ourselves in." She cast her gaze around the assembly, eyes burning. "The world we served isn't coming back," she said, and Teela thought she heard her voice break on the last word. "And we're foolish for waiting here, barely surviving, hoping something will miraculously change." Her voice was rising, and Malcolm reached for her shoulder again, but Locke shrugged him off, then turned and stormed from the funeral, back between the trees and toward the camp.

To Teela's shock, several others followed her. She locked eyes with Malcolm, who shook his head as if to say, *Ignore her.*

Silence fell over the assembly again. The sound of leaves crunching underfoot faded, and the forest grew so quiet Teela could hear the torch flames crackling. The dawn had turned to day, overcast light sparkling through the tree leaves.

Duncan looked down at the caskets laid out before him. He nodded once, then ran a hand over his face before he looked out at the crowd. Teela felt the air shift around him, like her father was returning to himself. Relief splashed through her. He was back. Everything would be all right. Duncan would tell them what to do.

But then he said, "She's right. Eternia will never be the same." Teela's heart sank, but then her father finished. "But it is up to us to rebuild it. Now. Let's honor our warriors as they deserve."

FIVE

Teela drove her knife into the trees under which the three fallen warriors were buried, dragging the sharp point along the bark as she painstakingly carved their names into the trunks in memorial. The bark was so thick she was afraid it would break the small blade, and she was sweating before she had finished the inscription for Ciza, her palm cramped. The air in the forest was steamy again, that strange charge making the air feel sticky and wet.

Malcolm had decided that, rather than bury the coffins beneath the earth, it would be better to push large stones over the open graves to keep wyverns from digging them up. He and Krass had rolled them from a nearby vale, and the three stones sat upright at the end of each still-open grave, waiting to be tipped into place.

On the final stroke of the *a* in Ciza's name, Teela's blade got stuck on a knot in the tree, and she couldn't get it free. She pulled as hard as she could, only succeeding in ripping open the blister on her palm. She slammed her fist into the trunk in frustration, a scream building in her throat.

"Side to side, Teela."

She swung around. Duncan was standing between the thick roots of the tree, watching her work. "Wiggle the blade side to side, not up and down," he said. "It will come free easier."

Teela followed his instructions, and after a moment of working it, the small knife came loose in her hand. "Thanks."

"Let me help you." Duncan pulled out his own knife from his boot and joined her at the trees, starting in on Zarbone's inscription while she started on Moxxu's. They worked for a while in silence. Duncan's work was faster and more precise than hers, and as he blew away the dust, she noticed he was carving the symbol of Eternos beneath the name.

Teela watched as he shifted his stance so he was sitting on one of the tree roots, one foot braced against the edge of the still-open grave so he didn't fall. They hadn't spoken much in the week since the funeral. Teela was afraid that Locke's dissenting outburst would inspire some kind of schism or obvious unrest, but nothing seemed to have changed. The camp had fallen back into their familiar routines, absent the added need of caring for the wounded from the raiding party. They woke at dawn, dividing into small parties that were sent out to hunt or collect water or try to shake a few of the hard, sour fruits from the dangerous heights of the canopy. Repairs were made on the structures and platforms they had built in the trees. They tended their garden of plants and herbs, Sigrid leading the others in trying to coax the leaves to grow green again after weeks of storm clouds without rain.

Teela wasn't sure if the eyes she felt on her were real or simply her imagination in the wake of the funeral. She wished she had never spoken—she should have trusted her father to collect himself and speak. She was too ready to protect him from nothing.

She wanted to tell him this now and weighed her words as they worked silently together on the inscriptions. But when she finally spoke, she found herself saying, "It's not your fault."

Duncan looked over at her, one eyebrow raised, and Teela clarified, "That they died."

Duncan ran a thumb over the rough edge of his carving. "Of course it is."

"They are warriors," Teela said. "They went with you knowing the risks."

"Any good leader feels the responsibility of the death of any soldier in his command. I would not trust a man-at-arms who does not feel the loss of each man in his charge, whether or not he was directly at fault. I was their leader. They followed me. In that way, they are my responsibility. As is everyone in this camp." He looked sideways, catching her eye. "You do not need to protect me, Teela," he said, and his voice was so gentle she realized that somehow he had turned this conversation around. *She* had meant to be reassuring *him*. Though well intended, his words made her feel young and silly, and her pride bumped up against them.

Teela dug her blade into the tree, scowling at the peeling bark. "I'm not trying to protect you," she said, sounding more petulant than she'd wanted to.

"Do you trust me?" Duncan asked.

A piece of wood popped off the tree and fell into Teela's lap. She brushed it off her pants. "Of course."

"Then you didn't need to speak for me at the funeral."

"That wasn't because I didn't trust you," she argued, "it's because I . . ."

She trailed off, and Duncan prompted, "You can tell me."

"I thought you had frozen. Or didn't know what to say. And I didn't want people to think there was something wrong. Locke was already being such a—"

"Teela," Duncan said, his voice edged with warning.

Teela gritted her teeth. It had never been so irritating to her how unwilling her father was to hear any slander among his warriors, particularly when one of them was speaking so openly against him. "I mean, she was starting to speak against you. And I didn't think that was fair. She doesn't understand how much you do for this company."

"And you felt the need to dissuade her of that notion because . . ."

Teela opened her mouth, realized any answer she could possibly give circled back to exactly what Duncan had led with. "Because," she said miserably, "I was trying to protect you."

Duncan nodded. He still wasn't looking at her, just patiently toiling away at the grave marker. "If I make mistakes—or if I'm unable to perform my duties—I will take the responsibility myself. It is not your job to protect me, Teela," he said again.

But I want to, she thought. Because the warriors of Eternos were her people, but Duncan was her family. Her father. He had raised her. Everything she stood for was because of him. Without him to teach her and guide her, she didn't know who she'd be.

"I thought you were still . . . recovering," she said quietly. "I thought I was helping."

"I know," Duncan said. "And I appreciate that. But I'm asking you not to anymore."

Teela nodded in reply. They went back to their work in silence for a moment. There was so much more Teela wanted to say. She wanted to tell him how interested Locke had seemed in the ship. About the wyvern she had tried to hunt, the frustration of failure. How tired she was of feeling like she was dangling on the precipice between child and adult, neither fitting her comfortably. She wanted to be young as much as she wanted to be grown. She wanted to fight. She wanted to hide. She wanted someone to protect her as fiercely as she wanted to protect everyone around her, and her father most of all.

"What happened at Snake Mountain?" she finally asked.

Duncan stopped working for a moment, then stuck his knife into the soft earth at his feet, turning fully to Teela and sitting back on his heels. "They spotted us as we were approaching from the banks of the Blood River. We were ambushed. We tried to run, but they gave chase. Next time, we won't approach from the west—they must have a guard tower."

"You're going to try again?" Teela asked, though she wasn't at all surprised hearing her father say this.

"Of course," Duncan replied. "The king and queen are still prisoners. We have to rescue them. It's our duty as their warriors."

Teela felt a tiny seed of fear beginning to take root in her heart. What would change if the king and queen were back among them? What could they be, other than symbols of a past long gone? Even if Skeletor was defeated and Adam was found and the Sorceress returned to Grayskull, life could never go back to the way it was before Eternos fell. If her father kept looking backward at restoring the world to what it once was, could they ever find a way to move forward under his leadership?

"Here." Duncan suddenly scooted over until he was beside Teela. "Try a push-and-pull cut instead."

"What does that mean?" she asked.

"Let me show you." Duncan took the knife gently from her. "Start with a notch—like this. Then work from there. It gives the blade something to grab on to."

Teela watched him work on the letters of Moxxu's name. "Why did I even try?" she moaned, dropping her head onto his shoulder. "Mine look terrible compared to yours."

Duncan chuckled—a soft puff of air through his nose. "So don't compare them."

He tried to hand her back the knife, but she shook her head. "You just do it for me."

"You're doing fine," he said. "Keep going."

"Pleeeeeease," she said, drawing out the word like she used to when she was younger and would beg him to let her leave training early to run around with Adam.

"Since when have you ever wanted things done for you?" He nudged her with his shoulder, and she nudged him back, hard enough that he almost tipped over. "Easy!" He laughed for real this time. "That's a bad idea when I have a knife!"

"So do I, so watch out!" Teela tried to make the V notch he had showed her, just below Moxxu's name, but only managed to take off a piece of bark. She let out a frustrated moan and rested her head against the trunk of the tree.

Duncan laughed. "You're so dramatic."

"I'm not dramatic, I'm just bad at this!"

"So practice. Here." Duncan put his hand around hers and began to guide her as together they traced the symbol of Eternos in the bark with just the tip of the knife. "No one ever got better at something by letting others do it for them."

“You’re so *wise*, Dad.” Duncan gave her a look. Teela made a face at him and was shocked and delighted when he made a face in return.

The sky overhead darkened suddenly, and Teela and Duncan both looked up. Teela expected to see a wyvern flying over the sun, or the canopy shifting in the wind, blotting out the light, but saw neither. The darkness felt complete and sudden, tinged with an unfamiliar green.

“What’s going on?” Teela asked. Duncan didn’t answer. He stood, face still to the sky. Teela stood, too, and went to his side, both of them standing on the lip of Ciza’s open grave. The closed casket gleamed white against the dark earth, deep below them.

Through the canopy, Teela could see fat black clouds rolling across the sun, moving preternaturally fast and dropping low. Rain, she thought at first with a surge of hope when she remembered the browning leaves of Sigrid’s herb garden. They needed rain. They could put out barrels and tins and bowls and collect it. They wouldn’t have to haul from the river every day. It would be clean and fresh and maybe, if it rained enough, Teela could bathe somewhere other than the silty river.

But then she noticed the bellies of the dark clouds were flushed an unnatural green that made her think of the poisonous frogs that lived in the Vine Jungle, their colors a warning to predators to stay away.

She looked to Duncan, hoping to use his expression to temper her own fear. If Duncan was calm, there was nothing for her to be afraid of. But Duncan’s face had creased with concern.

"What is it?" Teela asked. When Duncan didn't answer, she prompted, "Dad?"

"I don't know," Duncan said quietly. His hand was resting on the pommel of his sword hanging from his hip. The green flush of the clouds painted his skin an eerie emerald color, and for a moment, he looked luminous.

Teela felt the hairs on the back of her neck rise as she watched her father's face. Instantly, she remembered the night that Eternos fell, the way nothing had felt real or serious until she saw Duncan was afraid. Duncan had always been so stoic and unshakable, his fear a yardstick by which Teela measured her own.

Suddenly Teela became aware of shouting from the camp, and she and Duncan both turned to look back down the path they had cut between the cemetery and the clearing.

Through the trees, she could make out Malcolm. He had run out of his hut and was shouting to someone behind him, one hand thrust at the sky. "It's coming from the east!"

The east. Snake Mountain.

"Teela," Duncan said, "go back to the ship."

"But—"

"Teela," Duncan said, his voice frayed with fear. "Go now—"

The clouds on the opposite end of the camp from where Duncan and Teela stood by the graves opened in a flash, like a bag of heavy coins slit by a knife, and Teela watched as a torrent of rain was released. At least, the shape of it resembled rain—but the color was the same electric green of the undersides of the clouds, and as the drops fell, they seemed to shimmer like a courtly skirt midtwirl. It seemed heavier than rain, somehow neither liquid nor solid.

It seemed like something else entirely.

"Back to the ship now!" Duncan shouted, grabbing Teela by the back of her tunic and pushing her toward the path.

Then the first drop struck Teela's skin.

It felt like a sting, like the bite of an insect. She yelped, looking down at her wrist where the drop had landed. A red welt had risen where the rain had struck her. Teela swatted at her skin on instinct, as if it really were just a bug she might swat away.

From the camp, Teela could hear screaming. Shouting. The sound of frantic, racing footsteps. The camp wasn't far, but the rain had apparently already swept across it. By the time they made it back to the ship, they'd be soaked. Teela imagined her skin covered in these strange welts, her whole body pulsing and throbbing.

A sob of panic tore itself from her throat. "Dad—"

Duncan leaped forward and grabbed Teela around the waist, dragging her off the path. She wasn't sure what he was doing, but then he tossed Teela backward, as if she weighed nothing. She stumbled, her heart skipping a beat as her feet met empty air, landing hard enough the wind was knocked out of her, on a surface too flat and hard to be the soft forest ground.

Duncan had pushed her into Ciza's open grave.

"Dad!" she called, struggling to catch her breath and sit up, but

Duncan was already pushing the flat, heavy stone Malcolm had prepared over the top of the grave. The thick cords of his shoulder muscles strained against his shirt as he grappled with the boulder.

"Stay there!" Duncan shouted. "Stay covered!"

"DAD!" Teela shouted again, trying to get to her feet. But it was too late.

"Stay there!" she heard Duncan shout through the slim gap between the stone and the lip of the grave. "I'll come back for you!"

"Dad . . ." Teela's voice broke as, with one final shove, Duncan pushed the rock over the top of the grave, and Teela was plunged into darkness.

She could hear muted screams from the camp, heavy footsteps shaking the earth around her. Or perhaps that was the strange rain, falling in weighty bursts and tearing up the forest. It sounded like gunfire. Teela stood as much as she could in the cramped space and pushed against the rock. She didn't care what her father said—she had to help. If nothing else, she wanted him down here, protected with her. But the rock was too heavy for her to move. She pounded on it, fury that he had left her here, and fear and confusion muddling together into her chest and demanding release. The only thing she could do was pound her fists against the underside of the rock and scream in frustration. Her chest constricted, the fear of small, enclosed spaces that had always lived just below the surface of her skin rearing suddenly.

She thought of Adam, of a time when they had been playing hide-and-seek with the other palace children and, deciding to hide together, had accidentally locked themselves in one of the kitchen cellars. Teela had begun to panic at once, nearly breaking her nails clawing fruitlessly at the locked door. But Adam had stayed calm and assured her that the cooks would be by at any time to get provisions for dinner. He had made her sit beside him on the floor and told her how legendary this hiding spot would be—they were hide-and-seek champions, as no one would ever find them in here. When he had noticed her hand shaking, he had taken it. And when the cooks hadn't come as soon as she'd hoped, he had started to tell her stories about the warriors of Eternia from their favorite myth book, and though she had heard them all before, hearing his voice in the dark had calmed her heart.

When they were rescued, it was not by the cooks, but by the royal guards battering down every door in the palace looking for the missing prince. Adam had confessed to her only later that he knew the cellar was only used for feast day wine, and it was unlikely anyone would have found them for weeks if they weren't looking. But he had stayed calm, because one of them had to.

"And," he had told her teasingly, "I almost never get to be better at something than you are."

Now, as she sat in the dark, feeling herself start to shake and listening to the muted sounds of the world falling down over her head, she tried to imagine Adam here with her, his mop of blond hair and ears that stuck out too far.

Tell me all the stories again, she thought, sinking down onto the top of the casket and pulling her knees up to her chest. *The ones written long ago, where we already know the endings. We know everyone survives.*

SIX

The rain must have fallen for only a few minutes, but Teela's fear magnified it into what felt like hours as she sat alone in the darkness. She was too afraid to move—even after the sound of the rain stopped and the world outside the grave was silent. Partly because she wasn't sure what danger might be waiting outside, partly because she was afraid of the aftermath. Her skin felt hot and tight where the rain had struck her. She couldn't see it through the darkness, but she swore she could feel it throbbing so hard that it felt like the surface of her skin was rippling.

She strained to hear some sound from the camp, someone shouting it was safe to emerge, checking if everyone was all right, asking what had happened. The group had purposely chosen a location that was overhung with thick foliage to protect them from the sun—maybe the drops, too, had struggled to penetrate the canopy.

But there was nothing. The silence sent chills up her spine.

Teela wanted to wedge her fingers between the soil and the stone and push it back herself and escape—she wanted so desperately to see the sky that her lungs ached, shallow breaths tearing at her throat. She wouldn't be abandoned here, she knew that rationally—Duncan would come back for her when it was safe. She should wait. But the only thing she wanted more than to be free was to see Duncan. She wanted him to be the one to free her, to push back the stone and smile down at her and tell her everything was all right, it was just a strange passing storm, everything was all right.

But Duncan didn't come.

No one came.

The longer she sat in the dark, the more Teela's imagination began to spin increasingly catastrophic scenarios of what was waiting for her on the other side of the stone. The camp was flooded. Everyone had drowned. The huts had been leveled by the storm. Everyone who had been struck by the rain had melted like candle wax. She'd return to a camp full of nothing but bones.

She had to get out of here.

Teela stretched into a crouch, her heart thudding in her chest. Her legs ached after being pulled up to her chest for so long, muscles tensed in fear. When she stood, her head just brushed the stone, and she braced herself against it, hands flat. She expected to meet the resistance of the rock—she had seen how hard Malcolm had toiled to carry it to camp, and how Duncan had struggled to push it over the grave. But to her surprise, it started to slide away with ease.

Too easy, she thought with a sick lurch in her stomach.

She fit her fingers into the gap created between the stone and the earth and pushed the rock the rest of the way free, then hoisted herself up and out of the grave.

The first thing she noticed was the rock itself. Something—the rain, she assumed, whatever it was made up of, had left a pattern of deep indents in the stone, like there had been a long, steady drip that had worn it down over time, but done in a matter of minutes. So much of the rock had been eaten away, she had been able to move it on her own.

The ground wasn't wet, as she had expected it to be after such a storm. Everything felt weirdly dry, like desert earth. Overhead, the sky was again a vivid, cloudless blue, like the strange rain had never happened.

But the forest around her was different.

Branches had fallen from the trees, as though caught in a high wind, and their leaves had turned brown and shriveled. The bark was pocked like the rock, in places so deep that the trees seemed in danger of falling over. Tree roots seemed to have shrunk, withdrawing into the soil, and amid the tangled brambles where they had carved the names of the dead—names that, Teela noticed with horror, had vanished as if they were paint that had been washed away—she spotted a figure lying on his side.

"Dad!"

She sprinted over to where Duncan lay and rolled him over, relief flooding her when she saw he was still breathing. He had managed to take some kind of shelter beneath a thick overhanging tree, but his skin that had been exposed to the rain was covered in raised welts like the one still throbbing on Teela's arm. His clothes had been tattered by the acidic rainfall, and he was breathing heavily, each gasp wet like his lungs were a sponge.

"Dad, can you hear me? Dad!"

He didn't respond. His skin felt hot and slick.

Duncan was too tall and sturdy for Teela to get him back to camp alone if he was unconscious—she knew she needed help. "I'll be back," she said, though she wasn't sure he could hear her, then took off running down the short path back to camp.

Her progress was hindered by the branches and leaves that had tumbled from the trees, obscuring the ground the company had first cleared when they built their camp. Every step she took, the fragile ground seemed to collapse beneath her, throwing off her balance and sending her staggering. By the time she reached the camp, her shins were raw and bloody from twigs scraping them, the arches of her feet throbbing. Her calf muscles were shaking from staying curled in the grave for what felt like days.

The camp looked as if a fire had gone through it. Whole trees were toppled, one onto the shelter where they stored their provisions, and several of their treetop shelters had been knocked out of their branches. The ground was torn up like it had been plowed, and Sigrid's delicate garden was leveled, nothing left but the demarcated rows signaling where the plants had once been. The forest was eerily silent but for the sound of branches occasionally crashing through the canopy to the ground.

No birdsong, no animal calls back and forth.

And no sounds from her fellow refugees.

Teela looked around in horror at the camp members sprawled on the ground, caught in the open by the raindrops as Duncan had been. As she stood rooted to the ground, Teela saw the few members of their company who had managed to escape the rain as she had emerge from hiding, wide-eyed with shock. Teela spotted Krass struggling to stand, one hand on a fallen tree for support. His armor was pitted as if he had been pelted with rocks. She ran to him, reaching out to help him to his feet, though he sagged backward against the tree as soon as he was standing. His skin that wasn't covered by armor was pocked with the same red welts as Duncan's, and when he coughed, a black-green sludge speckled his lips. Teela had never seen the mountain of a warrior so hobbled—literally on his knees in the grip of whatever had soaked him.

"Teela!" someone called, and she turned to see Locke emerging from under the *Helios*'s gangplank. She must have ducked beneath it when the rain began. "Are you all right?"

"I'm okay," Teela said, the shudder in her voice surprising her. "But my dad . . . he's back in the woods, near the graves. He needs help."

Locke looked around the camp, and Teela realized the futility of such a statement—they all needed help.

"We need to get everyone who's hurt to shelter," Locke barked, her voice made of steel. Teela felt an immense relief that someone was taking control of the situation, and she remembered suddenly Locke on the training fields, bossing around the other cadets when they weren't listening or doing something dangerous or wrong. How had any of her fellow cadets ever ridiculed that willingness to take charge? "Let's rally anyone who's able to help at the *Helios*. Once we know how many of us are on our feet, we can figure out how everyone can be most useful."

"But what about—" Teela started, but Locke answered the question before she could fully ask.

"I'll get Duncan. You see who you can find." She glanced up again to the sky. "Quick—in case the rain comes back."

"What was it?" Teela asked. "The rain, the . . . was it rain? Whatever it was that fell from the sky."

Locke pushed her hair back from her face, staring around at their leveled camp with her jaw set. "I don't know," she said, "but I've never seen anything like it."

SEVEN

Three nights after the rainstorm, Malcolm and Andra, who had both escaped the worst of the drops, built a high fire for those who were able to gather around and report on the damage and repairs to the camp. They had all been assigned individual tasks, working hard and steadily to put things back together, and hadn't had time to discuss a longer-term plan than simply survival and the multitude of wounded. Teela had blisters on her hands from clearing branches and fallen walls of the huts. Her skin smelled faintly of the herbs Sigrid had used to mix a poultice for the wounded, though it had yet to help any of their welts heal. If anything, they were getting worse. The welt on Teela's arm had started to turn black around the edges, and it throbbed so badly it was hard to sleep. She couldn't imagine being covered in them, like so many others were. Including her dad, who was among the sickest of the company. Rain had splashed down from the leaves and drenched him where he lay, and he had struck his head when he collapsed, leaving him concussed and unable to drag himself to shelter.

"Maybe the rain was magic," Andra said, her soft voice almost drowned out by the crackling of the fire.

Sigrid sighed. "I wish I had my reference books. I can remember the most basic salves, but I'm not sure what else to do." Sigrid sat on the ground across from Teela, the contents of her satchel of dried herbs spread across her lap. Teela could almost feel the frustration radiating off the healer as she studied her supplies like she was hoping they would tell her the magic combination to heal the refugees. Teela had overheard Sigrid say quietly to Dian that she wasn't sure how long any of the wounded would survive.

Teela steepled her fingers together. Only a dozen members of the group who had managed to take shelter in time were completely unharmed by the acidic rain. Anyone who had been exposed to the rain for longer than a few drops, like those that struck Teela, were covered in the red welts that throbbed and wept, and inhaling the substance had left many with a heavy, wet cough that made it almost impossible to speak without wheezing, flecks of the green-hued phlegm dotting their mouths. Those who had been exposed the longest were developing fevers, their sleep sweaty and fitful. There wasn't room in the *Helios* to house everyone who needed medical attention, so Malcolm and Locke had assembled a quick lean-to under one of the wings to provide additional shelter.

On the edge of the firelight, Locke appeared, hauling their stewpot. "There's not much to eat," she said. "The food stores were mostly destroyed."

"You couldn't salvage anything?" Malcolm asked incredulously.

"I did what I could," Locke said. "But the rain caved in the roof of the hut, and then everything the rain touched turned rancid and rotten."

"The undergrowth is like that, too," Sigrid said. "Everything the rain touched is unusable."

"What about trying to hunt again?" Malcolm asked, looking to Dian, who had gone out with Andra that morning in search of wyverns.

Dian and Andra exchanged a look, then Dian shook her head. "They must all be gone. The river has turned to sludge, so if they weren't affected by the rainfall, they must have gone looking for water elsewhere."

Teela had seen the river for herself that morning, when she had gone to collect a bucketful and discovered the water had almost stopped flowing and instead had taken on a thick, tarry consistency. It burned her fingertips when she touched it, sizzling and fizzing green. The bloated carcasses of fish floated to the surface, bones sizzling through their skin. The camp had only two containers of fresh water stored in the *Helios*'s hull for emergencies. With so many unwell, it would quickly be used up.

Locke heaved the stewpot over the fire, then sank down on the ground beside Teela. "So," she said, "more than half our company is injured, with no known treatments. We've lost most of our food, and our water source and shelters have been destroyed." She looked around at the fire, then said with false cheer, "Did I miss anything?"

"If the rain *is* magic," Andra said, "what can we do? Can only magic stop magic?"

"And what magic do we even have available to us," Malcolm said, "without access to Grayskull's power?"

No one spoke. Teela's heart felt heavy in her chest. Had they come so far—survived for so long—only for it all to be snatched away from them in one freak weather occurrence? The unfairness of it made her want to throw something, the anger having no other outlet.

"I'll go out tomorrow morning," Locke said. "To see how far the destruction goes. If it's targeted just around our camp, that might tell us."

"I'll go with you," Teela said, and Locke shot her a quick, grateful look.

"For now, we can only wait and see," Sigrid said. "We will make the sick as comfortable as we can and keep trying different methods of relief. I'll see what other herbs I can salvage and if there is anything left in the med kit, though I think we used all those supplies when we left the Harmony Sea. It's going to be trial and error, I'm afraid, unless someone has some deep knowledge of magical cures they haven't yet shared."

"We need supplies, too," Malcolm said. "No one will be able to fully recover without proper nutrients."

"What if the rain comes back?" Teela asked. The thought sent fear twisting in her, like a heavy key turning in a lock.

"If it was an attack," Andra said, "it's probably behind us. We can wait to see if the water clears, and the ground can be planted anew."

"It still might happen again," Locke said. "Skeletor is not known for his restraint. If it did come from him, maybe they're retaliating against our attempt to rescue the king and queen."

"We don't even know what it was," Sigrid said, "or what caused it. Let's not make this into a crusade until we know for sure."

Locke raised her hands. "All I'm saying is I don't think it's wise to stay here and wait for it to return. Particularly if they know where we are. We should think about moving."

"And where do you propose we go?" Malcolm asked.

"And how?" Andra added. "More than half our company is too weak to move."

"Not if we take the ship," Locke said, motioning toward the wrecked *Helios*, in worse shape than ever after the rain.

"*That* ship?" Teela laughed before she could stop herself. "Even if you can get it to run, it wouldn't hold the whole company."

"It might run," Locke said. "I think I can make new solar panels from the spare parts I found in the cargo hold. It will take work and luck, but I think we can get it running again. And not everyone would need to get off the planet at the same time. If we send out an initial party—"

"When were you in the cargo hold?" Teela interrupted. She had snagged on the detail.

"Just before the rain," Locke replied. When Teela frowned, Locke added, "I wasn't in your quarters."

"But you were poking around—"

"That ship belongs to everyone," Locke said. "If your father is hiding something there—"

"He's not hiding anything!" Teela stared at her. The light from the fire danced across Locke's skin, and she looked as if she were cut from an amber gemstone. "He hasn't been keeping anything from you," Teela repeated, careful to keep her tone even as fury was bubbling up inside her. "Why would he do that?"

Locke shook her head. "I cannot pretend to understand Duncan's mind anymore."

"Okay, cool it, both of you," Malcolm said quietly, but Locke rounded on him.

"Do *you*?" she demanded. "Can any of you follow the logic that led him to muster a raiding party to take on Snake Mountain? That was a fool's errand—it's a miracle we only lost three men. Our whole company should have been killed in such a colossally stupid raid, but we followed our man-at-arms without question. And now this rain—what could it be if not retaliation? Skeletor must know where we are."

Teela noticed Sigrid and Malcolm glancing at each other. "Don't jump to conclusions," Sigrid said.

"Or make accusations," Teela muttered just loud enough to be sure Locke heard her. She could feel her hands balling into fists at her sides.

"How long," Locke said, "are we going to keep pretending that Eternia can sustain our existence any longer? Our city is destroyed. Our king and queen are captured—perhaps dead. The prince has vanished and magic is gone and we are now ruled by a megalomaniac intent on seizing the Power of Grayskull for himself and using it to control the world. If he manages to find the Sword, I don't want to be here to find out what he does with it. We don't have the numbers or strength or resources to stand against him. We may never—particularly if we keep getting bested just as we're gaining strength. We can let Skeletor's men chase us from camp to camp for the rest of our lives, or we can search for a solution that will last longer than the next time one of Snake Mountain's spies stumbles upon us."

"What are you proposing?" Andra asked.

"That we fix up the ship and use it to get off the planet," Locke said. "Perhaps Rintor would take us as refugees, or even our queen's home world. Or, my people come from Geolon—we could seek asylum there."

"That junker would never get us as far as Geolon," Malcolm said, "even if it *was* running. It's a hundred years old, at least."

"Primus, then," Locke said. "Somewhere closer. Anywhere else but here."

Teela stared at Locke, unable to believe what she was saying. Even more unbelievable, no one else around the campfire was laughing in her face at this insane suggestion. "We cannot leave Eternia," Teela said.

"Why not?" Locke demanded. "What is keeping us here?"

"This . . ." Teela looked around at the faces of her comrades, then felt her gaze drifting into the darkness toward the freighter, where the injured were, and to the trees, downed and decimated by the strange magic. And beyond that—the ruins of Eternos. The empty halls of Grayskull. She was finding it hard to find a concrete reason, so instead she said simply, "This is our home."

"Our home is a burned-out husk," Locke replied.

Teela thought of Duncan and his fierce loyalty to the royal family and the planet they ruled. If her father did not have something to strive for—if the last vestments of the job that had defined his life were taken from him—who would he be? And if the king and queen *were* alive, abandoning Eternia would mean leaving them behind to suffer at Skeletor's hands with no hope of rescue.

And what about Adam? If he came back—*when* he came back, from wherever it was he had disappeared to—the men and women of the Heroic Warriors had to be waiting for him. She couldn't imagine him returning only to find that his men had abandoned him and left his parents prisoner. That they had given up. She'd never be able to live with the shame. And if they left, she might as well give up on the hope of ever seeing him again.

"We can't leave," Teela said again. It was a feeble protest, and her voice sounded childish and pathetic, even to her.

"I think Locke is right," Andra said, and Teela gaped at her. Andra's eyes were downcast as she stared into the fire. "We have moved from place to place, trying to stay alive, and found each inhospitable. If the land does not reject us, Skeletor's men hunt us down. Remember they burned our camp in the Vine Jungle—they would have burned the whole jungle down just to smoke us out. They will not stop until we are eliminated or enslaved."

"We don't know that it will be a better-off world," Teela argued. "We don't even know if anyone would shelter us!"

"But we know it's bad here," Locke said. "I'd take even the cautious hope of the unknown over this feeling that we won't survive much longer on Eternia."

Teela looked wildly around the fire, hoping someone might meet her eyes and stand with her, but all she found were averted gazes. Even Malcolm looked away from her. "Perhaps," he said finally, his voice low, "we might regroup somewhere else. Find allies who would help us fight Skeletor."

"I'll look at the ship tomorrow, after we go scouting," Locke said, nodding as though something had been decided. She looked at Teela. "Maybe you could help me with that."

"I . . ." Teela stared at her. She wanted to argue. She wanted to shout, explain that they had to stay no matter how dire things seemed. But Malcolm and Andra and Sigrid—none of them had dismissed Locke's idea the way she had expected them to. It was only her, standing alone. “No. No, I’m not going to help you find a way to leave Eternia.”

“I’ll give you a hand, Locke,” Andra said quickly. “I don’t know much about engines, but I can pass tools as instructed.”

Sigrid rolled her pouch of herbs back up with a sigh and rose to stand. “I have to see to the wounded.”

“The ship shouldn’t be your priority, Locke,” Malcolm said. “At least not yet. Let’s get the camp put back together and the health of our company restored.” He glanced at Teela, then added, “Then we’ll decide what to do next.”

EIGHT

That night, Teela dreamed of Adam.

She had been thinking of him all day, missing him, wishing she could talk to him, so it wasn't a surprise to see him in her subconscious. She knew it was a dream as soon as she saw him, but it was still nice to be with him again, even if just in her head.

In the dream, she was on the training field, tasked by Duncan with scaling the climbing wall in the courtyard. He had told Teela that, once she was able to, he'd allow her to move up to the next class of cadets for sparring. The task seemed impossible, and Teela had fallen off the wall so many times she finally stayed on the ground, lying on her back, furious with everything—her father, the climbing wall, her own shaking muscles. She hadn't realized Adam had been watching her until he came and flopped onto the ground beside her. He looked somehow both older and younger than he would have been now. "You're in the Ice Mountains," he said.

"You're a weirdo," she replied, and he raised a hand.

"Hear me out. You're in the Ice Mountains, climbing with Ice Hackers on your tail."

Teela turned her head, frowning at him. "That's dumb. Why would anybody be climbing the Ice Mountains?"

"To ask the dragon Granamyr, oldest and wisest of all the dragons of Darksmoke, to grant you a single wish."

"Are you making this up?" she demanded.

"No, it's totally real," he said in that way he had that always left her unsure whether he was lying to her or not. "But Granamyr doesn't deal with puny humans like yourself!"

"Puny?" Teela scoffed. "I'm twice your size!"

Adam lunged suddenly, rolling over on top of her and pinning her to the ground. "Weak human!" he said in what she assumed was his best imitation of a dragon voice. "I shall cast you into the Pit of Shadows!"

"Get off me!" Teela pushed her feet into his stomach, and he rolled off her, laughing.

"Better climb the wall," he said, grabbing her by the ankle and pulling a foot out from under her as she began to stand. "Otherwise, the Hackers will get you!"

She kicked at him, laughing, but he dodged, grabbing a handful of climbing chalk and throwing it at her. "Ice bomb, watch out!"

Teela woke with a start. Had that been a dream or a memory? She couldn't be sure. The task had been real. As had Adam's patience, and him always knowing what to say. Of the two of them, she was always the one to get worked up first. She'd lose her patience over a drill she couldn't master or an obstacle too high to jump. She did not want to take the time to learn—she simply wanted to be able to do the thing, competent and steady from the first moment. While Adam was so much more accustomed to failure that he had learned to take it on the chin.

It took her a moment to blink away the shadows of Adam's teasing grin and remember where she was—in the *Helios*, lying beside her father as he slept, fitful and sweating through a fever. Duncan had not woken in earnest since the rain, his consciousness fleeting and precarious when he did stir. She had tried to get him to eat some of the mushrooms Andra had prepared, but the thin broth simply ran out from between his lips and down his chin.

Adam's voice was still in her ears. *You're in the Ice Mountains.*

The dragon Granamyr, oldest and wisest of all the dragons.

She remembered with a flash the reading the two of them had done in the palace library about the dragon's hoard, a legendary collection of magical artifacts, and the dragon himself, who possessed the deep knowledge of Eternia and its magic. The secrets he knew were second only to the Sorceress of Grayskull, and she was gone.

But the dragon Granamyr . . .

Teela laughed out loud at her own foolish delusions. She was so desperate, she was seeking answers in invented memories of mythical places. She wasn't even sure if the dragon Granamyr was just a legend or a real being who died long ago, his memory embroidered into a myth.

But if no one else could help them, maybe he could.

Teela pulled her knees to her chest, listening to Duncan's ragged breath.

She held her forearm up in front of her, staring at the welt against the darkness. The black-edged, bright-red bloom had throbbed worse when she tried to bandage it. Her skin felt as if it were rippling, though whether that was the aftereffects of the rain or simply her own emotions bubbling like a geyser against her vision, she wasn't sure. The Ice Mountains would be about a week's journey from their camp in the Evergreen Forest, but Teela knew she could make it. If the ancient dragon could offer some knowledge about the acidic rain—what had caused it and how to cure the sickness it had spread—there would be no reason to leave, even if Locke succeeded in repairing the *Helios*, or at least Duncan would be well enough to mount a defense against abandoning Eternia that would stand up to scrutiny. Surely Locke was in the minority—it was just the few survivors around the fire who, in the depths of despair, had agreed with her. Duncan could persuade the others to stay and fight. And Duncan himself would be restored, and not just from the sickness—he'd have something to lead them toward again.

Even if the dragon had nothing for her, she had to try. She couldn't bear to sit around drying out herbs and repairing shelters, pretending any of it was going to matter when their company was mostly sick and senseless, with no way forward.

A warrior knows how to wait.

But sometimes a warrior couldn't afford to.

"Dad?" she said quietly, though she knew he couldn't hear her. "Dad, I really wish you were here. I mean, I know you're here, but I wish you could tell me if I'm doing the right thing. I bet you'd say, *This is a bad idea, Teela. You don't have to protect me.* Except I do. I have to protect everyone. I have to protect Eternia. It's our home. We can't leave."

Who would stand against Skeletor if they left? Who would fight for Grayskull? They may be weakened and few in numbers, but they should stand. True warriors of Eternia would not flee in the face of a fight.

"You'd probably tell me not to go," she said, "but I would anyway. And I hope you understand that. I'll tell you all about it when I get back."

She leaned down and kissed him quickly on the forehead, his skin hot and slick. Then she climbed to her feet and began to ready for her journey.

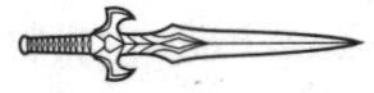

Teela didn't have much in the way of worldly possessions, but she still left half of them behind, taking only the essentials with her in her small pack. She picked her way quietly through the refugees sprawled on the floor of the *Helios* until she reached the cockpit and popped open the panel under the dashboard where her father kept the few artifacts he had saved from his old life—a pair of thin daggers the length of Teela's forearms, a gift from King Randor to celebrate his appointment as man-at-arms; a brass compass; and his thick gray cloak, lined in white fur, that Duncan had worn for courtly events in the winter. She took them all, strapping the knives onto her belt alongside her sword. She slung her father's cloak over her shoulders. It enveloped her like a tent, but she liked the weight of it, like her father's arms around her. She fastened the pin, taking a moment to run her fingers over the insignia of the Heroic Warriors inscribed there.

She stole quietly to the cargo hold of the ship and found a stun gun with a grappler that attached to the end, so rusted she wasn't sure if it would work, but it was better than nothing. She stole sandpaper from the repair kit—something she could use to get some of the rust off, then attach to the bottom of her shoes to grip the ice—and packed her bedroll and a mess kit. There was no extra food to take, but she filled her canteen from the water stores. She'd find more once she escaped the area that had been devastated by the rain. It didn't need to last her the whole way to the Ice Mountains.

She was out of the *Helios* and nearly to the edge of the camp when someone called from behind her, "Where are you going?"

Teela turned. In the dying glow of the fire, she could make out Locke's shape as she sat with her sword resting on her lap. Teela almost asked her what she was doing up, then remembered—Locke had the first watch shift. She cursed herself for being so focused on her determination to get to Darksmoke that she'd forgotten she'd have to avoid a watchman, especially Locke.

She felt suddenly foolish. How could she admit she was going to travel north in pursuit of what might be just a legend, because she was convinced it might save the camp?

"We need water," she said at last. "I'm going to see how far the devastation goes and find a new source."

"Can't it wait until morning?" Locke asked, and Teela could tell from her tone she didn't believe her.

"I have to help him," Teela said instead of answering. "And everyone else. I just . . . I have to do something."

Locke nodded, then patted the spot beside her. "Come sit with me," she said, and Teela reluctantly walked over. "Did you ever have to do the stair climb?"

Teela shook her head.

"I didn't think you would have been old enough. It's something all the cadets do before they enter their last form. Everyone gets up in the middle of the night before graduation and runs to the top of the Temple of the Snake Goddess in the hills outside the city."

"Isn't that, like, two million stairs?" Teela asked.

"At least, plus the rope bridges over the gorge." Locke's mouth twitched in a half smile. "The fastest got to ring the bell there, then everyone would toast to the new class and go to graduation together. It was this stupid initiation thing—everyone acted like it was secret and sacred and you couldn't talk about it, but it didn't matter. It was just a pride thing. So, to me, at seventeen, it felt deeply, deeply important. I was training for it more than I was training for my final exams."

Teela smiled, imagining young Locke, so serious about everything, approaching a graduation initiation ceremony as she did everything else. "No wonder you were popular."

Locke dug her elbow into Teela's side. "Look, I'm not exactly a natural warrior."

Teela began to protest, but Locke shook her head. "I just work hard. I never had control over anything except how hard I work, so I always did more than anyone else. I thought it meant I was tough."

"It did. It does," Teela said.

"No. It meant I was proud," Locke said, "and competitive, and unwilling to let anyone else best me without it feeling like a failure on my part. Not my best traits. But it's why I couldn't just finish the run, I had to win it. I had to be the one to ring the bell. And I was training every day for it, doing the stairs on my own over and over for practice, running myself so ragged that by the time the night came around, I slept right through it."

Teela laughed. "What?"

Locke nodded. "I woke up to someone else ringing the bell."

It was comforting to slip back into memory of a time and a place they both knew they could never go back to, but Teela was anxious to get going, aware of the light beginning to turn periwinkle with dawn over the tops of the trees. "Are you telling me this as some kind of extended metaphor? Can we just skip to the lesson I'm supposed to learn?"

Locke blew a breath through her nose—not quite a laugh, and Teela suddenly felt a prick of regret that she had interrupted instead of letting Locke finish the story the way she wanted to. When Locke spoke, her voice was a little rougher than before. "Look, you don't have to listen to me. Or learn anything from me. When I was your age, I know I didn't want to take advice from anyone. But I remember, when I showed up that day at graduation, Duncan asked how the run went, and I told him I slept through it, and he laughed and said, *You borrowed your strength from tomorrow.*"

Teela frowned. "What does that mean?"

"It meant I fought the wrong fight," Locke said. "I used my energy on the wrong thing."

"That doesn't . . ." Teela bit her lip to stop herself from saying anything more. If Locke knew what she was really doing, maybe she'd understand that there was nothing more important than saving the company and staying on Eternia to fight.

But then again, if Locke knew what she was about to do, she might try to stop her.

Locke stood suddenly and held out a hand to Teela to help her to her feet.

"It's not a metaphor," Locke said, and touched Teela lightly on the shoulder. "It's just the last time I remember seeing your father wear this cloak." Locke reached into her jacket and withdrew a packet of jerky, which she extended to Teela. "Do what you have to," she said. "But be careful."

Teela took the jerky. "I will. Will you tell everyone I'm safe?"

"Absolutely not," Locke replied. "Because I suspect you aren't. But I'll tell them I saw you leave, and they shouldn't worry. You're doing what you must."

"Thank you."

Locke clapped Teela on the shoulder, harder this time. "On Geolon, where my mother was born, they don't say *goodbye*. We say, *Until the circle closes.* It is not a goodbye, but a way to say that we will see each other again soon when the journey is finished."

Teela pressed her hand over the buckle of her father's cloak, where the crest of the Heroic Warriors was etched. "Until the circle closes."

Locke placed her hand over her own heart. "Until the circle closes. Travel safely, wherever it is you feel you must go."

NINE

The long, high arched bridge that led to Darksmoke—and, as legend had it, the dragon Granamyr's keep—emerged through the snow.

Teela's heart soared—a part of her had been afraid that it was all just a myth after all. The journey to the Ice Mountains had been difficult, but she'd managed to get most of the way there in only a week. On the edge of the Plain of Perpetua, she'd met a troupe of Avionian actors who let her ride along in their sky wagon to the feet of the Ice Mountains. She'd traded Duncan's compass for thick mittens, an ice axe, and toe picks for her boots to help with climbing, along with a package of dried meat and dehydrated fruit. As Teela passed the compass over, she'd said a silent apology to her father. It would all be worth it when she returned with a cure for the sickness.

Teela had secretly hoped the Ice Mountains might be misnamed, or at the very least exaggerated—more chilly hill than ice-covered mountain range. But the place was, in fact, aptly named. Within Teela's first hour of hiking, a ferocious wind kicked up loose snow, blowing it straight into her face, and she had to stop and shelter behind a border, freezing even though she was wrapped in her father's coat. When the gusts of wind finally abated and she stood, a drift of snow slid off her back.

It had taken Teela two days of scrambling up slick ice faces, the toe picks she'd attached to her boots the only thing keeping her from sliding back down the mountain more than once. Her toes grew so cold and stiff, even in her boots, that she had to keep stopping to find shelter just to rub feeling back into them. Her red hair turned white with frost, and each time she blinked, she could feel her eyelashes growing heavier with trapped flakes of snow.

At least she'd managed to avoid the Ice Hackers and trolls that roamed the mountains, though she'd often found the bones of their camps half-buried in the snow—and sometimes the literal bones of their prey. She saw a band of the marauders once from a distance while perched upon a cliff she had just scaled but was careful to keep her head ducked down and out of their sight. She vaguely remembered reading once that Ice Hackers had lost the ability to see color because of their overwhelmingly white world and relied on movement for hunting. She'd lain so still that, when she finally stood, a snow hare that had been twitching nearby took off in fright.

And now here she was at last, arrived at the final stage of her journey that would hopefully yield some answers.

But Teela's joy was quickly punctured when she took her first steps on the slick purple stone bridge, polished with ice and dusted in snow. Far below it, the black cliffs dropped into a long nothing, so deep and dark she couldn't see the ground. Her head spun, and she stepped backward before she realized it. Her foot slipped on the slick stone, and for a moment she teetered, off-balance, before she dropped onto her stomach on the stone, breathing hard.

She had not come this far to stop now. But the distance felt impossible. Teela pulled her pickax from her pack and hooked it into the ice ahead of her, pulling herself forward a few feet, then another. She made it halfway across the bridge using this method before her arms started to shake, and she could feel the ice soaking in through her trousers. Slowly, she eased herself to her feet, still staying low to the ground as she went, slow foot over slow foot, across the narrow bridge.

Granamyr's keep was a small dome built onto the hillside, like an astronomer's observatory. Teela could feel the heat emanating from it as soon as she tumbled gratefully off the bridge. She'd spent much of her journey worrying over how she'd approach Granamyr, if in fact the dragon of legend was even there and willing to commune with her. Teela had heard the same stories in her youth that all the children in

Eternos had heard of the dangers in dealing with dragons and their disdain for any beings that were not their own kind—particularly humans, who they had gone to war with thousands of years ago and never quite forgotten. How they loved a riddle and a trick and a quest—and, more than anything, a bargain.

Teela had no head for riddles and had expended all her questing strength getting here. She had nothing with which to bargain. But now that she had arrived at the keep, her body seemed to move forward on its own, despite her trepidation, pulled toward the heat before she could stop and take stock of her surroundings.

Then she was crossing the threshold.

The curved walls of Granamyr's keep were stacked high with treasures—gold and silver, precious stones, more jewels than the royal coffers of Eternos even at their height, Teela was sure. Ripples of heat emanated from a giant pit in the center of the floor, rising in shimmering waves toward the open oculus high above, through which the sky was visible. Teela stood motionless, her body gratefully soaking in the heat, relishing defrosting for the first time in what felt like years.

After several moments, Teela began to take stock of the treasures surrounding her, at the swords and chests and armor and piles and piles of what she was certain were ancient magical artifacts that had never been cataloged in any book of her youth. Did this vast collection contain a cure for the camp's sickness somewhere in its midst? It would take the full resources of the palace library to learn all their names and uses, where they had come from, and who had brought them as offerings to the great dragons. Teela wasn't sure whether to laugh or cry. She felt suddenly foolish for coming all this way only to realize now how overwhelmed she was by the treasures. What was she supposed to do? It would be insane to try to search through them, hoping she might find something carefully labeled with a helpful inscription like "*THIS WILL SAVE YOUR FRIENDS AND FAMILY.*"

Teela walked to the lip of the pit and peered down into the darkness. The heat scorched her face, and she reeled backward, coughing. There was no end to that darkness. It didn't even seem to begin. It was just one massive, undulating abyss, like a tunnel leading to the center of Eternia.

Teela sucked in a deep breath and steadied herself. She would do whatever it took. She couldn't return to the camp empty-handed.

"*Granamyr!*" she shouted, expecting her voice to echo around the curved room; but instead, it seemed to be swallowed by the darkness, snuffed into hardly a whisper. She cleared her throat and tried again, but it felt like the louder she tried to shout, the quieter her voice sounded in the giant room.

Teela waited, muscles quivering. Her hand strayed to the knife strapped to her thigh. Should she call out again? Had anyone heard her? Or was she just shouting an ancient legend's name into the darkness, a silly girl who thought she could help her people?

Then, from deep in the darkness, a seismic rumble.

She felt it more than heard it, the tremors moving up through her legs. Stones on the ground began to jump and dance. The darkness itself seemed to quiver, then part like a curtain, and suddenly before her loomed the great dragon, head thrown back, and jaws open to the sky. The dragon's skin appeared thick and leathery, the rosy color of the berries she and Adam used to pick wild from the fields around the palace and eat until their mouths were stained purple. His yellow eyes flashed, catlike, as he lowered himself onto his belly, his long snout nearly brushing Teela as he bent down to her eye level. She could have crawled inside his mouth without having to bend over, and when he rolled back his thick black lips, she saw the rows of teeth, as long as her forearm and yellowed with age. Bloody streaks of his last meal clung to the crevasses.

"Daughter of Eternos," Granamyr rumbled, his voice less a sound than a sensation traveling through her whole body. His hot breath smelled of blood, and Teela instinctively stepped backward, almost tripping over the long hem of her father's cloak. Another deep rumble, and Teela realized it was the dragon chuckling at her.

"You have come so far," he said, "just to die."

TEN

Teela felt her hand go once again to the blade at her thigh, but she resisted the urge to draw it. She was not here for a fight, and any hospitality the dragon might have toward her would likely evaporate upon seeing her blade. She came in peace, even if every muscle in her body was quivering with the urge to defend herself.

"Great dragon," she began, not sure how one was meant to address an eternal being, old as Eternia itself. She reconsidered, then tried again, "Your . . . your dragonship. I have come to ask for your help."

"My help?" Granamyr's nostrils flared, releasing two long coils of black smoke that twisted through the air like leaping dogs. "I have no allegiance to your kind. You petty, small-minded humans and your schoolyard games you call wars. I do not meddle in the affairs of humans, little one. Not unless there is something in it for me."

"There's nothing petty about the fact that Eternos has fallen to Skeletor!" Teela said before she could stop herself. She had no clue how up to date he was on the world outside his keep—or how much he cared. She had to make him care. "Without intervention, all of Eternia will be his."

"And why should this concern me?" Granamyr rumbled. "He may not be a man, but he is petty and small as the rest of you. I have no fear of that smug ossuary."

"Magic has vanished from Grayskull," Teela continued, not sure what would move the dragon but willing to throw every bleak statistic at him until one broke through the wall around his heart. "The king and queen of Eternia are prisoners of Snake Mountain, and the prince has vanished. And now, many of the remaining Heroic Warriors of Eternos are on the verge of death, and the rest ready to quit the planet unless I intervene."

One of the dragon's large eyes blinked slowly. "So let them go."

"I can't," Teela said, her voice rising.

"Why not?"

"Because I'm a warrior, too!" Teela said. "And this is my home. I will not abandon it."

"So is it mine," Granamyr said. "But your kind have so little regard for anyone beyond the walls of your cities. You would never think of me as a citizen of Eternia, would you? Otherwise, you would not have waited until you needed a favor to seek me out with this news."

Teela clenched her jaw. "In my defense," she said, "I thought there was a fifty percent chance you were imaginary."

The dragon stared at her. When he blinked, it felt like a cloud passing over the sun. Then the rumbling laugh once again. Teela felt it wash over her skin like the ripple of a stone thrown into a pond. The welt from the acidic rain on her forearm throbbed.

"Skeletor will not stop at Eternos," Teela continued, grasping at any straw, no matter how grand, that she might pull to tug on his sympathy. Did dragons feel sympathy? Did dragons feel anything other than contempt and hunger? "He will take the whole planet. He will bend you to his will or destroy you if you do not comply."

"He cannot touch me."

"He can with the Sword of Power."

Granamyr drummed his claws on the stone. The sound reminded her of the rain, and she almost ducked for cover. "And where is that Sword, small one?"

"I don't . . . no one knows," Teela said. "But if Skeletor finds it, the heroes of Eternos will be the only thing standing between him and complete control of Eternia. And now those warriors . . ." She was trying to speak grandly, like she imagined the Heroic Warriors of old would, but the facade was melting in the face of the dragon's indifference. "They're my people," Teela said, and her voice pitched. She hated how petulant it made her sound, but she couldn't help it. She *felt* petulant. "They're sick! If you don't help me, they might all die!"

"A sickness." The dragon rolled onto his side, using one of the massive talons extending from his front claws to scratch beneath his chin. "Surely, you have healers who can tend to them."

"It isn't an ordinary sickness," Teela said. "There was a rain—a strange rain that decimated the forest where we sought refuge and left our company injured and sick. The waters of the forest have been contaminated. The animals have all left. It might have been magic—I don't know. That is what I have come to ask you for—a cure, or a treatment. Something that might help my fellow warriors."

The dragon weaved his head back and forth in consideration, the frilled scales on his neck flaring. "A rain, you say?"

Teela nodded. "At least, I think so. I don't know what it was, but it fell from green clouds like rain. It burned the forest and left the company who was touched by it sick and burned, too." She yanked back her sleeve and showed him the black welt on her skin. "There is no cure that we have found, so we think it must be magic."

Granamyr hissed, his tongue darting from between his teeth toward her. Teela flinched, sure for a cold moment she was about to be eaten, resisting the urge to turn and flee. But all he did was touch the tip to the welt, then run his tongue over his black lips. He let out a low rumble, and Teela felt her teeth rattle in her head. "It would seem," the dragon said, "that someone has poisoned the well."

"What?" Teela asked, tilting her head back to look up at him. "What does that mean?"

Granamyr ignored her question. He raised himself to his full height, and the soft pink underside of his belly reminded Teela of the fluffy marshmallows the palace kitchens used to make every year for Adam's birthday cake. "What will you give me?" Granamyr asked. "In exchange for my help?"

So the legends were true. Despite her exhaustion, Teela wished Granamyr had mentioned a quest or riddle instead; she had so little on her—even less that might be valuable to a dragon. Nothing to trade or barter or wager that would be equal to that of her company's lives.

"I have nothing of value," she said quietly.

The dragon let out a hot purr, smoke rising from his nostrils. "All value is relative," he said, "so give me what is most precious to you, to show me what my gift would mean."

Teela looked down, her gaze landing on her father's inscribed cloak pin.

She unfastened the pin from her collarbone and laid it at her feet. The offering felt so small and pathetic, but still she said with as much strength in her voice as she could muster, "It belongs to my father, Duncan, the king's man-at-arms. It was forged in the pits of Stone Mountain and set with Coridite from the Widget Mines. It bears the insignia of the Heroic Warriors and has been worn by the king's man-at-arms for thousands of years. It might not seem like much to someone like you who has so much treasure. But my father is the most important thing to me." She swallowed. "He has value."

The dragon hooked a claw around the pin and raised it to his eye. In his giant talon, the pin looked almost comically insignificant, the side of a coin. "This gift is insufficient for what you ask of me," he said, and Teela felt her heart sink. But then the dragon continued, "However. I will give you what you seek. Do not thank me, child," he added as Teela felt her whole body sag with relief. "There's another price you must pay."

Teela swallowed. "What's . . . what's the price?"

The dragon's belly rumbled. "I have been waiting for someone like you. Someone who could close the door."

"What door?"

The dragon ignored her question and instead offered only the cryptic reply, "Close the door, or the wasting will never end."

Then the whole ground seemed to rumble with him again. There was a sudden flash of light, so bright as it reflected against the treasures lining the walls that Teela fell backward in surprise, arms thrown up over her face. When she opened her eyes, spots still danced across her vision, and she had to blink hard for a minute before she could see clearly.

Granamyr was gone.

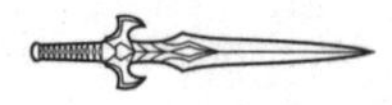

For a moment, Teela thought he had vanished with her father's cloak pin and left her nothing in return. Then she noticed, at the very edge of the black pit he had appeared from, a small bottle in a leather sling, a long chain attached to the edge pooled around it. The glass was the dark navy of twilight, but from deep inside a cloudy sparkle seemed to glow, like a galaxy across a midnight sky. Teela crawled forward to retrieve it, shocked that when her fingers brushed the surface, she found the glass cool to the touch despite the heat still shimmering from the pit. She found herself thinking of the first drink after a long bout of sparring, her muscles satisfyingly sore and her chest heaving.

She uncorked the bottle and raised it tentatively to her nose. There was no smell, and it was colorless. She wasn't foolish enough to touch it or, worse, taste it. She had no idea what it was or how this was meant to help. The bottle was barely as wide as her palm, the thin neck slightly longer than her index finger. She ran her fingers over the leather sling, then the chain, like some instructions might be etched there. But there was nothing.

She considered calling the dragon back and demanding to know what she was meant to do with his offering and what mysterious door she needed to be worried about closing, but she suspected there was a reason there were no stories about the men who asked Granamyr for special directions on what exactly they were supposed to do with his offerings. Something about looking a gift dragon in the mouth.

She hooked the chain around her neck and tucked the bottle under her cloak. The weight was somehow comforting in the absence of the heavy brooch on her shoulder. She knew her father would forgive her for the bargain—likely he would say there was nothing to forgive—but if she had traded away his precious insignia for nothing, she would not forgive herself. And if her father died . . .

Maybe Sigrid would know what to make of Granamyr's strange gift. She had to get back to the camp.

Outside the dragon's keep, a storm had risen, heavy winds kicking up drifts so thick that Teela was momentarily disoriented. The sky and the snow were the same color, and for a bewildering moment, she felt like she was underwater. The long, arched bridge that led from Darksmoke back to the Ice Mountains pass she had come from was covered in a soft white down, the polished stones rendered so slick she was afraid she'd slide off the side and into the darkness. There would be nothing to grab on to—the bridge had no railing, or even a lip of stone. It was just one long, smooth parabola. This time, when she tried to crawl on her belly as she had before, the winds seemed to hit her differently, and she felt like she was about to be lifted off the bridge like a leaf and carried away. She stood tentatively. The picks on her shoes helped with the grip, and she felt steadier this time. She started across, her face turned into the collar of her coat against the bitter wind.

She had reached the center of the bridge when she sensed something ahead of her, the snow thickening with shadows. She raised her head, her hair coming free of where she had tucked it into her collar and whipping around her face. Someone was standing on the bridge just ahead of her, a dark smudge through the snow like a spilled drop of ink.

Teela's stomach dropped. Was it one of the Ice Hackers? Or had the marauders finally found her, waiting for her to leave the dragon's keep, knowing there was nowhere else she could go?

Teela held up a hand, shielding her face from the snow. The figure stood tall, unbattered by the wind, one hand wrapped around a tall staff planted in the ice. A dark cape whipped around the figure's legs, and long white hair, the same color as the snow, was twisted into a column by the wind.

Teela stopped, though the wind nearly knocked her sideways. She knew this woman—both from ghoulish tales that she and Adam would exchange in whispers at night, and her own memory of dark boots striding over the bones of the dead the night Eternos fell to Skeletor. She had been liveried then just as she had been in every story, in her ebony armor, helmet concealing that long white hair, and Teela remembered feeling she was witnessing a villain rising from the pages of a storybook. She felt the same eerie uncanniness now as she stared again at those heavy-lidded eyes, the perpetual smirk on her plum lips.

"Well, well," Evil-Lyn said. "Daughter of Eternos, you are a long way from home."

ELEVEN

Skeletor's second-in-command sneered at Teela, the sloped planes of her face rearranging themselves into a mocking expression. Evil-Lyn took a step forward, cloak whipping around her ankles.

Teela groped for the knife strapped to her thigh, but just as her fingers closed on the hilt, Evil-Lyn said, "Oh, none of that." She tipped her staff, and Teela felt a sharp sting like the knife had burned her. The blade flew from her hand and landed point down on the bridge behind her, wobbling. She reached for her other knife, only to realize that Evil-Lyn had already enchanted it, and it stuck fast in its scabbard, unable to be pulled free.

"Let's see now." Evil-Lyn took another step toward Teela, head tilting back and forth like a serpent getting ready to strike. "Last I recall, you were just a little brat. Duncan's little brat, specifically."

"Get out of my way," Teela said, teeth clenched around the words. She could feel her muscles tightening, her body automatically dropping into her fighting stance, though she knew there was no possible fight she could put up against a sorceress like Evil-Lyn. Duncan's blades, if held at the right angle, could repel certain spells, but one was still stuck in its scabbard and the other was ten feet behind her, snow already piling around its hilt.

Evil-Lyn took another step. An icicle hanging from the bridge cracked and tumbled down into the darkness. Teela never heard it land. "You're a long way from home," Evil-Lyn purred. "What for, I wonder?"

The only weapon Teela had on her side was the element of surprise—and the hubris of a villain playing with her food. She wouldn't just stand here and wait for Evil-Lyn to decide she was tired of toying with Teela and shoot a spell her way. Instead, before the sorceress could continue her monologue, Teela lunged forward with a scream, catching Evil-Lyn around the waist and tackling her to the ground.

Evil-Lyn was more caught off guard than Teela had expected, and Teela hit her so hard they both went flying backward. Evil-Lyn's staff fell to the snow and was immediately buried in the soft powder. Teela felt the electric surge as the spell on her dagger broke, and she wrenched the blade from its sheath. She had Evil-Lyn pinned to the ground and raised the blade, ready to strike, but Evil-Lyn recovered quickly.

As Teela swung the knife down, Evil-Lyn threw up her wrist, encased in a metal gauntlet, and a spiked blade sprang free. Teela's knife bounced off it. She swung down again, but Evil-Lyn deflected once more, this time the teeth of her serrated blade hooking with Teela's. Evil-Lyn twisted her arm, and Teela felt the dagger tugged from her grip. It sailed through the air, off the edge of the bridge and into the deep pit below.

Evil-Lyn wedged a foot against Teela's abdomen and kicked. The breath was knocked from Teela's lungs as she hit the ground, sliding several feet backward on the slick bridge. Evil-Lyn was clawing frantically through the drifted snow, searching for her staff. Teela scrambled backward, her hand grazing something long and narrow and solid as she realized that she had landed directly atop Evil-Lyn's staff.

Teela yanked the staff from the snow beneath her and, not knowing what else to do with it, used it like a club, lunging forward and smacking Evil-Lyn hard in the side with the crystal orb that was set into one end. Evil-Lyn collapsed sideways, one of her wrist blades lodging in the stone, trapping her. She screamed in frustration but couldn't seem to muster a spell without the help of her staff. Sparks fizzed at her fingers, but nothing strong enough to be hurled. Teela swung the staff again, aiming for Evil-Lyn's head, but Evil-Lyn dodged, hooking an ankle around Teela's and sweeping her legs out from under her. Teela tumbled backward, throwing out her hands to catch herself but meeting only empty air. She was at the edge of the bridge, tumbling backward. She felt the bottle from Granamyr fly up from under her cape, the chain whipping around her neck as gravity suddenly shifted. She groped for something to catch herself, but the stone was slick and ridgeless, and she couldn't do anything as she slid off the edge of the bridge and into the empty air above the pit.

For a moment, she was weightless. She felt her arms windmilling helplessly, stomach in her throat. She had come all this way, only to die at the hand of Skeletor's lieutenant. The irony of it felt cruel. With so many natural forces against her—the snow, the ice, the dragon—her downfall would be at the hands of the very thing that had driven her here to begin with. If she had to die, she wanted a warrior's death, in the heat of battle, not feebly grappling and desperately outmatched on a bridge above the Pit of Shadows. Why hadn't she told Locke where she was really going? Or Malcolm—anyone? Everyone? Why had she come on her own? Why had Teela thought she, of all people, could be the one to keep the warriors on Eternia?

Suddenly, she felt a sharp jerk at her throat and realized her cloak had caught something, stopping her fall. She twisted around in midair, legs kicking helplessly, neck craned upward to see what it was that had stopped her fall.

Evil-Lyn was lying on her stomach, torso over the edge of the bridge, clutching Teela's cloak. Her teeth were clenched with exertion as she threw a hand down in offering to Teela. Teela could hear the fabric of the cloak ripping, and she knew she had only seconds. Whatever ulterior motive had led Evil-Lyn to push her off the bridge, then stop her from falling, was surely sinister, but Teela could deal with it when her feet were on solid ground. She'd take probable death over certain death any day.

She swung herself up and grabbed Evil-Lyn's hand, letting the sorceress help propel her upward and heave her back up onto the bridge.

Teela collapsed in the snow beside Evil-Lyn, her heart hammering. Her chest felt tight, and she struggled for breath. Her limbs shook so badly, she wasn't sure if she'd be able to stand, let alone fight, and she braced herself for a spell, or for Evil-Lyn to sucker punch her while she was down.

Instead, to her surprise, Evil-Lyn stayed sprawled in the snow beside her, both of them trying to catch their breath as the snow drifted around them.

After a moment, Evil-Lyn looked sideways at Teela. Her white hair blended with the snow like she was made of it. "You weren't supposed to die that quickly."

Teela heaved herself to her knees, scrambling backward toward the dragon's keep in the direction Evil-Lyn had sent her dagger flying. She yanked one glove off with her teeth and pawed through the snow, searching for the blade. The snow was so cold it burned her bare fingertips.

"Stop," she heard Evil-Lyn call. "Come, child, I don't want to hurt you. If I did, you'd be dead already."

Teela didn't turn. She kept fumbling through the snow for her blade. "I don't trust a word you say."

"Wise."

Teela's fingers brushed the cold hilt of the knife, and she sprang to her feet, turning to face the sorceress with the blade held before her. To her surprise, Evil-Lyn was still sitting on the snow, combing her fingers through the snarls the wind had tied her hair into. She flicked her gaze up to Teela, then rolled her eyes. "Put that away."

"Make me."

Evil-Lyn's mouth curled. "You know I can."

"Let me pass."

"Make me." Evil-Lyn retrieved her staff from the snow, using it to push herself to her feet. She surveyed Teela, and Teela braced herself for another spell, knife held before her defensively. But then Evil-Lyn said, "Do you want to get out of here?"

Teela felt the blade drop a few inches. "What?"

"It's just so cold." Evil-Lyn brushed the snow off the shoulders of her dark cloak. "I thought we might go somewhere a little warmer. What do you say?"

"I'm not going anywhere—" Teela started, but the orb on the end of Evil-Lyn's staff glowed suddenly, bright as staring into the sun. Teela was momentarily blinded, and a rushing sound filled her ears as if she'd been dropped into the ocean. For a moment, she thought Evil-Lyn had pushed her back into the pit after all.

But then her vision cleared, and she realized the snowy expanse was gone, replaced by the ruins of a white stone hallway, littered with hunks of rubble where the ceiling had collapsed inward. Stripes of bright sunlight fell in columns through the holes, illuminating black streaks of soot along the walls.

Teela felt her breath catch in her chest. She knew this place. She knew this hallway. If she closed her eyes, she could still feel her own footsteps running in syncopated time with Adam's down this hallway, slowing when they were scolded for running, then taking off again. She could hear Adam's laugh. She could smell the warm aroma of roasting meat from the kitchens mingling with the perfumes from the gardens.

"Where are we?" Teela asked, though she already knew.

"The Royal Palace of Eternos," Evil-Lyn replied. "Welcome home."

TWELVE

Teela could have stood there, rooted by memories, for hours if Evil-Lyn hadn't barked at her, "Come on, there are Shadow Beasts lurking and we've got things to do." Evil-Lyn started down the hallway, and when Teela didn't follow, the sorceress turned, arms folded in exasperation. "Shadow Beasts. Didn't they ever come up in your schooling, or did you mostly focus on punching?"

"I know what they are," Teela said hotly. The thought of facing a Shadow Beast made a shiver run through her, one that had nothing to do with the snow melting through her cloak. She had thought that, after everything she had been through, she couldn't be scared by the thought of monsters in the dark. But Shadow Beasts were more than just the villains of ghost stories told around the campfire. They were huge apes, with sharp teeth and a thirst for blood, that could dwell only in darkness. She stepped quickly into a beam of sunlight.

Evil-Lyn's mouth twisted. "That's the idea. Now, come on, before we lose the light."

The sorceress started down the hall once again, and despite herself, Teela felt her curiosity tugging her along. If Evil-Lyn meant to kill her, she would have let her fall into the yawning pit back on the bridge. If she wanted Teela as her prisoner, she would have transported her straight to the dungeons of Snake Mountain. But instead, she'd brought her here. She'd brought her home. Why?

Teela took off at a trot after Evil-Lyn.

The palace was somehow both exactly as Teela remembered and entirely different. Everything was coated in dust and grime. Walls had collapsed, and the fine furnishings had mostly been looted or tossed into piles and burned for warmth. The soot from the fires ran up the walls in cakey streaks, and sunlight filtered in through holes in the walls and windows.

It was in ruins, but it was still her home. The skeleton stripped of its flesh was still a familiar face. There was the classroom where Adam had once fallen asleep during a lecture and snored so loudly it had startled the professor. There was the closet they had hidden in after replacing the king's beard oil with indigo dye that hadn't washed away for weeks, though they had meant for it to last only a day. There was the corner where Teela had found Adam hiding from the dinner he didn't want to attend after his father had shouted at him.

"Brings back memories, doesn't it?" Evil-Lyn threw over her shoulder as she mounted a set of stairs leading up to a turret Teela couldn't quite remember the purpose of. "Well, probably different memories for us. You're thinking about feasts and dances, I'm thinking about decimating your friends and family. Weren't those the days! Ah, here we are."

They had reached a door, and Evil-Lyn pressed a finger to it, magicking the lock free. The door swung open, and Teela followed Evil-Lyn into a turret room. Teela recognized it suddenly. They must be above what had once been the palace infirmary. This would have been Sigrid's office. The furnishings had mostly been left untouched—part of the glass roof had broken and caved in, but the rows of pharmacy bottles and potions were still lined up neatly along the shelves over the desk. Teela remembered coming here once when she had broken her elbow during training. Duncan had been away, and she had been so young that his absence hurt more than the injury, so Sigrid had let Teela spend the day in her office beside her instead of in the infirmary itself.

It felt like stepping into a museum of her old life.

Except for the sorceress in the center of it.

Evil-Lyn leaned her staff against the wall, then swung her cape off her shoulders, shaking the snow off before she hung it on the top of the staff. "Please," she said, slinging herself into the chair behind the desk and kicking her feet up onto it. It looked too high to be comfortable, but the drama was undeniable. "Make yourself at . . . *home*." When Teela didn't move, Evil-Lyn sighed dramatically, then pointed a finger at Teela. A stool flew out from the corner and smacked against the back of Teela's legs, hard enough that she sat down.

"There you go." Evil-Lyn wrung the melting snow from her hair, then ran her fingers through it, pushing it into a magical arrangement on the top of her head. "So," she said, "how are things?"

Teela stared at her. She could taste blood filling her mouth from where she had bit her tongue when she'd been sat down. She considered spitting it at the sorceress's feet.

Evil-Lyn raised her hands in mock surrender. "Fine, we don't have to exchange pleasantries. We can skip right to the *what's a nice girl like you doing in a place like Darksmoke?*"

"That's not your concern," Teela said through gritted teeth.

"Debatable."

"Why were *you* there?"

"Wonderful—now you're grasping the concept of a dialogue. I was looking for that." She pointed at Teela, and Teela looked down, remembering suddenly the bottle the dragon had given her, still hanging around her neck. Instinctively, her hands closed around it. Evil-Lyn laughed. "I wouldn't take it from you."

"Yes, you would."

"Normally, sure. Good instincts." Her purple eyes flashed, the sunlight through the high windows splintering through them as if they were precious stones. "Do you want to take your cloak off? You're shivering."

Teela realized she was—the wet cloak was doing more harm than good.

"Or better yet." Evil-Lyn pointed a dark nail at the fireplace behind Teela, and a roaring fire sprang suddenly to life in the grate. Teela felt the warmth against her skin, though the wet cloak kept it from reaching her.

"Come on," Evil-Lyn said. "Don't be a martyr."

Slowly, Teela slid the cloak from her shoulders and let it fall to the floor. Evil-Lyn tutted. "Now, I know Duncan raised you better than that."

"What?"

Evil-Lyn snapped her fingers, and the cloak flew up like it was on a string and hung itself on the back of the door. "What's the point of fine things if you don't take care of them?"

Teela rolled her eyes but couldn't resist leaning into Evil-Lyn's fire, feeling a wash of relief as the warmth doused her. She winced at the pain in her fingers as they began to defrost. The snow had seeped through her cloak and into her clothes, and she plucked at the front of her tunic, trying to separate the wet material from where it touched her skin. Evil-Lyn noticed and flicked her fingers at Teela. There was a brief glow of magic, and Teela flinched reflexively, but all Evil-Lyn had cast was a spell to dry her clothes.

"Better?" Evil-Lyn asked.

"Are you going to offer me tea next?"

"Of course not. I don't touch the stuff. Though I'm sure I could rustle up something for you, if you insist. What is the recipe for tea? Just leaves and water, isn't it?"

"Why are you being nice to me?" Teela snapped.

Evil-Lyn pressed a hand to her chest. "Can't an evil sorceress have the daughter of her enemy over without being accused of having ulterior motives?"

"You've already revealed your ulterior motives." Teela held up the glass vial on the chain.

"Touché. Do you have any idea what that is?"

"Granamyr gave it to me," Teela replied, hoping her evasiveness would be mistaken for cunning and not, as Evil-Lyn had correctly guessed, lack of knowledge.

"Yes, but why? What did you ask him for?" When Teela didn't answer, Evil-Lyn flopped backward in her chair, rolling her eyes. "Go on, what would I possibly do with this information?"

"You'll tell your boss."

Evil-Lyn snorted. "Trust me, that faceless clown is far less of a threat than your crew seems to think. He has no idea where you and your little gang of misfits are hiding—and he doesn't care, by the way. You're a fly hardly worth swatting to him."

Teela thought back to Locke's assertion that the toxic rain had originated from Skeletor. "But *you* know where we're camped?" Teela asked.

"Oh, absolutely," Evil-Lyn replied. "The Evergreen Forest."

Teela felt all the cold that had left her seep back into her veins. "Will you tell Skeletor?"

"Why should I?" Evil-Lyn replied. "You're no threat. Even armed with *that*." She wiggled her fingers in the direction of the vial. Her nails were long and painted black, the tip of each inset with a small sparkling diamond.

Teela slid to the edge of her stool. "Fine, tell me. What is it?"

"I knew you'd warm up to me! Let's talk." Evil-Lyn crooked a finger, and the stool Teela was seated upon flew forward, dragging her along with it, around the desk until she was knee-to-knee with the sorceress. Evil-Lyn reached out and tapped one of those long, sparkling nails against the blue bottle. "So, what the generous beastie gave you is a sampling from the Wellspring of Eternia in the Whispering Valley. Did they teach you about that in battle school? No? Tell Duncan he really needs to beef up his geography curriculum."

"The Whispering Valley . . . it's . . . it's in the . . ." Teela struggled to remember. It felt like all the inane, extraneous knowledge she had picked up in school had been pushed from her mind in the shadows of survival.

"In the west, darling. Don't strain yourself. The Whispering Valley is a magical place, wherein burbles a magical spring, from which water can be drawn only in bottles made from the horn of a unicorn, of which there are precious few left. Tragic, isn't it, to be one of the last of your kind? Though you might know something about that." When Evil-Lyn turned her gaze away from the fire and toward Teela, her purple eyes looked black.

Teela gritted her teeth but ignored the barb. "What does the water do?"

"Oh, all kinds of things. Though I think you have one thing in particular in mind, don't you?"

It seemed pointless to keep playing dumb when the sorceress clearly knew more than Teela had hoped. "Our company is sick," she finally said, choosing her words carefully to reveal as little as possible. "I asked him for help."

"And he gave you this little vial you have no idea what to do with."

Evil-Lyn stood suddenly and crossed to the windowsill, where she selected the book on the top of the stack. It was coated with dust, which she blew directly into Teela's face, sending her doubling over, coughing.

"Sorry. Had to. Now let's see." Evil-Lyn flipped through the book, running her finger down the table of contents. "What sort of sickness are we curing here?"

"Welts," Teela said. "Like this." She held out her arm to show Evil-Lyn the blackened contusion.

Evil-Lyn clicked her tongue. "That looks like it hurts. Want me to make it better?" She flipped through the book until she seemed to find the page in question and, after dropping the book onto the desk and scanning it for a moment, turned to the potion cabinet, grabbing several bottles. She selected a clay jar from a cluster on the windowsill, blew inside it to clear out the dust, then began mixing her selected ingredients, periodically consulting the text. Teela watched, too confused by what was happening to process what she should be doing as the sorceress worked. Running? Keeping track of whatever she was mixing together? Trying to kill her somehow? The sorceress had implied she was going to help, but Teela knew better than to trust her. No help was given that freely, particularly from an enemy.

Evil-Lyn held up the poultice now congealing in the bottom of the jar for Teela to see. "All natural," she said. "Cure for warts and welts, here, look for yourself." She turned the book around so Teela could see the page. "Want to give it a try?"

Before Teela could answer, Evil-Lyn grabbed her by the wrist so that her sleeve fell backward, revealing the welt. Teela's muscles clenched, but she didn't move as Evil-Lyn spread the poultice over it.

Nothing happened. Evil-Lyn made a show of checking the book again. "Ah, here it says, apply twice daily for a week. You should start to notice results in two to three weeks."

Teela yanked her hand from Evil-Lyn's and stood. "We don't have time for two to three weeks. Why did you bring me here? Did you just want to torment me?"

Teela swiped the poultice off her arm, wiping it on her trousers, then turned for the door, determined to actually leave, but behind her, Evil-Lyn said, with theatrical wistfulness, "Oh, if only there was a way to help it along. Maybe a magical one, gifted by a dragon."

Teela stopped. Turned. Evil-Lyn had her chin resting on one hand, eyelashes fluttering, like a princess in a fairy tale sighing out a tower window as she waited for rescue.

"Why," Teela said, her tone rife with exasperation, "can't you just say what you mean?"

"Because being cryptic and coy is so much more fun!" Evil-Lyn pushed the jar across the table to Teela. "Want to add the final touch?"

Teela stared at the sorceress for a moment. This could all still be a trap—but what if it wasn't? What if this was the key to saving everyone who had been touched by the rain?

Without pausing further to think about what it meant that she was taking Evil-Lyn's word at face value, Teela undid the stopper on the blue bottle, then tipped a drop into the jar. The water inside the bottle was colorless but shimmered as it splashed forth, like a slick of oil in the sun, and Teela thought of the small galaxy she had seen trapped inside. The poultice sizzled and bubbled for a moment as if a fire had been lit under it, then settled, only slightly thicker than before.

Evil-Lyn scooped a dollop onto her finger, then took Teela's arm again, more gently this time. She spread it over the welt, then wiped it away again so quickly that at first, Teela thought she was clearing up a mistake.

Teela looked down at her arm and gasped. The black oozing welt had vanished, leaving her skin unblemished. She held up her arm, twisting it so the firelight fell on every inch of it.

Evil-Lyn made a gesture of presentation in the air beside Teela's arm. "Presto."

"How did you do that?"

"Followed the instructions. Then just add water."

"You said it wouldn't work for weeks."

"The thing about this water is that its magic is channeled through intention. It's already magic—it doesn't have to be wielded by a magician to work. But you have to tell it what you want it to do. In this case, I made something designed to cure welts. Just add water. It does the rest."

Evil-Lyn stood, cracking her neck, then stretched dramatically with her hands over her head. "Well, hasn't this been fun. Do you want a ride home, or are you too proud?"

Teela's fingers closed around the bottle. She couldn't believe she hadn't been more careful with it when she was scrapping with the sorceress on the bridge. She couldn't believe it was this simple—the journey had been arduous, but she had asked the dragon, and he had given her what she needed. Just like that? It was never so simple in the myths. There was always a cost. She had thought when she saw Evil-Lyn on the other side of the bridge waiting for her that her retribution had come calling in the form of the white-haired sorceress. But she'd been wrong.

Evil-Lyn strode to the door, running her hands down the furred interior of Duncan's cape. "Can I have this? For all the strengths of the Evil Horde, tailoring is not one of them."

"You expect me to believe you're just going to let me take this and go home?" Teela demanded. "Why not kill me and take the Wellspring water for yourself?"

"Well, I was only at Darksmoke hoping to get it for you."

Teela laughed before she could stop herself. "No you weren't."

Evil-Lyn raised her hands. "For your company! I was going to drop it anonymously out of the sky and see if you all started worshipping the sun when it cured your sickness."

Teela crossed her arms. "I can't trust anything you say."

"That's true," Evil-Lyn said with a shrug. "But this time, I'm being honest."

"Why would *you* help *us*?"

For the first time, Evil-Lyn's cavalier smirk dropped. "I want to see you and your company survive and retake Eternos."

Teela stared at her. "What?"

"Skeletor is an idiot. All bones but still spineless. He's been searching for the Sword of Power for years, and he's no closer to finding it than he was when he first took Eternos. The capture of the city was the only win he ever got, and look what he's let it turn to." She cast a hand toward the window, and Teela looked out at the crumbled ruins of the palace bailey. "Didn't even bother to keep it up. He'd rather rot in Snake Mountain. You think I like following him around the world, rooting through the rubble of cities he has leveled, looking for something he'll never find because he refuses to do anything that isn't his idea? That's the definition of insanity, darling. And I'm crazy, but I'm certainly not insane."

"You . . . want to overthrow Skeletor?" Teela asked.

Evil-Lyn's lips twisted into a smile. "Don't tell anyone, all right?"

"You're his second-in-command."

"I know, it's depressing to go this long without a promotion. See, that's the problem with this job, no room for growth. No dental insurance, either." Evil-Lyn dropped her head back. "Don't get me wrong, I'm not on your side. Not even close. But the enemy of my enemy is my friend, and all that. If the last heroes of Eternia die from some random pestilence, that's going to make my job a lot harder when I'm searching for allies to dethrone the gaunt ghoul who fancies himself a king. It's in my best interest to keep you all alive." She stared at Teela, one eyebrow ascending. "You still don't believe me."

"Why should I?" Teela demanded.

Evil-Lyn shrugged. "You needn't. I don't care. It's not my father who will die if I don't help him."

Teela's heartbeat quickened. It didn't make sense for Evil-Lyn to be in the Ice Mountains, then bring her here and tell her all this. Unless she was going to kill her . . . or she was telling the truth.

Teela didn't know much about the sorceress, but she thought she could hear a raw edge of frustration hidden behind breezy dismissiveness. But maybe that was put on, too. A double bluff? A triple bluff? But if this was a trick, to what end? What did Evil-Lyn have to gain in telling her this—truth or lie?

"How about this?" Evil-Lyn said. She had tipped the poultice into a jar, which she extended to Teela. "Take this little herbal remedy home to your friends and see if it works."

Teela ran her fingers over Sigrid's book. "And then in exchange, I suppose you want something from me?"

Evil-Lyn sighed dramatically. "Why does no one ever believe in my noble intentions?"

"You want something," Teela said again flatly.

"Fine, I want something. I want your company to ally with me when I make a stand against Skeletor, is that too much to ask?"

"They'll never go for it."

"Sounds like a you problem."

"You think I'd help you?"

"You might." Evil-Lyn wiggled her finger at the bottle of Wellspring water. "You know, that water you hold can do so much more for your people than just cure sickness. I can show you. I can help you. I want to help you, knowing that someday, you all will help me. I'll give you some time to heal your company and think. Then, we should meet again, you and I. And when we do, I'll give you another little lesson."

Teela chewed the inside of her cheek. She knew she was making a deal with a devil, but what choice did she have? If Evil-Lyn was telling the truth and the water was the key, not just to curing the camp's sickness but to improving their situation on all fronts, she had to see it through. Perhaps any talk of leaving Eternia would disappear right along with their many troubles. She drew in a breath. "All right."

"I knew you'd come around." Evil-Lyn clapped her hands together. "Shall we say three days' time? And if you don't want to, don't come. You can be rid of me right now. Consider this a freebie and then wash your hands of our association. The choice is yours." She glanced out the window, and Teela noticed for the first time the sun was beginning to set, the sky turning pink. "But now, it's almost your bedtime." Evil-Lyn picked up the jar on the table and handed it to Teela. "Go on, take this. Give it a try." She waved her hand. "And take the book, too. It may come in handy for our little get-togethers."

Teela scooped the jar and Sigrid's book into her arms. "Where would I meet you?" Teela asked. "If I wanted you to help me. Which, maybe I do, maybe I don't. I haven't decided yet."

Evil-Lyn retrieved her staff, then turned. "Oh, don't worry," she said, and tapped her staff twice on the ground. "We'll find each other."

The same flash of light from before burned Teela's eyes. When her vision cleared, it took her a moment to realize where she was—back in the Evergreen Forest, on the banks of the stream that had once been their water source. It was still thick and polluted with the rain. She could feel the weight of the vial around her neck, the pointed end digging into her ribs as she pressed the potion book she had taken from the palace against her chest. When she shifted, something crinkled, keeping the book from shutting completely, and when Teela opened it, she found a piece of paper twice-folded, nestled within the book's pages.

Teela unfolded it and read in a straight, spiky hand—"Midnight at the Skytree, three days. xx."

Teela knew in her bones she was a fool to trust Evil-Lyn. Duncan would have told her that without hesitation. There is no morality that exists in darkness—she remembered that from his lectures to the cadets.

THIRTEEN

When Teela arrived back at the camp, the stillness was eerie. The clearing that just days before would have been thrumming with activity at this time of day was quiet and empty. The shelters they had built looked small and liable to be blown over by a strong wind, the damage from the rain still not repaired entirely. The sun was just beginning to set, casting the trees in fiery light and lengthening the shadows.

Teela had hardly entered the clearing when she heard the sing of steel and felt the cold blade of a sword at her throat. "Who goes there?" a voice demanded, and Teela held up her hands.

"It's me."

"Teela?" The sword dropped—not just from her neck but all the way to the ground, and she turned to see Krass holding himself up against a tree. His skin was pale, and the black welts covering his arms had begun to spread like watercolors on a wet page. The whites of his eyes were stained black, a drop of ink spilled through water. "I'm so sorry, Teela. I can hardly see. The rain, it got in my eyes."

"Why are you on watch?" Teela asked, helping the great warrior to a nearby tree stump and guiding him to sit. "You should be resting."

"There's no one else—everyone is either sick or tending to—" His words broke into a fit of coughing. Teela unhooked the canteen dangling from her belt—there were still a few swigs of water she had melted from the snow of the Ice Mountains—and passed it to Krass. He gulped gratefully with his head tipped back to catch every drop.

"Where's Sigrid?" Teela asked, anxious to show the healer what she'd returned with.

"At the medical hut, I suspect."

"Come with me." Teela took Krass by the arm and led him back through the camp. Sigrid wasn't at the medical hut, but they found her dragging a bucket of river water she had been attempting to purify from the fire. She looked exhausted, her whole body curling around the bucket like it was too heavy to lift, though Teela had seen her carry heavier loads. She nearly dropped the bucket when she saw Teela approaching. “Teela!” she cried. “Where have you been?”

“I have something to help,” Teela said instead of answering. She held out the jar to Sigrid. “It will help cure the welts.”

Sigrid took the jar, sniffing it tentatively before asking, “Where did you get this?”

“I made it.” Teela held up the book.

Sigrid’s eyes widened, her dark brows shooting upward. “That’s mine. I recognize that stain from when I spilled my tea on it.” The healer’s wise gaze narrowed. “Where did you get this?”

“I . . . went to Darksmoke. To ask the dragon for help.”

“And he gave you my old medical book?”

Teela answered with something between a nod and a shrug. She wasn’t sure how she could explain making the trip from Darksmoke to the palace and back in such a short period of time without revealing Evil-Lyn’s intervention, and she wasn’t ready to tip the hand of her new ally just yet. Hopefully the results of the potion would be enough to distract Sigrid from where or how it had come about.

“It works! Look!” She took Krass by the arm and spread the poultice over one of his welts, just as Evil-Lyn had done to her. Sigrid started to protest—probably something about not having the two to three weeks needed to wait for it to work—but stopped when Teela wiped away the poultice with her hand, revealing the welt entirely healed. “That’s not possible,” Sigrid breathed. Krass stared at the spot where the welt had been, mouth agape.

"What is this? How does it work?" Sigrid demanded.

"Does that matter? I used the recipe in your book. It's all ingredients we can find in the forest."

Sigrid shook her head. "Teela, I tried that recipe. It did nothing. So how did you get it to work that fast?"

"I . . ." How could she explain? She'd have to tell Sigrid about the water. The dragon. The help from Evil-Lyn—how else would she explain where the idea of mixing the water into the poultice had come to her? She didn't have time to be cross-examined or for thorough, methodical Sigrid to waste the company's precious time interrogating the dangers of trusting the sorceress. No one would believe Evil-Lyn was hoping to overthrow Skeletor and had brokered a deal with Teela to help the camp. Even as Teela turned the story over in her mind again, debating how she could frame it, she knew how absurd it all sounded.

But none of that mattered. What mattered was that she had a cure. She had a solution. She couldn't let them stand around and waste more time.

So instead, all she said was, "I don't know, but I made it in the palace, and it works. We have to make more."

Sigrid paused for a moment, then nodded. "Let me get my kit," she said.

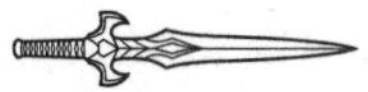

It was hard to harvest in the dark, but the cover gave Teela an opportunity to mix several drops of the Wellspring water into the large amount of poultice without Sigrid noticing. Sigrid still looked suspicious, but her eyes widened when they tried their new mixture on another of Krass's welts and it healed instantly. Teela was ready to grab the jar and run if Sigrid put up a fight—she'd take it around herself, alone—but all Sigrid said was, "We have to work as fast as possible. There aren't many of us well enough to help." Teela nodded quickly.

"I'll muster them," Sigrid said. "You start distributing this."

Teela ducked out of the circle of firelight and started across the camp, making a beeline for the *Helios*, where she assumed Duncan still was. She had to get the poultice to him. She was almost there when a voice called through the darkness.

"Teela."

She stopped. Locke emerged from the darkness. The sword strapped to her waist was stained with blood, and she had the carcass of a monkey thrown over her shoulder. Its pelt looked oily, and even from a distance, Teela could smell that its flesh was rotten.

"You're back! What happened? Did you find anything?"

Teela held up the jar. "A way to cure the welts."

Locke gaped at her. "How?"

"I went to Darksmoke."

"You went to Darksmoke?" Locke let out an astonished laugh. "Teela, that's on the other side of the continent. How did you make it there and back so quickly?"

"I caught a ride with some Avionians," she said, then added quickly before Locke could press the point further, "I saw the dragon Granamyr. He gave me a cure."

"You saw the dragon? And he didn't drag you down to the Pit of Shadows?"

"I bargained with him," Teela said. "I gave him my father's cloak pin. It works. I had a welt from the rain that wouldn't heal, and now look." Teela pulled up the sleeve of her tunic, showing Locke her clear skin. "It's gone."

Locke stared at Teela's unmarked skin, then grabbed her suddenly, pulling her into a fierce hug. "You," she said, taking Teela's face between her hands and kissing her on the forehead. "Are a marvel!"

Teela felt her cheeks pinking with pleasure. "I had to do something."

"You did *everything*. If I had known you were going to Darksmoke, I would have stopped you, you mad, wonderful girl. You really are your father's daughter."

"I was just going in to see him now," Teela said, starting again toward the *Helios*.

Locke took her arm. "He's not there." When she saw Teela's alarm, she added quickly, "We built a new shelter, a little ways off the clearing so it was in the shade of the trees. Come on, I'll show you."

Teela followed Locke across the clearing. The refugees had done what they could to clear the ground of branches that had fallen after the storm, but Teela suspected they were too weak with dehydration and hunger to do much, for the forest floor was still strewn with a thick layer of leaves and fallen branches. Most of what had been cleared was around the *Helios* wreck and the thin path she followed Locke down that led to a copse of trees, their overhanging branches roped and woven together to form a canopy, under which a fire was stoked and blazing. "We brought the most feverish here," Locke explained, "to keep them warm."

Teela pushed past Locke, running down the path to where her father lay, his skin raised with black welts. He was shivering, his teeth chattering, and his lids twitched as his eyes rolled behind them. She could feel the heat from his skin, warm as the fire at her back when she took his hand. "Dad," Teela whispered, but he didn't respond.

Maybe she was too late.

Teela started frantically applying the poultice to the welts on his arms, relieved as they began to instantly heal. It didn't ease her father's heavy, wet breath as much as she'd hoped it would, though, and in a fit of desperation, she tipped a drop of the Wellspring water straight from the bottle between his cracked lips.

Her father let out a wet rasp of breath.

Teela waited, holding her breath. *Please,* she thought, remembering what Evil-Lyn had told her about the water needing intention. *Please heal him. Make him well. He's all I have left in the world.*

But no matter how much intention she carried in her heart, it didn't seem to be enough. Duncan remained feverish and unconscious even as his skin cleared of the welts. Teela swallowed down the yawning pit of fear taking root in her stomach, checking on him frequently as she spent the rest of the night helping Sigrid and Locke apply the poultice to the wounded. The water had to work.

When she finally returned to the observation deck of the cargo hold several hours later, she immediately fell into a deep, dreamless sleep, boots on and sword at her side.

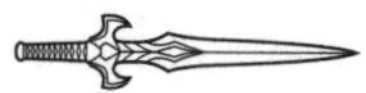

"Teela."

Teela woke with a start, so bleary and exhausted she wasn't sure what could have pulled her from her sleep. Was she still dreaming? Teela opened her eyes and found her father staring back at her, his eyes still glassy with fever but open.

Suddenly she was wide awake. "Dad?"

"Teela," Duncan said again, and Teela fell forward, arms around him. She could still feel the heat off his skin.

"You're awake."

"The welts." Duncan held up his hands in front of his face. "They're gone."

"Sigrid and I made a poultice that healed them." She scanned her father, not wanting to tell him that the water that was supposed to cure him hadn't seemed to be working. "How are you . . . feeling?"

"Not very well. But better."

Teela could see Duncan shaking slightly, a sheen of sweat glazing his forehead, and she realized the effort it must have taken for him to come find her in the ship. She jumped up and led him to his pallet. "Rest, Dad. I'll get you some water."

Teela practically flew down the steps, almost running smack into Sigrid, who was on the bridge of the *Helios*. "Sigrid, he's awake! Duncan's awake!"

"Yes," Sigrid murmured, sounding distracted. "I helped him get here. He was very eager to see you."

"What about the others?" Teela pressed. "Is everyone okay now?"

Sigrid's gaze stayed trained on the herbs she was measuring. "We made more of the salve, but it didn't work as well as the batch you made."

"I can help," Teela said quickly.

"And this isn't over yet. Many are still sick. They can't get well without enough food and water."

Teela's heart sank. She had noticed on her way back into the camp that the surrounding forest was still showing the effects of the rain, and of course there was the poisoned river. But surely the world would heal itself without intervention, magical or otherwise.

Or, she realized, maybe magical intervention was exactly what the world needed.

"Do you . . ." Teela started speaking without knowing what she was about to ask. When she fell silent, Sigrid at last looked up from her work.

"Do I what?"

Teela swallowed. "Have you ever used magic for healing?"

"Why?" Sigrid asked.

"I was just . . . I remember reading once . . . somewhere, I don't remember where . . . but that it takes intention."

Sigrid stared at her, nonplussed. "If that was all it took to heal someone, no one would ever be injured or ill. Every healer works with intention."

"Yes, but magic—"

"If only we had magic," Sigrid interrupted. "But until the sorceress returns to Grayskull, there's no point dwelling on hope." She returned to her work, but when Teela didn't move, she looked up again and sighed. "I'm sorry, I didn't mean to scold. It's been a long night. Do you need anything else, Teela?"

"Water," said Teela, "for father."

"There may be a canister left in the cargo hold," Sigrid said, "but we're running dangerously low."

When Teela was alone in the cargo hold, she unfolded the note from Evil-Lyn and read it again. She didn't want to associate with the sorceress anymore. Never seeing Evil-Lyn again would be preferable. But the sorceress may have been the only one who could help her. If the dragon's gift could be used to replenish all the supplies the camp needed—bring back their crops and restore their water supply—she would be foolish not to use it, and Evil-Lyn was the only one who could teach her how. Even just to banish the lingering effects of the sickness. When she had poured a drop of the water straight into Duncan's mouth, without some direction—more than just her willing it to heal him—it hadn't had enough of an effect. What was the point of magic water if she didn't know how to channel that magic into what she needed it to do? And once the camp was restored, if Evil-Lyn meant what she'd said about overthrowing Skeletor . . . Teela didn't dare hope that there might be an end to these years of running and barely surviving. But their failed raids on Snake Mountain had proved that they wouldn't get anywhere on their own. They needed help. They needed an ally.

She just never thought that ally would be Evil-Lyn.

Teela thought of what Evil-Lyn had told her about Skeletor's incompetence, that he was no closer to finding the Sword than he'd been when he felled Eternos. It would be crucial information for the warriors if they had to make the decision to stay or leave, but for now, it would be too complicated to explain where that intel had come from. She couldn't imagine the other refugees would be willing to trust Evil-Lyn or believe she was on their side. Teela still wasn't sure she believed it herself. The only thing she was sure of was that explaining her association with the sorceress wouldn't go over well, particularly with her father. Teela was sure that Duncan would never compromise his morals and stoop to an alliance with one of Skeletor's lieutenants, let alone one who had been the architect of so much of the destruction of their home.

And then there were the dragon's mysterious words to her before he vanished. She was supposed to seal a door. She still had no idea what that meant or how she was meant to do that, but it sounded final. Like there was a time limit on the magical effects of the water. Or at least a limited time to use them before the consequences came calling. And magic always had a price, didn't it?

She didn't know if it was a price they could pay. But she knew she had to try.

FOURTEEN

Two days later, Teela waited until the camp was asleep before she rose quietly.

Midnight at the Skytree.

She waited until Andra, on watch, had her back turned to the *Helios*, then stole out into the darkness of the Evergreen Forest. The moon was full and surprisingly bright. The trees around her looked dipped in resin, their branches pearled by the light.

Along with her sword, Teela had brought along one of the bows the hunting parties had fashioned to shoot down wyverns, and though she knew the forest well by now, she still found herself startling at every sound. She wasn't even certain where she was going; she'd just picked a path and started walking away from the camp. Evil-Lyn had simply told her she would find her, which now sounded absurd. The suspicion she was heading into a trap began to roil inside her, the hairs on the back of her neck standing up.

Something flashed on the ground at her feet, and she leaped backward, an arrow notched and bowstring pulled tight in reflex. But the forest around her was still, burbling only with the quiet sounds of twilight. Teela crept forward with the bow still extended before her, peering down at where she had seen the glimmer. There was a stone on the ground glowing bioluminescent blue. It wasn't natural—of that she was certain. The stone was enchanted.

Teela peered through the trees and spotted another soft throb of light a few yards ahead. Another glowing rock, she realized when she reached it. Then another. Leaves on the trees began to flash at her with the same eerie light, curling in around her path and urging her forward as though leading her through the forest. A cloud of insects flickered as they flew around her, their bellies flashing with light. Teela still kept the arrow notched in her bow, but lowered it to her side, the tip pointed toward the ground.

The Skytree appeared suddenly, the forest falling away and the entire clearing around it glowing softly.

"So glad you found the place."

Evil-Lyn stepped out from the shadow of the gargantuan tree. She didn't have her staff and was dressed in a simple black gown that fell to the ground in a column of fabric. Her white hair was wrapped at the base of her neck, and her face in the moonlight looked bare. As she drew closer, Teela noticed that the sorceress's eyes, usually accentuated with black, were unlined. Even her lips looked lighter than their usual dark slash.

Something about the lack of ceremony, the absence of the pageantry Teela had associated Evil-Lyn with before, made Teela relax for a moment—until she realized that the artifice was probably intended to have exactly that effect, and tightened her grip on her bow and arrow.

"So." Evil-Lyn seated herself on one of the knotted roots of the Skytree, ankles crossed delicately. "Did it work?" Her tone was that same flippant mocking as before, but Teela could hear the question and genuine curiosity beneath it.

"It worked," Teela said.

Evil-Lyn's eyes flashed with triumph. "Let me see your arm."

"It's already healed. You saw it at the palace."

"Humor me." Teela pulled back her sleeve and held up her arm for Evil-Lyn to see. Evil-Lyn crooked a finger at her. "Closer."

Teela took a tentative step forward, arm outstretched. She was surprised when Evil-Lyn seized her by the wrist and dragged her forward until their knees were pressed together. The bioluminescent light flared a bit brighter, and Evil-Lyn held Teela's wrist up to it, twisting her arm around to see it from all sides. She poked hard at the spot where the welt had been, and Teela yanked her hand away. "Stop."

"Does that hurt?"

"Only because you poked it!"

"And there were no side effects?" Evil-Lyn pressed. "You didn't have a toe fall off or something?"

"Was that ever a possibility?" Teela asked incredulously. "Is that how magic works?"

Evil-Lyn shrugged. "Sometimes. It's a tricky business."

"I'll take off my boots if you don't believe me."

"No need. I can't imagine the smell." Evil-Lyn leaned backward against the trunk, pulling her feet up onto the root so she was cradled in the curve of the Skytree.

"It didn't fix everything, though," Teela said.

"Magic rarely does."

"Some people are still sick. They're getting better, now that their welts are gone, but they need food and water and better supplies. They can't get well when they're starving. I tried . . . I tried to just give my father a dose of the water like it was medicine, thought about the water healing him and everything like you said, but it didn't do anything. Why didn't that work?"

"I told you," Evil-Lyn said. "But children never listen."

"I *was* listening," Teela protested hotly. "But I was also a little distracted by you kidnapping me."

"I did not kidnap you! I saved your life."

"After you ambushed me."

Evil-Lyn waved a hand. "Semantics bore me. Magic like that water needs intention."

"But I just told you, I thought about—"

"Not just thoughts," Evil-Lyn interrupted her. "It needs to be . . . directed. Through a proper channel. Otherwise, you're just spraying it around willy-nilly."

"Like the poultice," Teela said, and Evil-Lyn nodded.

"Yes, just like that. You add it to the recipe, and it enhances the effect. You see? Channel."

"So how do I channel it for things like food and water? I need to help my company."

"*Your* company, are they?" Evil-Lyn smirked.

"The whole of Eternia is mine because it is my home. I protect it with my life. I love it and all its people."

Evil-Lyn clapped lightly. "Engrave that on a plinth somewhere; that was pure poetry."

Teela ignored her. "There are more ways we can use the water, aren't there? Could it help give us food?" Teela asked. "Water? The supplies we need?"

"Maybe," Evil-Lyn said vaguely. "But we could find out together. If you're willing to trust me." A slow smile spread across her face. "And agree to our deal."

She could feel her toes bumping up against the invisible threshold between right and wrong. *What would Duncan do?* Teela thought, but the answer was her father wouldn't have gotten himself in this situation to begin with. He would have won the fight on the ice bridge or, if not, he wouldn't have told Evil-Lyn anything. He wouldn't take help from the most evil woman in Eternia, the one who had done more than her fair share of the work to take their home from them.

But Duncan wasn't here—just Teela and Evil-Lyn, staring at her with those dark, heavy-lidded eyes, expectantly. And Teela had to make a choice. She thought of the camp full of refugees she had left behind. She had to do *something*.

The world had always felt so black and white before Eternos fell. Good and bad, divided neatly. But now the lines were beginning to blur. Survival could only be seen in gray scale.

"I don't know if I can persuade the company to fight against Skeletor with you," Teela said finally. "But if I'm going to try, I need your word that the king and queen will be released to us. Safely. Alive."

"You really think I'm a woman of my word?"

"I don't know," Teela said. "But I'm willing to find out. For now."

Evil-Lyn tipped her head in acknowledgment of her own words parroted back to her. "Fine. You can have the king and queen. Unlike Skeletor, I don't see much point in figureheads. Any other conditions?"

"We want Eternos back," Teela said impulsively. She felt lightheaded with success. "The city."

"Absolutely not. You think I'm going to reign from the throne on Snake Mountain? Every inch of that place is either damp or ambiguously sticky. And you wouldn't believe the spiders. I'll take care of you. You won't be running from place to place like you are now. You have my word on that. Any more conditions?"

"No."

"Then go on."

Teela blew out a stream of air and stepped across the invisible line. "Will you teach me how to use the water?" she said.

Evil-Lyn clapped both hands to her chest with a sigh. "Darling, I thought you'd never ask."

FIFTEEN

Evil-Lyn must have known Teela would agree to the deal, because she'd come prepared with supplies.

Tumbled stones, ritual candles, spell jars, incense, vials, smudge sticks, black salt, pendulums, moon water, intention oils, feathers, shells—more items than Teela knew to think of as being used for magic. As Evil-Lyn laid them all out on one of the tall, flat roots of the Skytree, Teela said, "You brought so much . . . stuff."

Evil-Lyn fished a dead insect from one of the spell jars and flicked it off her fingers. "Didn't know exactly what we'd need, so

I thought it was better to be overprepared." She looked up at Teela. "What?"

"What?" Teela echoed.

"You're smirking. I don't like it. I'm usually the one who does the smirking."

"I just . . ." Teela sucked in her cheeks. "I thought you knew what you were doing."

Evil-Lyn blew out a sharp huff of breath. "If I admit I'm not entirely sure what I'm doing, it may undermine my authority."

"You know more than I do."

"Yes, well, that's not hard, tiny warrior."

"You know magic."

"Indisputably. But I've never worked much with anything like . . ." Her eyes strayed to the vial around Teela's neck. "*That.*" Evil-Lyn finished her setup and stood, the skirts of her dress swishing around her. "Believe it or not, my stroke of brilliance with the poultice back at the palace was something of an . . . educated guess."

"But what makes the water so different from any other magic you use?" Teela asked, tamping down the flare of indignance she felt that Evil-Lyn had taken an "educated guess" with Teela's limb, of all things. She pulled the bottle out from beneath her tunic and let it hang at the end of its chain around her neck. In the dark, the faint sheen of light in its depths was almost as bright as the bioluminescent rocks Evil-Lyn had laid out around them to see by.

"There is magic in everything available to those who are able to channel it. But there are items whose magic exists whether or not it is channeled, whether or not it ever interacts with a magical channel. I have not had as much experience with the latter. They're rare and hard to find and no one . . ." She trailed off.

"No one what?" Teela prompted.

"No one ever trusted me with one before," Evil-Lyn said.

"Well," Teela replied, "your name doesn't really inspire trust."

Evil-Lyn rolled her eyes, and Teela laughed, surprising herself with how easy it felt. She quickly rearranged her features into something more serious. "Is your staff a channel?" she asked.

"Yes," Evil-Lyn said, "but it's a channel for my own inherent magic. I don't know the particulars of how to maximize the magic of something outside of me and so . . . powerful. I'm more used to having to coax the power forth. It's hard to explain."

Teela picked up a soft bundle of dried herbs, smudged black and charred on one end. "So we'll run some tests—"

"I'd be careful about wild experimentation if I were you," Evil-Lyn interrupted, tapping a fingernail against the vial. "This is a finite resource. It won't stay full forever."

Teela frowned. Magic never seemed like something that could be gone. Even Grayskull hadn't been emptied of magic when the Sorceress and the Sword of Power vanished. It was just in stasis, waiting. "Can the horn be refilled?" Teela asked.

Evil-Lyn shrugged. "Sure, if you can get to the Whispering Valley."

"I made it to Darksmoke."

"Believe me, I'm not underestimating your abilities." Evil-Lyn gave her an appraising up and down. "Undertaking that journey on your own was . . . impressive."

Teela felt a small bubble of pride swell in her chest. "Thanks."

Evil-Lyn picked up several of the polished stones and rearranged them. "I didn't know any of you had it in you to do more than just move your camp around and hope Skeletor walks off a cliff."

The bubble burst, irritation a sharp pin. "You think we wouldn't fight harder if we could?" Teela asked. "It takes so much energy just to survive."

"Well, you're hobbled by poor leadership, just as I am."

Teela frowned. "What are you talking about?"

"Your sweet father—a dead man walking."

Teela's hand closed instinctively around the bundle of herbs, crushing the broken stems in her palm. "He's not."

Evil-Lyn gave her a pitying smile, which made Teela angrier. "He's a ghost, darling. A shell of who he was. That's the problem with men whose entire existence is defined by their work. Take that away and what do they have? Nothing. Who is he without his duty—a duty he failed to carry out, you'll remember. He had one job and he failed at it, and now he's finding it difficult to pick himself up and move on."

"You will not speak this way about my father," Teela snapped, trying to snuff the small flame of doubt that had ignited in her chest: his drunkenness on the way home from the failed rescue mission, his hesitation over the three warriors' graves. Teela hadn't wanted to believe it. She had told herself anyone would suffer beneath the weight her father carried. Even the strongest stones would erode over time, under constant pressure. But she had thought he was holding up. And if he wasn't, that was what Teela was for. She could help buoy him up where he needed it.

Evil-Lyn rolled her eyes. "Don't get your tunic in a twist. You can tell me it's not true, but I'm an objective witness. Your group needs new leadership. As do the forces assembled at Snake Mountain. Which is where you and I come in."

"I'm not . . . I don't want to be a leader," Teela said, shaking her head.

"Yes," Evil-Lyn said. "That's probably the thing that makes you uniquely qualified for it. Now." She clapped her hands together and looked down at her spread of magical talismans. "What's your familiarity with the arcane language? Ancient runes? None at all, I assume?"

"I've heard of them."

"In history class?"

"In . . . novels."

Evil-Lyn nodded. "Better than nothing, I suppose. So, runes are used to channel magical purpose. Like, say, if you have a magical vial of water—instead of just pouring it randomly on things and hoping it has the desired effect. It's like what I told you about intention—adding the water to the poultice gave it an intention. A purpose. That is, if you're an accomplished sorceress like me."

"Brag," Teela muttered.

Evil-Lyn ignored her. "You can, with time and training and many years of study, learn to create that intention with only your thoughts. But since we don't have time—and you don't have the skills—you can use runes to channel an already existing magical source. Runes are just a clearer, easier way to let magic know what you want it to do. It improves your success rate."

"Then I need to learn them."

Evil-Lyn pointed to Teela, her eyes flashing. "She's quick! Unfortunately, there are thousands of different characters."

"Then I need to learn . . . some of them."

Evil-Lyn selected several of the stones from the pile, and Teela noticed they were each etched with a different symbol. "The more specific the rune, the more specific the instruction given to the magic. It's the difference between telling a seed to grow and to grow to exactly seven feet tall and produce three pods."

"I just need them to grow."

"Well then." Evil-Lyn crouched in the dirt and dug out a small crater with her fingers. She glanced around the roots of the Skytree until she found what she was looking for and retrieved a fallen branch with a bristle cone still clinging to the end, still small and green and the size of her thumb. She snapped the cone from the end of the stick, then placed it inside the hole she had dug and covered it with soft earth. "If you want something to grow, you use this." She selected a stone from her collection and placed it on top of the earth. Engraved on the flat top were three vertical lines stacked on top of one another. "Think you can remember that?"

"Will there be a test at the end of class?"

"Yes, but I don't want you to just study for the test. Now, the water." Evil-Lyn held out her hand for the bottle of Wellspring water. Teela hesitated, her instincts telling her she should not be passing over her most precious, finite resource to the right hand of her enemy. Evil-Lyn could take it and vanish. She could smash it. She could empty the whole thing into the ground. Maybe the rune didn't mean *grow* at all—maybe this was all a ploy to summon some sleeping demon that would eat the refugee camp whole.

But Evil-Lyn was here. If she'd wanted the water, she would have ripped it from Teela's throat, then pushed her off the bridge back at Darksmoke. Surely, they wouldn't have come this far.

Teela lifted the chain over her head and passed the vial to Evil-Lyn. The sorceress tipped the bottle slowly until a single drop fell on top of the rune stone. Instead of beading and sliding off into the soil, the water spread, running the length of the rune as if it were a streambed until every crevice was filled. The rune pulsed softly with light, then was sucked into the stone, leaving its surface polished and dry as before.

Teela and Evil-Lyn both stared at it.

"How long does it take?" Teela asked.

"No clue," Evil-Lyn replied.

Teela looked sideways at her. "I thought you knew everything."

"I do. You just witnessed the rare phenomenon of me admitting ignorance."

"Lucky me."

Evil-Lyn's mouth curled. "You know, you're not as much of a drip as I thought you'd be."

"What?" Teela laughed before she could stop herself. "Why did you think I was a drip?"

"All the warriors of Eternos I've ever met are such bores. They drill the sense of humor out of you."

"Not everyone," Teela protested.

"Like who? Your father? He's always been humorless. He didn't even find it funny when I turned him into a toad. Which was objectively hilarious."

Teela wanted to argue, to tell Evil-Lyn about the yearslong cabbage wars between her father and Prince Adam, hiding them in each other's beds for reasons long ago forgotten. Or the time he had convinced Teela the shells they found on the shores of Harmony Beach spoke to him and he would hold them up to his ear and listen very sincerely, insisting they were just shy when Teela picked them up and heard nothing. But that version of her father felt like someone she had known so long ago. She could hardly recall the sound of his laughter.

Evil-Lyn swept her white hair over her shoulder, combing her fingers through the ends. "Honestly, the sense of humor was a big factor in why I joined Skeletor to begin with. He's an imbecile, but at least he knows how to crack a joke."

"You never would have fought for Eternos," Teela said.

"How do you know?"

Teela gave her a pointed look. "Like I said earlier—*Evil*-Lyn."

Evil-Lyn's mouth curled. "Yes, well, I added the 'Evil' bit myself. I could have picked something else."

"Like 'Good-Lyn'?"

"Doesn't roll off the tongue."

"'Benevolent-Lyn.' 'Hero-Lyn.'"

Evil-Lyn rolled her eyes. "Don't make me sick."

"Look!" Teela gasped as a small green bud burst from the soil just beside the rune rock. She watched, heart racing, as the vine began to creep toward the sky, a whole growing season happening at top speed. Leaves sprang from the stalk, peeling open and fanning their fronds. Shoots turned to vines, which sprouted leaves of their own. Trembling buds turning into fronds the size of Teela's hand in seconds. Pink blossoms budded, then opened, then just as quickly wilted and fell, leaving behind swollen nubs that grew into a bulbous yellow fruit, skin mirrored and shining in the moonlight.

"Well," Evil-Lyn said after a moment.

Teela glanced sideways at her. Evil-Lyn was staring at the stalk, her mouth a little open and her eyes wide. She looked as human—as real—as Teela had ever seen her, her usual mask of cocky apathy replaced by sincere wonder. "I didn't think anything could impress you," Teela remarked.

"You wouldn't think so. But sometimes magic is just . . . cool." Evil-Lyn retrieved a knife from her belt and sliced the yellow pod from the vine, then sliced it open. The fruit inside was white as moonlight, studded with black seeds. Juice ran down her wrist as she cut off a piece for herself, then another, which she handed to Teela. "Well. Cheers, darling."

Teela placed the fruit on her tongue. The flavor exploded across her senses, sweet as sugar, the delicate pulp so tender it almost felt as though it was dissolving in her mouth. The seeds popped in her mouth, tart and juicy. The fruit sated her thirst for the first time in what felt like ages.

She swallowed, glancing at Evil-Lyn, wondering if she, too, was overwhelmed by the sweetness, but Evil-Lyn was still holding her slice, watching Teela.

"It's good," Teela said.

"I'm sure," Evil-Lyn said.

Teela swallowed, the fruit suddenly sticking in her throat. "Did you . . . is it poisoned?"

Evil-Lyn threw back her head and laughed. "Oh, please. Darling, if I wanted you dead, I'd have killed you long ago." Evil-Lyn held the fruit up to examine it in the light of one of her glowing stones. "But magic is unpredictable. I just wanted to make sure you didn't drop dead before I tried it."

Of course Evil-Lyn would offer up Teela as sacrifice before she'd risk endangering herself. But Teela was too exulted to be mad about that as she looked down in awe at the piece of yellow rind in her hand. It actually felt like food, none of the thin broths or tacky seeds they had eaten since the rain. Even the supplies before then—the wyvern jerky and chewy bread—had never really made her feel sated.

Teela licked the juices from her fingers. Three more of the bulbous fruits had appeared on the vine, and it took all her willpower not to tear into another. "What else can the runes be used for?"

"Start with that. Do you want to try it?" Teela held out her hand for the rune stone, but Evil-Lyn slipped it back into the pouch. "No, darling, these are *mine*. You can draw the rune yourself in the soil."

"So what does the stone do?" Teela asked.

"Reference images. When the runes are trickier, it's important to make sure you draw them just right. But I'm sure you can handle three lines." Evil-Lyn pointed her toe at the ground. "You try it."

Evil-Lyn cut another cone off the tree branch, and Teela copied what Evil-Lyn had done, burying it in a shallow trough in the soil before drawing three vertical lines over the dirt. Evil-Lyn passed her the vial, and Teela carefully tipped a drop of water onto the ground. The water ran along the lines of the rune before being sucked up, leaving the ground dry.

This time, the sprout burst from the ground almost at once, and Teela and Evil-Lyn both leaped backward out of its way. Teela tripped over one of the Skytree roots and fell hard on her backside. She stared up as the tree kept growing, twice the size of the previous one and producing a dozen fat fruits.

"Well," Evil-Lyn said, standing on her toes to pick one of the fruits. "Who needs stones?"

She tossed the fruit to Teela, who caught it. The smell from the skin was like the earth after rain.

“Take the fruits back to your camp,” Evil-Lyn said, turning to begin packing up the supplies she had spread across the root of the Skytree. “Then we’ll meet back here in a week, and I’ll teach you more.”

“A week?” Teela said. “Why not sooner?”

Evil-Lyn glanced over her shoulder at Teela. “My whole life doesn’t revolve around teaching you magic, you know.”

“Then what does it revolve around?”

“Well,” Evil-Lyn said, and gave Teela that pointed grin that, Teela was shocked to discover, didn’t frighten her as much as it had just a few days ago when she saw it from across the bridge at Darksmoke. “Right now, I’m neck-deep in planning an assassination.” Evil-Lyn wiggled her fingers at Teela. “Ta-ta, darling,” she said, then vanished.

SIXTEEN

Teela was prepared for questions when she returned to camp in the morning, her arms full of the sweet yellow fruit. She had rehearsed answers on the way as to what it was and how she'd found it and was it safe to eat and how had they not encountered it before when they had combed the forest for food sources?

She'd spent the walk back to the camp concocting a thin but technically plausible story about happening on a grove of fruit trees they'd somehow missed until now. Not the most airtight alibi, but she knew that, if she told the truth, there were members of the camp who would immediately distrust any help given them by one of Skeletor's men, and their recovery would be stalled before it had even begun. She needed them to see the benefits of the water without knowing what they were benefiting from. Eventually, she'd reveal the source of their good fortune, after they had already become accustomed to the effects of the water and knew it was safe and necessary. Only then would she tell them where it had come from and who had taught her to use it and float the idea of aiding said individual in a coup against Skeletor.

Effect then cause, that was the way to soften the blow. Otherwise, their trust might be shattered before Evil-Lyn had a chance to present her plan to ally the two enemies.

The company was so excited to see food—not just food, but sweet, juicy, and delicious fruit—that most of the questions Teela had anticipated went unasked, and when they came up, they were delivered between giant mouthfuls of pulp, Teela's answers less important than the sudden bounty.

"Where did you find these?" Malcolm was the first to ask, his beard studded with the white pulp of the fruit.

Teela shrugged. "I was walking last night looking for water, and I got lost. I found this clearing with fruit trees, and they were all covered in these pods. I took as many as I could carry."

Krass tore off a huge bite as if he were tearing meat off a carcass with his teeth. "Do you think you can find it again?"

Locke spit a mouthful of seeds into her hand, scrubbing the pulp off with her nail. "What are they? I've never tasted anything like it."

"Can we plant them?" Malcolm asked, picking one of the seeds from his teeth. "Do you think they'll grow?"

"We can try," Sigrid said. "Do you remember if they were in shade or shadow?" she asked Teela. "Or how damp the soil was?"

Teela opened her mouth to answer, but Locke spoke before she could. "Trees will take time to grow from seed."

"That was the strangest part." Teela swallowed. Here was possibly the trickiest of the lies she had been practicing—though there had been no way to rehearse looking Locke dead in the eye while she delivered it. "Every time I picked one of the pods, another grew back right away. I even pulled a few leaves off just to see, and those grew back, too. I didn't try planting them anew, though—maybe they'll also grow fast."

Locke's granite gaze felt heavy on her shoulders. Teela swallowed. If Locke found out that their survival now hinged on an alliance with an evil sorceress, Teela suspected she would spin it into another reason they should leave Eternia—there was nothing left for them except alliances with enemies. If there was anyone Teela had to keep the water from for now, it was her.

"I've never heard of any fruit tree like that," Locke finally said, each word sounding carefully selected as berries plucked off a vine.

But before Teela could muster a reply, Malcolm cut in. "Don't question it. We're overdue for some good luck." He picked up another piece of the fruit and sucked the pulp from the rind in one bite. "The forest has finally given us something we can use. Do you think you can find your way back to where the trees were and harvest more?" he asked Teela.

"I don't think so," Teela said. "It was so dark, and I was so lost. But let's plant these seeds first and see if they grow."

"That doesn't seem—" Locke said, but Krass cut her off.

"I'll clear some land."

"There's already a tilled corner of the garden you can use," Andra said. "I pulled up the dead wheat and haven't planted anything else yet."

Teela held out her hand, and Locke tipped the seeds she had scrubbed clean into them.

"We should distribute the rest," Sigrid said. "Make sure everyone gets some. I might try and boil some down for those who are still too sick to have much of an appetite. It will be easier to keep down."

"I'm going to take some to my father," Teela said, and Sigrid nodded.

As Teela stood, a pod of fruit tucked under one arm, Locke stood up, too. "I'll come with you. I have work to do on the ship."

"How are the repairs going?" Teela asked as they started across the camp together toward the *Helios*, trying to sound casual and not like she was keeping her fingers crossed for a report of failure.

"Better than you probably hope," Locke said.

"Can I see what you've done so far?" Teela asked.

Locke raised an eyebrow. "You really want to?"

"I promise I won't stick a wrench in the control panel on purpose."

Locke laughed. "Come on, then."

Teela held up the pod of fruit. "Let me just put this by my dad, in case he wakes up."

Teela left the fruit next to Duncan's sleeping form, then returned to the cockpit of the *Helios,* which was strewn with wires and circuit boards. Locke had pulled apart the underside, and wires dangled in long threads from under it. She had cleaned an emergency tool kit they had found on board when they first stumbled upon the wreck and laid the tools across the pilot's seat.

Teela stood in the doorway as Locke slid under the control panel, fiddling with the loose wires. "I haven't had much time, with . . . you know, everything. And I know it doesn't look like progress."

"You've done a great job taking it apart," Teela said.

Locke laughed. "I was always better at that first bit. So much easier to take things apart." She patted the floor beside her, and Teela lay down, staring up at the underside of the control panel as Locke pointed out the wires she was fiddling with. "These here are what connects the engine to the control panels. Something's chewed through them, but I think that some of the other couplers that control things like the cargo bay doors might be able to be repurposed. The anodes will have to be inverted, and if the solar panels won't hold the charge, we might be out of luck, but here."

She detached one of the wires and held it toward Teela. Teela unhooked the wire Locke indicated and touched their raw ends together. A light flashed bright red on the control panel overhead, and one of the dials began to spin.

Teela let out a surprised laugh, forgetting for a moment that she was rooting against the success of the ship running again. Locke grinned back at her. "Pretty cool, right?"

"Once you get it running," Teela said, "we can use it to harvest supplies outside the forest. Or trade with nearby villages. We won't be so dependent on what we can hunt and forage just from the forest."

Locke looked sideways at Teela. "You know that's not what we're planning to use it for."

"I'm just saying." Teela stared up at the mess of wires. "There might be other uses besides leaving Eternia."

"So we trade and get supplies from farther afield," Locke said. "How long can we just keep surviving?"

"How long have you been thinking about leaving?" Teela asked her.

"Honestly." Locke rubbed sweat from her brow with the back of her wrist. "Since we found the ship."

Teela thought back to the day they had found the clearing with the downed *Helios*, the way Locke had advocated almost manically for them to stay here, promising the ship could provide at least some measure of shelter. They could start with a place to stay instead of all sleeping out in the open, waiting to be found in the time it took them to build one.

"That's why you were so keen to settle here," Teela muttered. She climbed out from under the control panel and pulled herself up into the copilot's seat, legs crossed under her.

"Not the only reason." Locke pulled herself up after Teela. She slid one of the tools toward her with the toe of her boot. When she noticed Teela was still staring at her, she sighed. "Look, it was so incredibly brave and incredibly stupid of you to go to Darksmoke. And, clearly, you're not just a fine warrior but a fine negotiator, if you were able to get the dragon to gift the antidote to you. You saved the camp, Teela. Nothing changes that, and I hope you know how grateful and proud everyone is."

"I feel like there's a *but* coming."

Locke's mouth quirked. "*But* it's going to take more than that cure to save us."

"We were doing fine—" Teela started, but Locke interrupted her.

"Fine? We haven't been fine since Eternos fell. When was the last time any of us had enough to eat? Or didn't have to keep watch for an attack? We've been driven out of all our previous camps. Are we meant to just stay on the run forever? We are the last warriors of Eternos and we're wasting away. As we are now, we have no chance of rescuing the king and queen, to say nothing of making a stand against Snake Mountain. Skeletor doesn't have to find the Sword of Power to defeat us—but he will. And what will we do then?"

Teela opened her mouth to argue, though she wasn't exactly sure how she was going to refute any of these sensible, fact-based points, but they were interrupted when behind her someone said, "Teela."

Both Teela and Locke turned to the door of the cockpit. Duncan stood there, the blanket from his sleeping pallet thrown over his shoulders, the fruit Teela had left by his bedside in one hand. His skin still had a clammy, feverish sheen to it, and Teela thought she could see the shadows of where the welts had healed. But he was up, and he looked tired in the same way he had looked tired for years, rather than the bone-deep exhaustion of illness. "I thought I heard your voice."

"You're up," Teela said. She motioned toward the yellow fruit in his hand. "Try it, Dad. I brought some back to camp this morning. Everyone has been eating it."

Duncan turned the fruit over in his hand, running his thumb over the skin. "Where did you find this?"

"In the forest," Teela said. "It just . . . appeared overnight."

Duncan gave her a look, and Teela quickly cast around for some distraction. The others might not be as attuned to the fact that she was lying, but she was sure Duncan would be able to tell right away. Her father had always had a knack for being able to tell when the cadets were lying—about running all their laps, or finishing their reading, or who had glued another student's shoes to the changing room floor. Teela wasn't sure if her father had a particularly keen sense with her, or if she just crumpled under his gaze faster than the others.

"How strange," Duncan said, his tone inscrutable, but then he took a bite. His eyes widened.

"It's good, isn't it?" Teela prompted. "It reminds me of the sweets you used to bring Adam and me back from Targa. Do you remember? When you went with the king on the diplomatic mission? And you were caught in that storm on your way home, so they were all coated in sand, but we still ate them all?"

"I remember," Duncan said. He took another bite, heartier than the first, then looked around the cockpit at the mess of strewn wires and Locke sitting cross-legged on the floor. "What are you doing with the ship?"

"I thought maybe I could get her to run," Locke said.

"So we could get supplies from outside the forest," Teela said, and Locke shot her a look.

"Or," Locke said, "maybe so we could leave Eternia. See if any of the nearby worlds will take us as refugees."

Teela glanced at Duncan, prepared for him to laugh at this or tell her off. Finally, finally someone would speak up against this insane idea and call it what it was. It wouldn't just be Teela fighting for them to stay.

But Duncan's face remained impassive. "Have you made any progress?"

"Some," Locke replied. She, too, looked tense, braced for a scolding, though it didn't seem to be coming. "It's an old ship."

"Teela can help you," Duncan said, "if you need it."

"I . . . what?" Teela stared at him, unable to believe what she was hearing.

"Why not?" Duncan said. "It looks like a big job."

"I don't . . ." Teela looked from Duncan to Locke. ". . . know anything about mechanics."

"Then you can learn." Duncan put a hand on her shoulder as he turned again to the cockpit ladder. "I'm going back to bed. I'm still not feeling quite . . . myself."

"Do you need any—" Teela started, but Duncan waved her away.

"I'm fine. Stay here and help Locke. And thank you for the fruit."

As he climbed back down the ladder, Teela looked to Locke. She expected her to look triumphant at Duncan's mild reaction to the news she was trying to find a way to leave the planet, but she looked as surprised as Teela felt.

"You don't have to help," Locke said quickly. She dipped her head, staring down at her hands. Her nail beds were stained with grease.

"I . . ." Teela looked from Locke to where Duncan was retreating down the *Helios* bridge. "I'll be right back."

Teela scrambled down the cockpit ladder after her father, following him across the bridge and up the other ladder to the observation deck and hauling herself up after him. "Dad. What Locke was saying about leaving Eternia . . . you can't think that's a good idea."

Duncan sat down heavily on his sleeping pallet with a deep sigh. "It's something we should discuss."

Teela stared at him. She felt as if her father had been replaced by an impostor, a version of him that looked and moved and sounded real, but spouted nonsense her real father would never say. The king's man-at-arms would never give up on Eternia. "What about the king and queen?" Teela asked. "We have to rescue them. We have to fight Skeletor and retake the city. You can't . . . we can't just leave. That's like giving up."

"Is it?" Duncan asked lightly. "It sounds to me like doing what has to be done to survive." Teela started to argue, but Duncan held up a hand. "We can talk about this later. And with the rest of the company."

"But what about—"

"Teela," he said, a creeping note of warning in his voice, and she fell silent. Duncan ran a hand over his face. "I'm sorry. I'm still so tired."

"Do you need me to get you anything?"

"I just need to rest." He lay down on his back, staring up at the ceiling.

Teela hesitated, then lay beside him. He wrapped an arm around her, and she leaned her head on his shoulder. "I'm glad you're okay," she said quietly. It felt like an impossibly small thing to say, considering how deep she felt the relief, like a current through her bones.

Duncan touched his chin to the top of her head but didn't say anything.

"Isn't this the part," Teela said, "where you tell me everything's going to be okay?"

She felt the quiet laugh in Duncan's chest more than she heard it. "It may not be," he said. "But we'll get through it together."

SEVENTEEN

Teela helped Sigrid and Andra plant the seeds in the patch of earth Andra had prepared for wheat. Teela waited until the cover of darkness before she stole back on her own to draw the rune Evil-Lyn had taught her. If anyone saw the rune, Teela would have to explain where she had learned it.

After her conversation with Locke in the *Helios*'s cockpit, Teela was more motivated to keep the truth of the water from the others for as long as she could, and especially from Locke—if she found out the truth, she might want to use the water to try to fix the ship. Teela didn't know if that was possible—or what rune would be needed to give life to the

Helios—or if one even existed—but she wasn't going to waste her limited supply to find out either way. The neck of the bottle was already empty, leaving only the round belly full of water. She had to use it carefully.

She followed Evil-Lyn's instructions—at the corner of the tilled earth, she drew the three vertical lines and let a drop of water pool in its grooves. She waited, but nothing happened. *Grow*, she thought, remembering Evil-Lyn's admonition that the water needed intention. Her heart thrummed with panic. Did she need more runes? One for every seed? Or every row? How much magic water was needed to supply a whole bed of crops?

She drew a copy of the rune at each corner of the patch to be safe and dribbled in the water—a little more than she had with Evil-Lyn. As she finished the last, she noticed small green shoots beginning to push their way through the soil, leaves breaking from the stems and uncurling in the moonlight.

Teela let out a stream of air she hadn't known she'd been holding in. She'd been worried she wouldn't be able to do it without Evil-Lyn—or that, somehow, the sorceress had tricked her. It still felt dangerous to trust Evil-Lyn, but if they were going to continue their alliance, Teela needed to start. The sorceress had given Teela no reason to doubt her. And if they were going to stand together against Skeletor—and if it was going to be Teela presenting her to the camp as an ally—she had to make sure her trust was ironclad. She owed it to herself, and the refugees—and, she thought, even to Evil-Lyn. She had proved herself reliable so far. Perhaps people—even bad ones—could change.

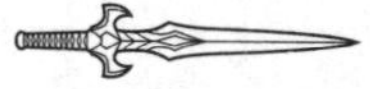

The next morning, Teela was awakened by shouts in the camp. She sprang out of bed, reaching for the knife she kept under her pillow. On his pallet on the opposite side of the ship's observation deck, Duncan was already sitting up, but he held up a hand to Teela to still her rushed movements. He was peering out the window and down onto the camp, and beckoned Teela over to join him. As she crossed the deck, Teela realized the shouts weren't warnings of danger, but joy. The sound was foreign and unfamiliar after so long.

Teela peered out the window next to Duncan and saw that during the night the camp had been almost overtaken with the wild, luscious vines spilling over the edges of their tilled patch, each stem bursting with pods of ripe fruit.

Teela released a breath. "It worked."

Duncan looked sideways at her. "What worked?"

"Uh . . . nature," Teela said quickly. "I was worried that maybe it was a fluke in the forest, or we planted it wrong, or it wouldn't . . ." She trailed off. Duncan was staring at her—not suspiciously, but with something searching in his gaze that made her want to tell him everything. But not yet.

"Come on!" She punched him lightly on the arm, then sprang to her feet, retrieving her boots from where she had kicked them off the night before. "I'm starving."

"You go," Duncan said.

Teela turned back to him as she fastened her cloak. "Aren't you coming?"

"I need to go to the medical tent."

"Do you need me to bring you something?" Teela asked. "Or I can have Sigrid come to you?"

But Duncan shook his head. "I was going to see if she needed any help."

Teela hesitated. "But . . . you're still sick."

"So are many others," Duncan said. "I'm well enough to help."

"Come on, Dad," Teela said. "Come have something to eat first."

Duncan smiled at her as he retrieved his own boots from the end of his pallet. "I'd say save some for me," he said, "but I don't think there's any risk of us running out."

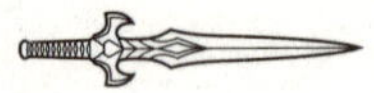

Flowering vines crept across the forest floor, twisting through the whole clearing. The stalks had even grown up and around the fuselage of the *Helios*, woven their way through the branches assembled into lean-tos and up the trunks of the trees. Every few seconds, there was a plop as a fat yellow fruit fell from somewhere on the vine to the ground.

Might have overdone it with the runes and the water, Teela thought as she picked her way through the vines.

"Teela!" Malcolm appeared suddenly beside her and crushed her into a hug so tight he lifted her off her feet.

She laughed. "I can't believe they grew!"

"More than that. Look!" He led her over to the patch of crops, and Teela realized that not only had the strange, sweet fruit grown overnight, but the crops that had been destroyed by the rain had begun to grow back in abundance, stalks of wheat and barley already knee-high and vivid green, healthier than they had ever been.

"That's . . . how?" she said, not having to fake the stunned note in her voice.

"Because of you!"

Teela felt a flare of panic in her chest as she turned to Malcolm. Did he know? Did everyone know?

But then he clarified, "You found the fruit!"

"Oh, right." She tried to laugh again. *If you feel this guilty*, her father's voice said in her head, *it probably means you shouldn't be doing it.*

Malcolm ruffled her hair with his massive fist, nearly pushing her over. "Take the credit. You've saved us twice now. Now here." He picked one of the pods and ripped it in half, then handed it to Teela. "Eat!"

Teela tore into the fruit, letting the juice drip down her chin. It was so fresh and sweet she groaned aloud.

Andra appeared suddenly at Teela's shoulder, hands shining and sticky with juice. She held them a distance out from her sides to avoid the mess. "Do we need to pick them?" she asked.

"How long do they last on the vine?" Malcolm added.

"I don't know," Teela said. "But there's got to be a way to preserve them." She looked around, noticing that Malcolm, Andra, and several other members of the camp nearby seemed to be looking at her, waiting. She swallowed, unsure what they were all staring at her for, but sure either she had said something incriminating that revealed her allegiance with Evil-Lyn or they had all just suddenly realized how weird this was and almost definitely not just a mixture of nature and luck.

But then Andra prompted, “Teela. What should we do?”

“Oh. Um.” They were looking to her for *instructions.*

She almost told them all to wait here while she went and got her father—he’d know what to do next. But this was her responsibility. She looked around at the mess of vines, then said, “We need to cut back some of the vines to keep the paths clear and so the weight doesn’t break the shelters we’ve built. Let’s get a fire going and boil them down to preserves, something that won’t rot and that we can use to flavor other things.”

“Should we pick it all?” Andra said.

“No,” Teela replied, “let’s leave some on the vine to see how long they last before they rot. That way we can work out a schedule. And we need someone seeing to the other crops as well and making sure they don’t get choked out.”

“All right!” Malcolm clapped his hands together, then pointed to Krass and the pair of refugees standing beside him. “You three with me. We’ll start the harvest.”

“I’ll get a fire going,” Andra offered.

“I can start cutting back the vines,” Teela said. “Whoever wants to join me, grab any blades you have.”

As the group began to break up, Teela noticed Locke standing at the edge of the garden. She had a piece of uneaten fruit in one hand, and the other was pushing back the thick vines, peering down at the soil. Teela felt her pulse spike.

Locke had seen the runes. She knew this wasn't just naturally occurring good luck. She would demand to know where Teela had learned about the runes and what had happened at Darksmoke. What exactly the nature of the magical cure was that she had brought back to the camp. Who had taught her what it was and how to use it.

But then Locke straightened up, letting the leaves fall back over the soil. "I think shovels will work as well," she called to Teela. "The stalks are thick, but they break easily. We should take some of the fruits to Sigrid, for those who are still sick."

"Do you want to handle that?" Teela asked.

"Are you giving me orders?" Locke asked. Teela suddenly felt sheepish. What authority did she have? None that wasn't rooted in deceit. But then Locke grinned at her. She still didn't seem to be entirely teasing, but she gave Teela a mock salute and said, "Aye, aye, Commander."

Teela rolled her eyes and tried to pretend it didn't feel like Locke was the only one who thought Teela had no idea what she was doing.

EIGHTEEN

The vines fruited abundantly for two days, then began to brown and curl back on themselves. The wheat's growth slowed, and Teela wondered if she should risk another drop of water in the runes to revive them—or if that would even work. Maybe magic salted the earth.

But the yellow fruit had raised the company's morale—and filled their bellies for the first time in weeks. The camp felt like it was coming back to life. The air smelled like smoke and honey as they boiled the fruit down over the fire into a paste, and the work was accompanied by happy chatter and even singing.

Andra was the first to call the yellow fruit "lucky fruit," and the name stuck. They used the lucky fruit to flavor their remaining supply of mushrooms. Andra dried the skin and used it to make crunchy chips that sated with only a few bites, and they filled every available jar, pot, and bowl with the boiled-down preserves, sweet and filling and full of enough water that their thirst began to abate with the hunger. They dug another garden bed and sprinkled the seeds strained from the paste. Teela didn't use the Wellspring water on them at first, wondering if they'd grow prolifically on their own, but a few days later, when the sprouts finally broke through the thick soil looking anemic and fragile, she used her turn on watch to place a rune in the center of the patch and water it. The next morning, the lucky fruit vines were waist-high, flowers bursting along them. Teela thought about stamping out the rune in the dirt in case someone spotted it but wasn't sure whether that could counteract the effect of the water.

There was one person who would know the answer, and Teela asked her several nights later when they met once again at the Skytree.

"Why would you want to erase the runes?" Evil-Lyn asked. It was a moonless night, and Evil-Lyn had conjured an orb of light to illuminate the clearing where they worked. It hung above them, casting an eerie blue sheen over the world, and in the light, Teela noticed that the sorceress looked tired. Her eyes were shadowed, and her skin had lost some of the lustrous shine that always made her look dusted in sparkling sand.

Teela hesitated, debating how to answer, but Evil-Lyn must have sensed the truth in her silence. "Aha. Is there something wrong with your company knowing you're getting magic advice from their mortal enemy?"

"I . . ." Had she actually managed to offend the impenetrable sorceress?

But then Evil-Lyn's mouth quirked into a smile. "Kidding. Don't worry, you're not the first person who hasn't wanted to have to explain me to their parents. To be honest, I'm not sure. If I work with runes, it's usually through the stones, and you can pack those up as soon as you're done, but you don't erase the rune itself. We can do some experiments tonight and find out. Ah, a bonding opportunity! Soon I'll be thinking of you as the daughter I never wanted."

Evil-Lyn sat back against one of the tree roots. Teela joined her, the shifting weight in her cloak reminding her suddenly. "I brought you something." From under her cloak, Teela withdrew a small flask filled with the lucky fruit paste and handed it to Evil-Lyn.

Evil-Lyn took the flask as if she were being handed a dead rat by the tail. "Charming." She uncapped the flask and sniffed it. Her forehead wrinkled. "What exactly am I meant to do with this . . . goo?"

"It's from the fruit," Teela said.

"Well, that's a relief. I was a little worried you handed me a jar of wyvern pee."

Teela let out a bark of surprised laughter. "We've been eating it for days. It's saved us."

"Thrilled to hear it. The physical evidence wasn't really necessary." She tried to hand the flask back to Teela, but Teela shook her head.

"It's for you."

Evil-Lyn scoffed. "Surely you need it more than me."

"Probably, but I want you to have it. I'm sure it's better than whatever Skeletor is serving you."

"Oh. Thank you." Evil-Lyn carefully recapped the flask, then stared at it for a moment before tucking it into her dress. "The food *is* terrible at Snake Mountain. No one knows how to cook anything without burning it." She raised a sculpted eyebrow at Teela. "So, it seems the water is definitely doing its job."

Teela nodded. "But what other runes can you teach me? We need meat. Water. Better shelter from the elements. We need our supplies repaired—we've been using the same tools for years, only what we could salvage from Eternos, and they're mostly broken and battered. Do you think the water will work on nonorganic material?"

The sorceress waved at Teela to pause her monologue. "So many demands! I'm already exhausted." Evil-Lyn closed her eyes, pressing her elegant fingers to her temples. She was wearing silk gloves the color of twilight. She was putting on a theatrical show, but Teela could hear a real note of weariness in her voice.

"Has something happened?" Teela asked.

Evil-Lyn's eyes snapped open. "What?"

"You look tired."

Evil-Lyn snorted. "The one day a girl doesn't wear makeup."

"I was just asking," Teela said. "You don't have to tell me."

Silence for a moment. Evil-Lyn took a long breath in through her nose, then let it out in a slow hiss through her teeth. Then, without looking at Teela, she said, "A double life is exhausting. And my dear liege is starting to catch on to something. He's been trying to get it out of me."

"What do you mean?" Teela asked.

Evil-Lyn pursed her lips, and Teela could almost feel her considering whether it was wise to tell her more. Then she pulled off one of her gloves with her teeth. Teela gasped. Evil-Lyn's fingers were bruised and crooked, like they had been smashed.

"He's torturing you."

"No, no, that makes it sound fun. He's testing me."

"Use the water."

"What?"

"Use the water—it will heal you."

"No thank you." Evil-Lyn slid her glove back on, wincing slightly as her fingers bent. "I prefer to deal with my problems without magical intervention."

"Please." Teela unhooked the vial from her neck and extended it to Evil-Lyn. "Use it."

"That," Evil-Lyn said, "would be a waste of your precious resource."

"You're not a waste."

In the darkness, Evil-Lyn's gaze was inscrutable. "It's yours," she said. "And I will not be beholden to you."

“You wouldn’t be beholden—”

“We have a deal. I help you make your sad, little warriors strong again, and you bring them to fight Skeletor for me. I’m not going to owe you anything,” Evil-Lyn said, her tone firm enough that Teela knew the conversation was over. “Not you, not anyone.”

Teela set the water on the root between them. The light from the orb over their heads made the liquid look shot through with lightning. “I’m sorry he treats you that way,” Teela said quietly.

“I knew what I signed up for.” Evil-Lyn sighed. “When you pledge yourself to a lunatic, you’d be a fool to think you’ll be immune to his cruelty.”

“Why did you ever join him to begin with?” Teela asked.

“Oh, I can hardly recall anymore. Youthful rebellion—did your father ever tell you not to date someone and that only made you want to date him harder?”

“Not a lot of opportunities to date, currently.”

“Metaphorical dating. Please. I have standards.” She wrapped her hair around her hand, then let it unfurl around her shoulders. “And when you aren’t getting anywhere on your own, you hitch your wagon indiscriminately to the most insane star. My father was a sorcerer, too. I lived in his shadow, and he liked it that way. He made sure I never knew how to be my own person, thinking I’d always be reliant on him and that way he could control me. An alliance with Skeletor freed me of my father—and gave me a chance to be more powerful than he ever was.”

They sat in silence for a moment. Teela realized that the forest around them sounded alive again, for the first time since the acidic rain. She could hear the low thrum of insects, the call of wyverns from the canopy, the rustling of branches as water dripped from the leaves. It seemed nature was beginning to heal itself, all on its own.

Teela was about to say something—offer some sort of solidarity or sympathy or even a follow-up question—when Evil-Lyn grinned. "How's that for a compelling backstory? I've been working on it for a while. What do you think, is it too—" she wiggled her fingers "—something?"

Teela rolled her eyes. "Fine. Lie to me." Teela knew that within every lie was at least a kernel of truth. She studied the sorceress for a moment. "You don't have to stay with him, you know," Teela said.

"I'm taking him down from the inside, remember?"

"I mean, right now. You don't have to stay and fight—you could just go. I would help you."

"And go where? Back to camp with you?" Evil-Lyn snorted. "I'm sure your friends would welcome my defection with swords."

"They'd come around," Teela protested. "Or you could go off on your own. You're powerful and smart. You'd be fine."

Evil-Lyn shook her head. "No, darling, I'm not made to be alone. I'd never survive it. Now." She stood suddenly and stretched her arms over her head before shaking out her hands. "Stop therapizing me. We have runes to study."

NINETEEN

No one questioned the sudden outpouring of good luck that had fallen upon the camp. Teela suspected that, after so long of getting kicked while they were down, what might have otherwise been spotted at once to be some kind of suspiciously fruitful intervention instead just felt like a long-overdue change in fortunes.

With food and water, better sleep beneath stronger, safter shelters, the refugees were the strongest and healthiest they'd been since they were driven from Eternos. The forest seemed to be healing, too, though Teela wasn't sure if that was because of the magical influence or that nature had simply found a way to will itself back to life. The damage done to the trees by the rain began to heal, and the sludgy river cleared with the current. Wyverns began to dot the trees again, and Teela began to wake to the sound of the monkeys calling to one another from the highest branches again. The world began to feel like it was coming back to life around them.

The only person who seemed unaffected by the sudden bounty was Duncan. Teela brought him dinner every night at the medical tent, where he had started staying all the time, tending to those still recovering from the storm and the failed raid on Snake Mountain. He hardly ever emerged anymore, even sleeping there instead of joining Teela in the *Helios*. It felt, Teela thought, like hiding, albeit in the most righteous way possible. No one could accuse him of checking out when he was helping the wounded, but he was able to stay hidden away from the camp's real problems—and could sit wallowing in his own guilt about the failed raid on Snake Mountain.

"Malcolm thinks with the stronger lumber I found, he might be able to repair the broken spears we lost when we left the dunes," Teela said as they shared dinner one night. She made a point of keeping Duncan updated on what was happening in the rest of the camp, in hopes that something she said might inspire him to come out and see for himself. "He has the spearheads. Arlo wants to try to make a forge—something he can do rudimentary blacksmithing in."

Duncan didn't reply as silence fell between them. Teela picked at the piece of lucky fruit in front of her.

"I think we might be ready to try something more proactive again," she said after a moment. "Like maybe another rescue mission."

"Rescue mission?" Duncan repeated.

"Another raid on Snake Mountain," she said, knowing she was pressing on a bruise. "We could send a company to pilfer some of the supplies we need from Skeletor's men. Or . . . we could try to rescue the king and queen again."

She watched her father's face for a reaction. Seeding the idea now that they needed to make another stand against Skeletor might make it easier to swallow when Teela was forced to finally reveal her alliance with Evil-Lyn and what she had promised her. And giving the camp something to work toward—something that would keep them on Eternia—would distract them from Locke's continued tinkering with the ship and the plan unfolding around it. Teela had been avoiding the *Helios* whenever she could, but several days ago she had overheard Dian and Locke in the cockpit discussing the benefits of trying to relocate the refugees to Trolla instead of Primus—and felt her heart sink.

Duncan picked at a piece of fruit stuck to the front of his tunic. "I'm not sure that's a realistic thing to aim for."

"Why not? We're regrouping. We could have a chance this time. And we can't leave them there. They'll think we've given up." Duncan started to speak, but Teela pressed on. "You should start thinking about it. Making a plan. You know what went wrong the last time, so it won't happen again. Maybe Malcolm could help you."

"Teela," Duncan said quietly.

"If you want to stay shut up in here, you don't get a say in what the rest of the company does," she said, her voice rising. "You have no idea what's happening in the camp anymore."

"A company takes many kinds of leaders. Not all work can be forward facing and visible."

"But not all work can keep you hidden away," Teela snapped. Duncan didn't take the bait, which didn't surprise her. She'd never known her father to rise to anyone's temper. He stared at her, his gaze even, which just made her more furious. "You're not even doing anything to try to stop Locke's plan to get us off the planet," Teela all but shouted.

"Stop it?" Duncan repeated. "You want me to stop her?"

"Why wouldn't you?" Teela said. "We can't leave! If we rescue the king and queen, we have a chance to stay and fight. And we can't just abandon them!"

"It's not my choice," Duncan said dully. "If the majority of the company wants to leave, I'll respect that."

"These are the Heroic Warriors of Eternos, and you are still their commander! Command them to stay! Command them to fight!"

"You cannot force people to do anything, Teela. And you cannot force them to be just and decent. Such qualities must arise from within. Forcing obedience makes us no better than Skeletor."

"It's not forcing anyone if they choose to follow you because you are their leader!"

Duncan was quiet for a long moment, and Teela thought she may have lost him entirely. But then he drew in a deep breath and began to speak. "I think," he said, "the days of a man-at-arms are behind us. We are all in this together now, all of us equally invested in our survival and our choices. Whatever the company decides to do now, it should not be just my choice. It should be all of us. And if everyone wants to leave, I will respect that. I hope you will, too."

"Would you go with them?" Teela asked. "If they left."

"I don't know," Duncan said quietly. "What do you think is left for us here, Teela?"

The question unexpectedly pricked tears in the corners of Teela's eyes. Perhaps it was the smallness of the question in the face of all the things she held close about her home. The smell of the mist off the mountains. The color of the sky at sunset, the way the pink and purple refracted off the walls of the Royal Palace of Eternos. Their myths. Their stories. Their histories. She knew nothing about those things would change if they went somewhere else—their history was theirs, no matter where they were—but Teela didn't know who she would be if she wasn't a warrior of Eternos. Perhaps that was why she wanted to stay so badly—she still clung to the hope that someday, the world would right itself. The court and the castle and the city would be restored, and she could take her place in the only destiny she had ever considered. She'd never wanted anything else or thought she'd ever have to consider it.

"Would you leave Eternia, Teela?" Duncan prompted.

"I . . ." Teela's voice broke, and she pressed her fists against her cheeks. "I don't know." The sob stuck in her throat splintered into a sad laugh. "I don't know anything. I don't know what I'm doing."

Duncan reached out and put a hand on top of hers. "No one ever does," he said with the first smile she had seen from him in days. "We're all just pretending."

"The escape pods are running."

Teela didn't know what to say, or what exactly the implications of this announcement were, so she just swallowed and said, "Oh."

"Sorry," Locke said. "I'm just really excited and wanted to tell someone, and you were the first person I saw."

"That's . . . exciting," Teela said, trying to infuse her voice with enthusiasm she didn't feel.

Locke nodded vigorously, either immune to or purposely ignoring Teela's lackluster response. "I pulled some of the old solar panels off, and Dian and I cleaned them, then hooked them up to the pods. I wasn't sure if the engines were even still able to hold a charge, but it looks like they're charging."

"How big are the escape pods?" Teela asked.

"Oh, tiny," Locke replied. "Like three people max. Or one, if you're Malcolm-sized." She grinned at Teela. "But I might be able to retrofit them to carry more weight."

"Great. I'm thrilled for you." Teela turned back to her work, but Locke didn't leave.

"Actually, can you come help me?" Locke asked.

"With what?" Teela said.

"I want to boot up the engines. Dian's off hunting, and I don't want to wait," said Locke.

"I don't know anything about engines," Teela said.

"Neither does Dian," Locke replied. "I just need you to hold things in place for me. And your dad said you should help, remember?" Was it just Teela's imagination, or was that a spark of triumph in Locke's eyes?

"Okaaay." Teela reluctantly laid down her spade and climbed to her feet, brushing the dirt from her hands on the knees of her pants.

She followed Locke across the clearing and around the *Helios*. The two escape pods had been carved out from the belly of the ship, leaving two cavernous grooves Teela hadn't noticed since they were on the side of the ship farthest from the clearing. Locke had rigged the solar panels up in the trees to catch more of the light filtering through the canopy, wires running down the trunks like vines to connect to the open panels of the pods. Through the mirrored plexiglass windscreens, Teela could make out the dashboard of one of the pods, the navigation screen lit up and displaying a fuzzy map with their location marked in a blinking red dot.

Locke had thrown a thick cord of rope over a heavy tree branch and secured it to the top of the pod. "So what I need you to do," she said, "is provide a counterweight. The thrusters still aren't great, so the pod will need a little encouragement to get it off the ground."

"I do not weigh as much as this pod," Teela said.

"I know," Locke said. "You just need to give it some momentum, once I turn the engine on."

Teela tied the rope around her waist as Locke hoisted herself into the cockpit of the pod, windscreen cracked open so Teela heard her shout, "Ready?" Teela gave her a thumbs-up, and Locke started flipping switches on the dashboard. *Please,* Teela thought as the engine flicked and stuttered, flaring and spitting gray smoke. *Please, don't work. Don't work.*

The engine suddenly roared to life with a blast of hot, dusty air. Teela took an involuntary step back, her hand rising to cover her eyes. "Now!" Locke shouted, and Teela leaned backward, throwing all her weight counter to the pod.

There was a creak, and then, with a sudden jerk, the pod was airborne, hovering several feet off the ground. Teela stepped back, unfastening the rope from around her waist as she watched the pod rise. It hovered to the height of the *Helios,* then seemed to stall out before it went any higher. The base of the pod wobbled. In the clearing, Teela heard someone shout in excitement. They must have seen the pod.

There was a stuttering, coughing noise, then the light of the engine died, and the pod crashed back to the earth, leaving a groove in the soft dirt.

Teela ran forward as Locke hauled herself out of the smoky cockpit, coughing. "Are you all right?" Teela asked.

Locke was doubled over, but flashed Teela a thumbs-up and a triumphant smile. "It worked!" she finally managed between hacking coughs.

Before Teela could reply, Malcolm came jogging around the side of the *Helios*, a jar of the lucky fruit juice in one hand. "Anyone hurt?" he asked, thrusting the jar into Locke's hands so she could take a grateful drink.

"Did you see it?" Locke asked him after taking a long gulp.

Malcolm nodded. "I can't believe you got it running."

"An engine that little will never lift the whole ship," Teela said.

"But it proves the solar panels work," Locke said. "And I think the main engine has some of the same problems the pods did."

"What if you make something else out of them?" Teela suggested, as though the thought had just popped into her head. Really, she'd been trying for days to come up with any way to distract Locke from working on the ship itself. "If we had something like a Sky Sled? That would be more practical. And helpful."

"A Sky Sled!" Malcolm clapped his hands together, a clang sounding out when he struck his metal gauntlet. "It would be brilliant to have something like that."

Locke didn't look convinced. She was staring down at the engine, studying it, then looked up suddenly at Teela. Teela felt a creep down the back of her neck like a cold stream of water. "Unless you don't think that's possible," Teela added. She felt a flash of guilt, knowing Locke would never back down from a challenge.

"Oh, it's possible," Locke said, and she turned back to her engine. "But I might need to take apart the *Helios* for things like a steering mechanism and a base."

"So?" Teela said, trying not to sound as hopeful as she felt. "A Sky Sled could help us with hunting and trade and fetching water. We could get outside the forest. It would help."

Locke ran a hand over her face, leaving a smear of grease. "I'm just not sure that's . . ." She trailed off, staring down at the engine again.

"Not sure of what?" Malcolm prompted.

Locke shook her head. "Nothing. I can do it," she said, already reaching again for her tools. Then she murmured, so softly Teela wasn't sure they were supposed to hear, "But that's not what's going to save us."

TWENTY

"What if I want to use the water to destroy something? Is there a rune for that?"

Evil-Lyn shot Teela a scornful look, domed by one perfectly arched eyebrow, from her perch on one of the low branches of the Skytree. She had her face painted again tonight, her long hair swept up, and she wasn't wearing the silken gloves. There were still faint bruises on her knuckles, but she looked entirely more herself than she had the last time they met—which was to say, composed and terrifying. "Whose life are you looking to ruin?" Evil-Lyn asked.

"No one's," Teela said quickly. "But this ship—the one Locke wants to use to get off this planet—she's getting closer to getting it running."

Evil-Lyn leveled her steely gaze on Teela. "So you want to . . . kill Locke?"

"What? No, of course not!" Teela threw a handful of leaves from the forest floor at her. "You're so creepy."

Evil-Lyn waved a hand, and the leaves turned to bubbles, floating lazily through the air until she reached up and popped them with several flicks of a long black nail. "What is your intention then, exactly?"

"I was just thinking maybe there was a way to . . . make sure the ship didn't run."

Evil-Lyn considered this for a moment, then slid down from her perch. "Well, let's see." She cleared a patch of earth with the toe of her boot, then spread her collection of rune stones there. Teela scooted closer to her, staring at the stones as if she knew what they meant as Evil-Lyn began to pick through them, mixing and matching with no explanation.

"Are you sure you don't want to kill her?" Evil-Lyn finally asked. "It's so much easier to devise a spell."

"No," Teela said.

"And it would make for an interesting experiment in the limits of the Wellspring water."

"Limits?" Teela hadn't considered there *could* be a limit to the water's abilities.

"Some magical items can be used only for good intentions. It's why spelled items are more fickle than magic alone. I wouldn't recommend chopping vegetables with a cursed blade, for example. I learned that the hard way."

"So the water can't be used for bad things?" Teela asked.

"I don't know," Evil-Lyn said. "But sometimes there's . . . a cost."

"A cost?" Teela repeated.

"Magic is a give-and-take. Spells are exhausting. Others will physically hurt whoever casts them." Evil-Lyn shrugged. "It's energy transference, darling."

"So what's the cost of using the water?"

"Maybe nothing," Evil-Lyn replied. "You and your little camp seem to be doing fine thus far. It may be so small it doesn't even register. Or maybe there is none. Sometimes channeling magic through an object means the object itself absorbs the cost. The water being a finite resource—maybe that alone is the cost."

"Is that why you were worried the fruit was poisonous?" Teela asked. "Why you wouldn't eat it?"

"Now you're catching on." The sorceress considered her rune stones for a moment, then said, "Are you sure you don't want to kill this mechanic?"

"No," Teela said firmly.

"Well, then I guess we'll never know. Let's see." She tapped a finger to her lips. "I can only think of runes for dismemberment; poison; slow, painful, agonizing death. Any of those work?"

"You're so morbid."

She selected several rune stones and handed them to Teela, listing each use in turn. "This is a rune for freezing—I don't know if it will work on machines, but you could cast it on what's-her-name. Or this one, for darkness, if it's solar-powered—or you might be able to pair darkness with something else to get the point across that it's a metaphorical darkness that should shut down the engines. There's also always the option of using a small explosion." When Teela didn't reply, Evil-Lyn said, "I'm impressed you're going down the path of sabotage."

"It's not sabotage," Teela huffed.

Evil-Lyn laughed. "Darling, this is *textbook* sabotage. If you looked up *sabotage* in the dictionary, you'd find a picture of you drawing a rune on that ship to try to blow it up."

Teela tossed the rocks into the dirt. "Don't make fun of me."

"I'm not."

"You need us to stay here, too."

"I know. I just use humor to cope." Evil-Lyn waved her hand, and the rocks gathered themselves into a neat pile. "Well, good luck not breaking up your camp."

"What do you mean?"

"Do you think if you sabotage this ship, they'll just let the idea drop?" Evil-Lyn asked. "As certain *you* are that staying is the right thing to do, they're certain they're doing what's right, too. That's the thing about people—you can't really change their mind once it's fixed. I mean, look at you. You won't even consider their idea."

"Do you want me to?" Teela asked.

"No, of course not," Evil-Lyn replied, knotting the pouch of rocks at her belt. "I'm just making a point."

"Show me the rune for darkness," Teela said, then added quickly, "Just in case."

Evil-Lyn's lips quirked. "Of course," she said, and bent down, drawing the rune in the dirt. "Just in case."

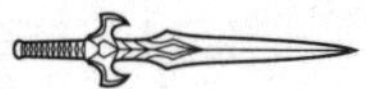

Teela stole back into the camp in the navy hours before dawn, just as she was supposed to replace Andra on the watch. Andra was posted up in the highest branches of one of their tree houses, looking out through the forest with an old set of binoculars they had recovered from the *Helios*'s cargo hold, and didn't notice Teela until she climbed up the ladder to take her place. "Hey," Teela said quietly, and Andra jumped.

"Oh, you *are* here."

"Why wouldn't I be? It's my turn on watch."

"Locke said she's taking your spot."

"What?"

"She came up about an hour ago and said you weren't in your bed, and she didn't know if you'd make the shift—she's got the first one tomorrow, so she said she'd swap you."

"Why was she looking for me?"

Andra shrugged. "I don't know. I didn't ask." She raised the binoculars again. "Go back to bed. Locke should be up soon."

Teela climbed back down the ladder, uneasiness fluttering in her belly. Why would Locke have been checking in on her? Had she been keeping track of Teela's comings and goings?

Teela forced herself to stop and take a deep breath. Worrying was pointless—it just meant you lived the worst-case scenario in your own head before you knew the truth. Better to prepare than fret. And she wasn't doing anything wrong. The opposite—she'd been the one to save the camp. Righteousness flared inside her like a struck match. So what if it was Evil-Lyn who was teaching her? No one else could. She had to learn where she could, and since the water had saved them, Locke had nothing to complain about.

Teela started up the gangplank of the *Helios*, but stopped halfway when she noticed the snapped-off solar panel resting against the side of the ship beside the shape of the Sky Sled she had assembled from the dismantled escape pod. Absently, Teela traced the rune for darkness Evil-Lyn had shown her on her palm with her thumb. *Sabotage.* Was it sabotage if she was just trying to do what she knew was best for the refugees, even if they couldn't all see it?

Teela hopped down off the gangplank and stood in front of the solar panel. She wouldn't do it, she thought, even as she felt herself reaching out and tracing the shape in the pollen and dust that had settled on the panel. She could feel the vial of water around her neck. It suddenly felt heavier and colder than it ever had before.

If she did this, she would be falling into the exact trap she had promised herself she would avoid. The necessities of survival had already made Teela's morals somewhat elastic—Teela would never have considered any situation where it was acceptable to steal before Eternos fell, yet here she was, having cleaned out the abandoned remains of other camps and even taken what she needed from a group of travelers they had met on the coast of the Harmony Sea, when her stomach was folding in on itself with hunger. You did what you had to.

But this fell outside the bounds of necessity. This wasn't survival.

But if doing it meant staying, maybe they were the same thing.

Before her mind tied itself up in any more knots, Teela forced herself to reach out and wipe away the rune. She was still a warrior of Eternos. She wouldn't stoop to the levels of Evil-Lyn.

"What are you doing?" someone said behind her, and Teela jumped, so startled she almost knocked the solar panel over.

Locke was standing behind her, wrapped in a black cloak, her hands in the pockets of her cargo pants. Her eyes strayed from Teela to the smear in the dust on the front of the solar panel, and Teela resisted the urge to look, too, and make sure the rune really had been entirely scrubbed away.

"I . . . thought I heard something," Teela said.

"What kind of something?" Locke asked.

"Something . . . growling. In the forest. It woke me up. I went to investigate."

"I came looking for you—I thought I'd wake you up for your watch so you could eat something first. But you weren't in bed."

"Right. I was out . . ." Teela waved a hand vaguely at the forest. "Investigating."

Locke didn't say anything, just stared at Teela. Teela knew the tactic; she had seen Duncan let cadets stew and sweat in silence until they confessed to their crimes. People gave themselves away in silence. Teela felt herself struggling not to fill the quiet with more explanations.

Finally, Locke said, "I'll take your watch shift. Go back to bed."

"Oh. Thanks. Can I take yours tomorrow?"

Locke waved a hand. "Don't worry about it. I don't sleep much anyway."

"Are you okay?" Teela asked.

Locke nodded. "Just a lot on my mind."

"Yeah," Teela said. "I get it."

Locke gave Teela a wan smile. "Do you have it, too? Insomnia?"

"Every night," Teela said. "And if I do fall asleep, all I have are nightmares."

Locke nodded. "About the night the city fell?"

"Sometimes," Teela said. "Sometimes other things."

"Like what?"

Teela took a deep breath. A breeze whispered through the trees, lifting her hair off her neck. "About something bad happening to the camp," she said. "Or my dad. Sometimes I dream about . . ." She swallowed. "Adam. Wherever he is now—I dream that he's in danger or in pain and I can't do anything to help him."

"That's hard." Locke dug the toe of her boot into the dirt that had been kicked up from the test flight. Drifts of it had settled against the ship's landing gear and the base of the gangplank. "I have nightmares about cats."

Teela laughed before she could stop herself and clapped a hand to her mouth. "Cats?"

Locke shuddered. "I hate cats."

"How can you hate cats? They're so sweet."

"They have weird slitted eyes, and they're unpredictable and have no loyalty to anyone."

"Well, clearly you've met the wrong cats."

"I don't ever want to meet any more."

Teela grinned. "Noted. No cats."

"No cats. Are you going back to bed?"

"Probably not," Teela said. She felt too wired and restless to sleep. "I might start making breakfast. Or go see if my dad needs anything."

The wind rose around them again, and Teela shivered. "Here." Locke unwound the cloak from around her shoulders and extended it to Teela.

"It's fine—"

"Take it. I was going to drop it off at the ship anyway."

"Are you sure?"

"I run hot." She shook the cloak. "Take it."

Teela took the cloak and wrapped it around her shoulders. "Thanks. I'll give it back soon."

Locke shrugged. "Use it as long as you need it. It will always keep you warm."

TWENTY-ONE

Sigrid was the first one to notice that the river had dried up.

She came running back from the riverbank several days after the escape pod engine had run, empty bucket slapping against her thighs. "The water! The water is gone!"

Malcolm, who had been sitting with Teela by the remnants of the morning cook fire, set aside the handle of the spear he had been carving. "Gone?" he called as Sigrid stopped next to them, breathing heavily. "What do you mean gone?"

"It's dried up," Sigrid said, quieter but with the same urgency in her tone. "There's no more water."

"It can't be dried up," Teela said. "It's a river. It doesn't just disappear overnight."

"Come see for yourself."

Teela and Malcolm followed Sigrid down to the riverbank to find that, in fact, the streambed—which had been swollen with fast-moving water the day before—was dry.

"See? Bone-dry," Sigrid said, hopping down into the empty bank and picking up a smooth rock that was just at the bottom of the river. "Like there was never any water here at all. You'd think it would be muddy or damp or something, but it's just . . . gone."

"Did you notice anything yesterday?" Malcolm asked Teela. "You were the one who went for water, weren't you?"

"It was all normal," Teela said. She bent down to the streambed and picked up a handful of dust, then let it fall between her fingers in a fine mist.

"Maybe the source was cut off somehow, or someone dammed it," Malcolm said. "Let's send a party upstream." He didn't sound too optimistic, but Sigrid nodded.

"I'll go check it out," Teela offered.

"By yourself?"

"I'll just follow the riverbed until midday, then turn around. Nothing bad will happen."

Malcolm looked skeptical but nodded. "Fine. Be careful. And take this." He handed Teela his knife, and she stuck it into her boot.

Teela started to hike up the streambed, staring down at her feet and hoping to find any hint that water had been there—a squelch of mud or a trickle of liquid. She kicked over stones, searching for undersides dark and damp, but nothing. As if there had never been water to begin with.

She had hiked nearly a mile when, finally, the evidence of water appeared. A trickle of water, though as Teela watched, she noticed it was retreating, like something was sucking it back into its source, its retreat so slow it almost wasn't noticeable unless you stared hard. It couldn't be the sun or the soil sopping it up. It was like, drop by drop, the river was simply, slowly vanishing. When she turned and hiked the other way, she found the same thing happening a mile in the opposite direction from their camp. It was as if both ends of the river had been stopped with an invisible dam, leaving their camp in a desert in the middle of the forest. Teela wondered if it was something they were doing—some irrigation that might be drawing too much from the river. But she couldn't think of anything. Someone collected water three times a day, no more than what they needed. It didn't make any sense.

Teela stopped walking and cleared a spot of stones in the dusty bottom of the riverbed. She drew a rune Evil-Lyn taught her in the dirt—a command to refresh—that she had used to keep their food stores protected from rot. *Intention*, she thought, and held in her head the image of the flowing stream, thick water swelling around her legs and carrying her back to the camp. She imagined herself wringing out her clothes from all the water, dripping and drenched and cool as she pulled out the vial from under her shirt and let several drops fall into the rune.

But instead of the usual electric-blue flash as it filled the strokes of the rune, the water turned black when it struck the ground. It bubbled, then was sucked into the dirt. Teela waited, but nothing happened. She tried again, and again the water turned black before disappearing into the earth. She ran her fingers over the rune. Was there a better one? A different one? Had she misremembered it? She had held the intention in her mind, directed the magic with a rune.

And nothing.

There had to be a different way.

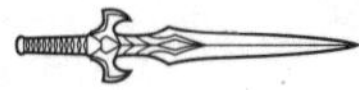

"We need water," she said as soon as Evil-Lyn appeared among the branches of the Skytree that night.

Evil-Lyn stopped dramatically, giving Teela a careful up-and-down look. "Hello to you, too."

Teela didn't have the patience for the sorceress's antics tonight. "The river dried up."

"Sounds tragic."

"And the rune I used to refresh it didn't work."

Evil-Lyn's eyebrows knitted, a flash of concern creasing her face. "What do you mean it didn't work?"

"I mean, I drew the rune, the one used to refresh," she said. "Just like you showed me. I used the Wellspring water in it, and nothing happened."

"Are you sure you drew it right?" Evil-Lyn asked, fishing the stone from her pouch and handing it to Teela.

Teela nodded. "I did it right. It must just not have been the right rune. There's got to be a better one, one for water or hydration or something." She paused, noting Evil-Lyn's inscrutable gaze. "Why are you looking at me like that?"

"Just wondering how much is user error," Evil-Lyn said.

"I didn't mess it up!" Teela growled. "It just didn't work. And the water is completely gone, overnight, like it was never there. Come on, I'll show you." She grabbed Evil-Lyn by the wrist and started to drag her away from the Skytree.

"Unhand me!" Teela felt a sharp zap like electricity, and she let go of Evil-Lyn with a yelp. Evil-Lyn glared at her. "We don't have that kind of relationship, kid. Just because I show up to our meetings doesn't mean you get to boss me around."

Teela gritted her teeth. "Then help me."

"Then respect me."

"I don't," Teela snapped. "And if you're going to throw a fit about it, then our partnership should end here. I'll figure out the magic myself."

Evil-Lyn's face darkened. Her fingers flexed at her side, and Teela wondered if the sorceress was about to curse her. Or just walk away.

But then Evil-Lyn's eyes darted to the vial hanging around Teela's neck. Teela had the sudden feeling Evil-Lyn was about to snatch it—something she couldn't remember feeling since that first meeting at the Skytree—and she closed her hand reflexively around the bottle.

Evil-Lyn rolled her eyes. "Fine. Show me this river magic doesn't work on."

Evil-Lyn followed Teela as they hiked through the forest to the dry streambed that had fed the camp the day before. Evil-Lyn hopped down after Teela into the dry bed and pressed her hand into the dirt.

"See?" Teela said, motioning toward the packed earth. "No water. Nothing."

"Water sources dry up all the time."

"Not like this."

"No," Evil-Lyn agreed, "not like this." She dug a toe into the dirt, digging up a dried stem of moss. It crumbled into dust.

"We can't survive without water," Teela said.

"Obviously."

"You have to help me."

"I don't think there's anything to be done."

"But you said—"

"This isn't natural," Evil-Lyn interrupted, kicking her heel into the dirt so that a cloud bloomed around them. "This is magical intervention."

Teela felt her chest constrict. "You think someone's done this to us intentionally?"

"Not necessarily," Evil-Lyn said, tossing one of the streambed rocks between her hands. "But I did tell you—magic often comes at a price."

Teela stared at Evil-Lyn, mouth agape. "*This* is the price?" she said. "This is because I've been using the water? You said there might not even be a price! Or if there would be, it would be small! You didn't say it could be a full-blown, dried-up river."

Evil-Lyn turned to her, head cocked as one eyebrow ascended. "I said I didn't know what the cost would be. Are you blaming me for the laws of the universe?"

"You knew something like this could happen!"

"I didn't know *this* could happen."

Teela looked around at the dry bed of the stream. A breeze rose through the trees, kicking up a swirl of dust from between the stones. She felt nauseated. What was the point of the water healing the camp if they were all going to die of dehydration?

"So what do we do?"

"You find another water source," Evil-Lyn replied.

"We can't," Teela said. "We can't move the camp again. That was . . . that was the whole point of this! Locke will want our next home to be on a different planet. Others will agree with her. I thought you cared."

"About what, exactly?"

"About . . . us," she said, though the first thing she thought—the stupidest thought that had maybe ever crossed her mind—*about me*. "About us regrouping so we could help you stand against Skeletor."

Evil-Lyn picked up a handful of dust and let it run through her fingers. Then she brushed her hands off on her skirt as she stood and gave Teela a withering look. "Care?" She snorted. "Don't be naive."

TWENTY-TWO

It felt like the forest was turning on them.

Three days after the river dried up, all the leaves began to fall in clumps from the trees surrounding their camp. It was not a gradual, seasonal fall, but rather like a giant hand had taken the branches and given them a good shake, sending all the leaves floating to the ground at once. The next day, they woke to discover the trunks had begun to shed thick chunks of bark, revealing hearts that were ashy and crumbling. The trees themselves began to lean on one another like drunks at a bar. One night, a fallen tree flattened the shelter where the lucky fruit preserves were stored. No one was hurt, but the rations were destroyed.

The rapid growth of the initial plants Teela had sprinkled with the Wellspring water had slowed until it felt more sluggish than even normal plants. The vines no longer produced endless fruit overnight. The wyverns had stopped flying low enough to be hunted, now that the river was dry, and the lucky fruit stopped being satisfying on its own. The lucky fruit was hydrating, but they still needed water.

She racked her brain, trying to puzzle out a solution for how she could fix what was happening—Evil-Lyn had said all magic had a cost, but how was the river tied to using the magic for things like healing the camp and growing food? She couldn't make the connection, but if this was the price of using the Wellspring water, it was starting to feel too high.

Thirst and hunger began to claw at Teela and the rest of the camp, which manifested into frustration with one another. Everyone was quick to snap and short on patience. Locke and Malcolm got into an argument that almost came to blows over what Malcolm claimed was Locke not doing her part in the camp, instead tinkering incessantly with the Sky Sled. A demonstration of the work she'd been doing—the way the base of the sled hovered on its own even as Locke was still working on attaching a steering mechanism—almost calmed him, until Locke chose to make a quip about how a meathead like him couldn't understand the work she was doing, and they had to be separated.

Teela thought about using the runes to help the lucky fruit grow again, but the contents of the bottle were running dangerously low. She didn't want to risk using up the final drops on something that might not even work. The camp didn't even want more of the fruit—there were so many other things crowding ahead of it on the list of needs. Teela found herself worrying about whether she should save the water for some more pressing but still unknown need in the future, and the futility of such train of thought didn't stop her from dwelling on it.

Evil-Lyn taught her runes to protect the camp from the falling trees, and another to restore the crumbling bark and fallen leaves, but the Wellspring water had no effect on them. Two more trees fell the night after Teela performed the spell, and the trees continued to crumble, like they were smoldering from the inside, turning slowly to ash.

More and more trees began to lose their leaves. The crops that had begun to grow back in after the rain withered. The grass and moss that had softened the ground and spangled the trunks of the trees began to mortify and die.

How, Teela thought as she crawled back onto her pallet on the *Helios* at the end of yet another fruitless lesson with Evil-Lyn that had done nothing to bring back the river, *did things go so wrong so fast?*

She was exhausted—she had been sleeping less and less as she spent more time with Evil-Lyn, trying to find a solution, then on her own, testing out those solutions, pouring drop after drop of her precious water into runes that wouldn't channel it, and neither of them knew why.

Maybe their luck had just run out, Teela thought as she began to drift off to sleep, throat burning with lack of water. Nothing good could last forever.

Crrraaacckkkkkk.

Teela sat up, disoriented in the darkness for a moment, thinking at first it was another tree falling and unsure whether she had only dreamed the sounds. But then she heard them again—but this time, inside the ship itself. The click of hard steps on the floor of the ship, like studded boots, then a snuffling sound. Something inside the ship fell—a can, or a pan, with a metallic ping and grind as it rolled away.

"Dad—" Teela turned, but her father pressed a finger to his lips, already sitting up on his pallet. He retrieved his weapon from where it was hanging on the wall beside him, and Teela wondered if it would work after so long collecting dust. She pulled her own knife from under her pillow and pushed herself to her feet, following Duncan as he crept through the darkness of the ship.

They followed the strange chittering sounds to the cargo hold, their backs pressed to the ship's hallways. Duncan's steps were silent on the floor, and Teela tried to place her feet in the same spots to avoid creaking. As they approached the cargo hold, Duncan held up his hand and they both stopped. Ahead, Teela could see a shape, a patch of darkness shifting and twisting. Someone was on board with them, rooting through the bag of tools Locke had collected or fashioned and left in the cargo hold. In the darkness, she couldn't recognize them, though their silhouette was so distinct—a rounded back and shoulders that tapered into thin arms and bulbous hands—she thought they must be a stranger or else they would have sparked some recognition. They seemed to be struggling to open the bag of tools, like it wasn't made for them.

Duncan put a hand on Teela's shoulder, pushing her gently backward into the darkness, then holding up a hand for her to stay. Teela waited, holding her breath, as Duncan crept toward whatever it was rooting through their supplies. The figure finally succeeded in tearing the bag open, scattering the tools and knocking something off the counter—a can of oil, Teela realized, which bounced against the ground once before rolling to a stop against the toe of Duncan's boot.

The creature raised its head as the sound stopped abruptly, turning toward Duncan just as he fired. The bullet bounced off the intruder, pinging into the ceiling of the ship, but the flare was enough to illuminate its face for a moment—a thick shell on its back, bulbous arms that ended in claws. A Karikoni, Teela realized, one of the crustacean warriors from the Orkas Islands. For a moment, Teela was so surprised she forgot to be scared. What was a Karikoni doing on the mainland, away from the coral islands they called home? Not only that, but what was he doing here, in their ship, looting the *Helios* like it was abandoned, though surely he had seen the camp full of warriors sleeping all around it?

The crustacean warrior roared, swinging a massive claw at Duncan.

"Teela," Duncan shouted. "Wake the camp!"

Teela darted for the ship's door, but the Karikoni lunged past Duncan toward her. He battered her backward into the hallway from where she'd come. She felt the razor claw clip her shoulder as the Karikoni tossed her into the wall with such force that her neck wrenched. She shook her head, trying to clear the stars from her eyes as the Karikoni bore down on her again, claws clacking like sword blades connecting. He was in between her and the gangplank now, so instead of trying to leave, Teela scrambled back the way she had come, up into the cockpit. The Karikoni chased after her, but the space was too small for his wide shell to fit through the door. He managed to grab one of Teela's feet in his claw, trying to pull her back, but there was another blast and the Karikoni reared back, letting go of her. Teela flew forward, crashing into the dashboard.

The Karikoni roared again in frustration from the hallway, but this time she heard her father's yell, too. Another blast echoed around the ship, followed by the crack of a body hitting the wall.

Teela flipped every switch on the dashboard, and the ship roared to life. Lights flared, engines woke with a throaty growl, even the wipers started, squeaking over the cracked windshield. Was that alarm enough? *Does this ship have a horn?* she thought hysterically. The ship's high beams illuminated the clearing, and in their glare, she could see the camp was crawling with Karikoni. They had heavy nets strung over their shells, filled with the lucky fruit and weapons and whatever they could find.

The camp was being robbed.

The refugees were beginning to emerge from their shelters, blinking in the beam of the ship's lights. A shout of warning began to pass through the camp as the Karikoni were spotted. Teela saw several of the Heroic Warriors jumping to the ground from their tree houses, swords and knives and whatever else they could find in hand. The

Karikoni, too, were armed with coral-studded clubs and fishing tridents, and Teela could hear the clash of metal on metal even through the windshield.

The floor behind Teela buckled suddenly, and she spun around just as the Karikoni burst into the cockpit, the metal plates around the door splintering. He swung at Teela, and she dodged, letting the weight of his swing carry him forward crashing into the pilot's seat as she slipped behind him and buried her knife in the soft flesh between his shell and shoulder. He roared in pain. Teela tried to pull her knife free but realized it was stuck, the hilt wedged underneath the shell. She braced herself against it, trying to release it, but the Karikoni's elbow collided with her face, and she staggered backward, collapsing into the wall. The Karikoni swung again, this time knocking Teela into the dashboard and pinning her there with his crusher claw. She fought for air, vision narrowing as his claw tightened on her throat. She could feel blood trickling into her eyes. The Karikoni was pressing her into the windshield so hard she could feel the plexiglass bowing beneath her. The bottle of Wellspring water was digging into her rib cage under her shirt. She imagined it shattering, the shards burying themselves in her heart.

"Teela!" She raised her head just as Duncan dragged himself up into the cockpit. In the light filtering in through the windshield, she could see the front of his tunic was sopping with blood. She thought he was going to take another futile shot at the Karikoni, just in hopes of distracting him into letting her go. But instead, Duncan aimed his weapon and shot directly into the windshield.

The windshield shattered when the beam hit it, and Teela tumbled backward through the opening, sliding down the nose of the ship. She managed to grab the edge of the windshield, the shards of glass slicing her hand but stopping her before she fell. The Karikoni tumbled past her, off-balance, and crashed to the ground, landing on his face with a crunch.

Teela tried to pull herself back into the cockpit, but the nose of the ship was too slippery, and she couldn't get enough traction. She waited, hoping Duncan would appear and pull her back in, but there had been so much blood soaking through his shirt. It wasn't a long fall to the ground—the Karikoni had landed badly, but if she could control her descent, it would be easier. She let go of the windshield and slid down to the edge of the ship before jumping to the ground. The fall was longer than she hoped, and on impact, she felt the tremors up through her legs so hard, she staggered and dropped into a crouch before she fell.

She only had a moment to catch her breath before another Karikoni scrambled toward her. The net on his back was wrapped around one of the camp's last jugs of water, and he was running for the edge of the camp. He swiped a claw at her as he passed, but missed, and Teela shot up, racing after him. She took a flying leap, arms windmilling, and jumped onto his back. She clung to the net, even as the Karikoni began to thrash, trying to swipe her off. Her knife was still stuck in the other Karikoni's back, but when this warrior's claw brushed against one of the ropes, it snapped. The next time he swiped for her, Teela latched onto his forearm, pulling it down with all her weight.

The Karikoni's shoulder twisted in his socket, and he howled in pain. His pincer clicked helplessly, and Teela used it to clip two more lines on the net. It was enough that when she yanked, the net broke, and the water jug tumbled free.

The Karikoni lunged for the jug, but Teela grabbed for it, too. The Karikoni snarled as they grappled, then jammed his crusher claw into the side of the jug, dousing them both in water. The sudden change in weight sent Teela tumbling backward, landing hard. Her palms stung as she skinned them on the ground.

"There," the Karikoni spit, his voice raspy. "Now no one gets it."

Something struck the Karikoni on the back of his skull and he slumped to the ground, dazed. Locke stood behind the crab, wielding a metal bar that looked like it had come from the *Helios*'s landing gear. A cupped piece of metal still clung to one end, shielding a mess of raw wires. Locke threw out a hand to Teela and pulled her to her feet. "Where's Duncan?" Locke asked, her voice ragged.

"The ship," Teela said. "He's hurt."

"Are you armed?"

Teela shook her head. "I lost my knife."

"Here." Locke reached into her own boot and pulled out a knife, which she handed to Teela. It was half the size of Teela's dagger, barely as long as her palm, but it was better than nothing. "What are Karikoni doing on the mainland?" Locke asked, but before Teela could answer, another crab warrior dropped from the tree overhead with a yowl. Locke and Teela leaped apart. The Karikoni sprang to his feet, squaring off with them. He had a bundle of the lucky fruit strapped to his shell. The skin looked gold-leafed in the light from the ship.

The Karikoni lunged with a bellow, but Locke dug the rounded end of her weapon into the ground, tossing dirt and dry leaves into the Karikoni's face. The crab-man stumbled, making a choking noise like a beached fish gasping through its gills, which Teela realized was a cough. "Get the fruit," Locke said, and Teela used the moment of distraction to cut the lucky fruit from the net on the Karikoni's back. The Karikoni snapped at her with a growl, but Locke swung her club again and the Karikoni's claw caught that instead. They locked, sparks flying as the metal ground against the hard shell. The Karikoni twisted his claw, and Locke gritted her teeth as her shoulder bent in its socket. She was clinging with both hands to the base of the club, feet planted on the ground.

Teela cut the final rope, then reared back, driving the dagger into the shoulder of the Karikoni. The blade hardly pierced the thick skin, but it was enough that the Karikoni's grip broke, and Locke stumbled, blade released. The Karikoni snatched up as many pieces of the lucky fruit as he could carry, then took off running toward the edge of the woods.

"I'm going after him," Locke called, already running.

"What? No! Don't!"

"We have to find out where they're coming from!" Locke called over her shoulder. All she had was the club—Teela wasn't sure if it would be enough. She looked behind her at the camp—the warriors seemed to be holding their own against the Karikoni. There weren't as many of the crab-men as Teela had initially thought, or perhaps more of them had been felled.

For a fleeting moment, she had the thought that it would all be easier if she let Locke chase the Karikoni on her own. She was virtually unarmed, but she was a warrior of Eternos. Surely she could hold her own. And if she couldn't . . .

Teela sighed, then took off into the trees on Locke's heels.

TWENTY-THREE

Teela hadn't been prepared for how dark the forest was.

The path to the Skytree had become so familiar she could walk it with her eyes closed. But here, in the thick woods that turned away from the river, as soon as she was out of the circle of light cast by the *Helios*, Teela had to slow almost immediately to avoid running into low-hanging branches. She stumbled on the uneven ground, unable to see the peaks and valleys of the forest floor. Ahead of her, she could hear the crashing of the Karikoni as it charged through the trees, knocking down anything in its path, but she couldn't see Locke anywhere.

She reached one hand out, steadying herself against one of the forest trees. Under her fingers, the bark felt chalky, and when she held her hand up to her face, she could see the palm of her hand was black, like she had touched a charred trunk after a forest fire. She pressed her hand into the trunk again, and this time a chunk broke off, as easily as if it were made of snow.

She followed the husks, realizing after a few minutes of tracking progress that they made a perimeter around the camp. Their camp was the epicenter of the wilderness wasting away.

A deep unease crept through Teela. She could feel the weight of the bottle of Wellspring water heavy around her neck, the glass suddenly cold against her feverish skin.

Then, to her left, through the darkness, something crashed, and she snapped to attention.

Locke.

Teela drew her knife and charged forward into the darkness. The heavy down of broken branches slapped at her legs, tearing her trousers and cutting her shins. It was hard to work out exactly where the noise was coming from—it seemed to echo around the forest, bouncing off the trees and rising into the sky like smoke from a campfire.

Teela heard a scream, high and primal, though she couldn't decide if the rough edge to it came from pain or because it originated from a creature that wasn't human. But it oriented her enough that she turned to follow the sound, tearing through the forest until she stumbled into a clearing.

The trees hung low over the riverbed, as dry here as it was near the camp. In the stony basin, Teela could see Locke and the Karikoni warrior facing off. The crab-man had dropped the stolen fruit on the riverbank as he snapped his claws at Locke. He was bleeding from a wound to his knee, but it hardly slowed him down. Locke swung her blade, and the Karikoni batted it aside with his crusher claw. The sword lodged in the soft bank of the dry river, throwing Locke off-balance. The Karikoni lunged, and Locke had to let go of her blade in order to dodge the blow from his claw.

Teela wasn't close enough to draw her own blade, so she grabbed one of the lucky fruits from the riverbank and threw it as hard as she could at the Karikoni. It splattered against his shell, spraying pulp and juice. It was enough to distract him, and he turned to Teela with a roar that gave Locke enough time to retrieve another knife from her boot and lunge forward, burying the blade in the soft meat behind the Karikoni's knee. He shrieked in pain, dropping to one knee, and Locke caught him under the chin with a hard punch, flipping him backward onto his shell. His legs pinwheeled as he struggled to rock himself back onto his feet.

Locke jumped onto his crusher claw, pinning it into the ground as Teela slid down the riverbank to join her.

"Are you all right?" Locke asked, her voice punctuated by heavy breaths.

Teela nodded. "You?"

Before Locke could answer, the crab-man let out a howl, swiping at Teela with his free claw, and Teela jumped backward.

Locke gritted her teeth, straddling the Karikoni with one foot on each of his claws. "How did you get here?" she demanded. "What do you want?"

The Karikoni spat at her. She spat back at him. He bucked suddenly, and Locke lost her balance. She was thrown from the Karikoni and landed hard on the riverbed. Teela lunged for Locke's sword, still buried in the riverbank, but the Karikoni didn't stay to fight. Instead, he took off scrabbling down the riverbank, away from their camp.

"Here." Teela handed Locke her sword back, and Locke took it, looking sideways at Teela.

"Thanks for the help."

"All I did was throw fruit."

"You have good aim and a good arm." Locke grinned. "For a second there I thought . . ."

"What?" Teela asked.

"Nothing," Locke said. "Forget I said it. I should know that you would never leave me on my own, no matter how much we disagree."

Teela nodded, though her stomach twisted with guilt when she thought of how close she had come to using the water to sabotage Locke's attempts to fix the *Helios*. But that wasn't the same, she assured herself. When it mattered, she'd never leave someone behind.

"We've got to take care of each other," Teela said, and she squeezed Locke's arm. "We're all we have."

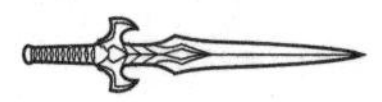

It appeared the Karikoni had been run out of the camp by the time Locke and Teela returned. A few crumpled bodies littered the ground around the ship, shells gleaming in the moonlight. Locke stopped to confer with Malcolm about the damage, but Teela ran past them both and up the gangplank of the *Helios*.

Duncan was still in the ship where Teela had last seen him. Sigrid was with him and had him propped up against the wall as she bandaged the wound. The Karikoni's claw had caught him in the side, and though Sigrid had stitched and bandaged it, his shirt was so soaked with blood Teela felt her stomach turn. She wasn't sure how there was any left in him.

"Dad," Teela said quietly, dropping to her knees beside him.

Duncan cracked his eyes open and smiled. "Teela. You were . . . magnificent."

Her eyes filled with tears, and she looked to Sigrid, hoping to find some clue in her face as to how worried she should be. Sigrid looked grim, and Teela's stomach twisted. She thought briefly of the poultice that had cured the camp of their sickness and whether it could work on a wound like this. But they no longer had the supplies needed to create the mixture or, based on how Duncan was looking, the time.

But what if she just used the water on its own?

But how could she give Duncan the last of the water without raising suspicion or having to explain herself to Sigrid, to everyone? She shook her head back and forth as though to clear her mind of that thought. What did it matter whether people judged her for what she'd done? If it was her father's life or her own pride, she knew which she would sacrifice.

"Teela," someone said behind her, and she turned to see Malcolm standing on the gangplank to the ship. Teela pressed the heels of her hands into her eyes quickly, then stood up. He ducked his head as she approached. "It doesn't seem he'll be able to help us, I suppose."

"Help you with what?" said Teela.

"We captured two of the crab-men. They want to parlay with our leader. I was hoping Duncan could speak to them but . . ." He gestured helplessly toward Duncan's slumped form.

"I can do it," Teela said automatically.

"You'll interrogate captured warriors? Do you think that's . . ." He trailed off, and Teela heard the unvoiced conclusion, *wise*.

"I can do it," she said again, fixing him with her best hardened stare. Maybe it was a rush of undeserved confidence. Maybe she just felt, in that moment, more her father's daughter than she ever had before. She had watched Duncan. She knew him. She knew what made him strong—the way he spoke to his friends, but, more important, the way he spoke to his enemies.

And she wasn't the same stammering, uncertain girl she'd been at the funeral of the three warriors a little while back. The past weeks of bringing salvation to the camp and having them look up to her for instruction and decision-making had changed her; she could feel it.

She could do this. She could be her father's surrogate when he wasn't able. "Trust me."

"All right," Malcolm said. "Come on."

"I just need a minute," Teela said. She could feel the heavy weight of the water vial against her chest. "I'll be right there."

Malcolm nodded. As he turned back to the gangplank, Teela ran back to where Sigrid was kneeling on the ground beside a now-unconscious Duncan and unhooked the vial of water from around her neck. Sigrid looked up from the needle she was sterilizing over a candle flame as Teela dropped down beside them. "Teela," she said, and her voice sounded half warning, half wary. "What are you doing?"

"I can help," Teela said. It was the only way she could explain it without having to explain it. She tried to remember the runes Evil-Lyn had taught her, but her mind was racing; it was hard to pin any of them down. Had she showed her one for healing? Was there a rune for healing? Or a general, catch-all *fix this*!

Restoration. She remembered Evil-Lyn drawing a rune on the bottom of the dried-up riverbed. A rune for restoration. It hadn't worked then, but maybe this was different.

Her fingers were wet with her father's blood, and before Sigrid could stop her, or even ask, Teela traced the rune on his skin, then uncapped the bottle and poured out the last drops of water. The drops flowed straight to the rune, flooding the lines Teela had drawn as if they were grooves in stone.

Please, Teela thought. *Please.*

She felt a hand on her shoulder and turned. Malcolm had returned for her. "It can't wait," he said. "We have to do this now."

"All right." Teela shoved the now-practically-empty vial back down her shirt, but not before she saw Sigrid staring at it. Teela stood, feeling Sigrid's eyes burning a hole through her back as she trailed Malcolm out of the ship.

TWENTY-FOUR

The two captured Karikoni warriors had been bound to trees at the edge of the camp, their claws wrapped tightly in canvas to keep them from snapping. Krass stood guard between them, swinging his sword at his side, though both warriors seemed too battered to fight anymore, let alone stage an escape attempt. One of them had a ferocious gash across his forehead, blood flooding one slitted eye. Teela noticed a smear of blue paint across his chest, like a designation of rank that had been washed away. As she approached, she noticed the other soldier look to his comrade as though in deference.

Teela stopped in front of the two Karikoni. Some of her earlier confidence in the *Helios* had dissipated, but she stood straight, a hand on her knife as though in that moment she felt like a warrior and not like an exhausted child.

"Who are you?" she demanded, trying to sound like her father or like King Randor had when he addressed the city of Eternos from his Throne Room.

The Karikoni leader twisted his head around to face her, blinking blood out of his eye. "I have no allegiance to you, daughter of Eternos." His voice was gravelly, like rocks tumbling over one another. He blinked hard again, his face twitching against the glare of the morning sun. "Who is this child?" he said to his fellow, then to Krass, "I asked to speak to your leaders, not this girl."

"She speaks for us," Krass said. "Treat her with respect or you will not be given the chance to speak at all."

The Karikoni snarled, and Krass cracked his thick neck in return.

"Stop," Teela said, holding up a hand.

"Stay out of this, little girl."

"Bold to name-call," Teela said, "when you're our prisoner."

The Karikoni tossed his head with a laugh. "I have nothing to say to you."

Teela wanted to argue. She wanted to snap back at him, let the struck match of her temper flare and burn. But she was here as a representative of her father. What would Duncan do? He wouldn't take the bait. She remembered suddenly him telling her once that anger was the mask that fear wore to hide itself. This warrior was afraid.

And he was injured. Teela noticed it again as the Karikoni tossed his head. He was still squinting, the sun in both eyes and one filled with blood.

"Will you bring me a cloth and some clean rags?" Teela turned toward Krass with a hushed tone.

Krass frowned. "What?"

"Something to clean his eye—he can't see anything."

"Teela," Krass said, his voice low as though imparting a secret. "You don't have to do that. He's a prisoner."

"He should be treated with respect. It's what my father would do."

Krass looked like he wanted to argue, but after a moment he nodded. "As you wish."

When Krass returned, Teela cleaned the wound over the Karikoni's eye, then used the rags to bandage it as best she could. "Could you stand to the left?" she asked Krass. "To block the sun from his eyes."

Krass sighed dramatically but stepped to the side.

The Karikoni commander blinked several times, then nodded. "Thank you."

"What's your name?" Teela asked.

"Pinchent, daughter of Eternos."

"Teela," she said. "My name is Teela. Are you a soldier?"

"I am a lieutenant in the ranks of the Orkas Infantry."

Teela crouched down in front of him so he didn't have to crane his neck to look up at her. "I would bring you water if I had it, but it would seem your men took ours."

Pinchent's chin jutted out, and when he spoke again, Teela heard the defensive edge creeping back into his voice. "Because ours is gone."

"What happened?"

"Our water has been polluted," Pinchent said. "It is no longer safe for us to drink from or hunt fish from or even swim in. We followed it to its source, then up the river, and found your camp."

"Our river?" Teela said. "It's all dried up."

"It feeds into the sea, where we live," Pinchent replied. "We thought if we followed the river, we could find where the pollution was coming from."

"Did this happen slowly?" Teela asked.

Pinchent shook his head. "In a single night. The coastline had been crystal clear that day, then the next morning it was black and sludgy, and my men who drank from it grew ill. The fish have all died. They've been washing up bloated and rotting on our shore. All the water on the island has either dried up or been poisoned."

"Our water source has dried up, too," Teela said. "Is that why you came to the mainland?"

Pinchent nodded. "Only half of our party survived the journey here. We were already so weak and dehydrated. We have to bring food back to our tribe or the rest will not survive."

"But when we got here, we found that the forest was dying, too," his subordinate piped up. Teela thought of the charred trunks and falling trees that appeared to be worsening by the minutes; even just before, when she'd stepped outside the *Helios* to interrogate the Karikoni, Teela had realized all the leaves on the trees surrounding their camp had fallen to the ground. "We hoped to hunt. But your skies are empty. There are no wyverns. When we found your camp, we made a decision to take what we needed to survive. We were hungry. And desperate."

"And are you sorry?" Krass said from behind Teela.

"Not for trying to protect my people," Pinchent interjected fiercely.

"We would have done the same," Teela acknowledged, "if it came to that."

"Punish us if you want," Pinchent said, "but we will not apologize. Nor return what was taken."

"No punishment," Teela said quickly. "Keep what you stole."

"Teela—" Krass said, but Teela ignored him.

"Cut them free," she said. All the unsurety she had felt before the interrogation began had evaporated. She knew what she needed to do—not as a leader, but as a citizen of Eternia. There was no question. When Krass didn't move, she said again, "Let them go."

"Are you sure?" Krass asked, his tone making it clear he wasn't convinced.

"Something is killing Eternia," Teela said. "There is no point in fighting each other, because we are all victims of it."

Krass's brow furrowed, but he withdrew the small knife from his belt and used it to cut the two warriors free. Teela used her small knife to cut the canvas wrapped around their claws, and the two Karikoni climbed to their feet, shaking out their stiff limbs.

"You should return to your company," Teela said. "And get the supplies back to your people."

Pinchent offered her one giant claw, and Teela touched her hand to it. "I thank you for your kindness, daughter of Eternos. And your mercy."

"We are all survivors," Teela answered. "We should not fight each other. I hope you exercise the same mercy and kindness next time the opportunity arises."

Pinchent nodded. "In thanks, I offer you this." The Karikoni unhooked the plate of armor from his back that was covering his shell. "Forged by our Karikoni blacksmiths from coral of the Sea of Rakash. It serves our men as both armor and a boat, for the coral is less dense than water. Should your water return, or should you move your camp to somewhere with a new source, it will help you in fishing, as the creatures of the sea are drawn to it. It is also strong enough to protect you from the blow of a blade. Take it, with our thanks for the fruit."

Teela bowed her head as she accepted the armor, turning its heft over in her hands. It was concave and seemed to be carved from some pearled black shell. The first thing Teela thought was how much Adam would have liked using it for sledding down the foothills outside Eternos during the winter snows. "Thank you," she said.

"We wish you and your warriors luck," Pinchent said. "We wish you survival. We wish that for all of Eternia."

TWENTY-FIVE

As soon as the crab-men had been released, Teela returned to the *Helios* to check on Duncan, her heart in her throat as she wondered whether the water and rune had worked on him.

She found him on the observation deck, asleep on his pallet. *Asleep*, Teela confirmed, checking his breath—and, it seemed, asleep deeply and untroubled by pain. This was nothing like the fitful, feverish sleep he had endured after the rain. Tentatively, Teela pulled up his shirt for a look at the wound, but it had been wrapped in a clean bandage. She thought about unwrapping it, when, from behind her, someone said,

"Teela." Teela turned. Sigrid was standing at the opposite end of the observation deck, holding a bowl and cloth. A prickle of apprehension ran up her spine when she saw how Sigrid was looking at her—warily, like Teela might spring at her.

Teela stood up. "How is he?" she asked. "He looks . . . he looks better."

Sigrid came to stand beside her, setting the bowl on the ground and not meeting Teela's eyes. "He's fine."

"Fine?" Teela repeated. She felt like they were stepping around the subject—what they both really wanted to be saying—like a spilled drink puddled on the floor. "He's . . . he's fine?"

Sigrid nodded. "Miraculously. Improbably. He's fine." She knelt beside Duncan, and Teela watched with bated breath as Sigrid unwrapped the bandage from Duncan's torso.

The wound was gone. Healed—not even a scar, as if it had never been there.

Teela's heart skipped with relief, then she realized Sigrid was finally looking at her, only with a heavy, accusatory gaze.

"What did you give him?" Sigrid asked.

"I . . . what?" Teela's mind raced. It was so improbable—the idea that Teela might have done something to heal a mortal wound in seconds—that maybe she could convince Sigrid it hadn't happened. She hadn't gotten a good look at the wound to begin with. It was blood from the crab warrior. He'd never been wounded at all.

But then Sigrid stood, crossing her arms, and Teela felt herself wilting. "You drew a rune on him, Teela. And gave him something."

"Do you know runes?" Teela asked, unable to keep the surprise from her voice, though she knew it betrayed her.

"I don't know what it meant, but yes, Teela, as a healer I recognize the ancient language of magic channels," Sigrid replied testily. "So tell me what it was you were channeling."

Teela felt the truth pressing itself against the back of her teeth. She couldn't talk her way around this; she would just have to reveal as much as she could without mentioning Evil-Lyn.

"When I went to Darksmoke," Teela began, her words halting and tone wobblier than she would have liked, "after the company fell ill from the rain, Granamyr gave me this." She pulled the bottle out from under her shirt and showed it to Sigrid. "He said it's water from the Wellspring of Eternia. It has restorative properties. That's why the healing salve I made worked when yours didn't—I mixed the water into the poultice."

Sigrid took the bottle, tipping it toward the light so it refracted blue against the wall. "Why didn't you tell me?" Sigrid asked, her tone inscrutable. "I could have used this."

"There wasn't . . . that much. And you can't just pour it on things."

Sigrid nodded. "The rune you drew on Duncan . . . How did you know how to do that?"

"I . . ." This was what she had to keep quiet. She couldn't tell anyone the truth about where she'd learned the runes. Even sharing anything more about how the magic worked felt like tipping her hand. "I . . . the dragon showed me a few before I left Darksmoke," Teela said feebly. She held her breath.

Sigrid stared at her for a moment, then, to Teela's immense relief, she nodded. "And does Duncan know about this magic water?" she asked. Teela thought about lying but knew she'd be exposed as soon as Duncan woke. She shook her head. Sigrid frowned. "Why didn't you tell anyone about this?"

"I didn't think I needed to. It was working. It was helping!"

"Working on what?"

"Well, you know, it helped heal the welts from the rain. And it . . . helped the crops grow."

"It's not just healing magic?"

"No, it's restorative. At least, that's what . . . the Granamyr told me."

Sigrid looked grim. "We need to tell the others."

"No, don't, please," Teela said quickly. "It's gone—there's nothing left." She offered the bottle to Sigrid so she could shake it back and forth and hear there was no liquid sloshing in the vial. "What's the point, if it's too late?"

"We should see if anyone else knows anything about the properties of the Wellspring."

"But why?"

"Magic usually has a cost, Teela," Sigrid said. "Especially magic that powerful. I haven't done much work with magical treatments for exactly that reason. There's always a scale that needs to be balanced. Sometimes it costs the patient and—" she paused, as though weighing her next words "—sometimes the magician."

"It hasn't affected me," Teela said. "And everyone's fine. The company got better. The welts didn't come back."

But Sigrid was shaking her head. "Then there must be something else. We should ask the camp—someone else might know more than I do about magic, or the source. I've never even heard of the Wellspring of Eternia. Did Granamyr tell you anything else about it? Where it comes from or what it is?"

Teela shook her head. But she knew she couldn't let the whole camp find out. Someone would surely know something—enough that she would have to reveal where she'd learned the runes, and who had been teaching her about them.

"I'll tell Duncan," Teela said quickly. "When he wakes up. If anyone will know something, it will be him. I'll let you know what he says, but you don't have to worry about it."

Sigrid stared at her for a moment, then nodded. "All right." She dropped the bottle, and it fell back to the end of its chain around Teela's neck. "Teela . . . why didn't you tell me any of this sooner?" she asked.

"I thought maybe you wouldn't trust it," Teela said, relieved at finally being able to be fully honest. "Or let me use it. And we really needed it."

"Why wouldn't we trust it?" Sigrid asked.

"Because of where it came from."

"Darksmoke?"

"Yes. Of course. Dragons are . . . suspicious. Let me talk to my father. He'll know what to do. And maybe he'll know more about the Wellspring."

Sigrid sighed like she wanted to keep scolding Teela, but then she looked down and said, "Can I give you something for your hands?"

"What?" Teela looked down at her palms. She'd forgotten she'd skinned them when the crab-men attacked. It felt like such a small injury in proportion to the fight, and she had washed the blood from between her fingers. But her palms were scraped and red, and now that she'd paused to catch her breath, she could feel her pulse throbbing in the open cuts.

Sigrid turned to leave. "Come with me. I've got something that will help."

Teela followed Sigrid from the *Helios* and to the hut Sigrid used to store her medical supplies. Her brain was riffling through possible ideas of what to do next, interrupted only by the small voice in the back of her head berating her for her stupidity. If only it was true that the knowledge of how to use the water had come from Granamyr and not from Evil-Lyn. What had she been thinking, promising the camp would help the sorceress overthrow Skeletor? A common enemy didn't make them allies. She had been blinded by desperation, by the desire to help, to do something, to save the king and queen and prevent another raid on Snake Mountain from ending in tragedy. To save their camp from the rain. She'd had to do *something.* She just was no longer sure that she had done the right thing.

And something was undeniably happening to the natural world around them. From the rain, to the river, to the trees. Evil-Lyn had told her magic comes with a cost, just like Sigrid had said. Could the two be linked? And if they were, how could she stop it? Or control it? Or—if possible—reverse it?

She needed answers, and she couldn't get them from within the camp unless she was prepared to reveal the extent of her runic magic knowledge, where it had come from, and the pact with Evil-Lyn.

Teela followed Sigrid into the medical hut, waiting while Sigrid rooted around in her trunk for the supplies.

"Oh." She straightened, holding up a book to Teela. "Did you want this back?"

It took Teela a moment to realize what it was and why Sigrid was giving it to her—it was the book of remedies Evil-Lyn had taken from Sigrid's old office in the palace. The one that had provided the recipe for the salve that had cured the welts once the water was added to it.

"No, no. It's yours." But even as she spoke the words, an idea was taking shape in Teela's mind. From what she had been able to tell from her visit with Evil-Lyn, the Royal Palace of Eternos was in pieces, but that didn't mean there was nothing there that might help. Evil-Lyn had gone there to find what she needed. Maybe the information Teela needed was there, too. She thought of the enormous palace library, with books on every subject on the planet. She had spent time there studying for exams, poring over books on combat and history. But she and Adam had also gone to read fairy tales and fat encyclopedias with illustrations of animals, real and fictional. Novels, poetry, history,

Books on Eternos. Books on magic.

Maybe she could keep the water—and her alliance with Evil-Lyn—secret for just a little longer if she had the answers to how exactly the magic around the water worked, and why, and what it cost. And how she could get more, now that her vial was dry, and also fix whatever it was that had gone so terribly wrong.

It would take her a day to trek to Eternos, unless she took Locke's cobbled-together Sky Sled—she could be there and back in not even that long if she flew. As Sigrid carefully applied a paste to the cuts on Teela's hands and wrapped them in clean cloth, Teela's stomach twisted with a strange combination of fear and dread and excitement when she thought of returning to the burned-out husk of her home.

But Teela needed answers, for herself, for the camp, and for the well-being of all Eternia. And she knew where to find them.

TWENTY-SIX

Teela rose in the earliest pink hours of dawn and stole down from the *Helios*. She took her sword and two knives, which she carried in her boot. Under her tunic, she wore the empty vial of water, bumping against her heart with every step. The Sky Sled's engine would be loud—not loud enough to wake the camp, but at least enough to alert whoever was on watch. She'd have to move quickly.

The Sky Sled felt flimsy as she climbed aboard. She had ridden real Sky Sleds before, always behind her father or one of the older cadets back at the palace. Those machines were light and fast, with a seat behind the handlebars and a solid plate for passenger and pilot to rest their feet on. Teela had never felt crowded on a Sky Sled, but now, as she straddled Locke's contraption, she felt like the whole thing was about to fall apart beneath her. Instead of a sturdy running board holding it all together, the steering and engine were connected by a narrow strip of metal peeled from the *Helios* without stripping too much from the hull. There was nowhere to sit, so she had to balance precariously with her feet sideways on the narrow beam.

Teela took a deep breath. How hard could it be to steer a sky bike through dense forest?

She flipped the switch on the console and the engine flared to life. The bike frame shook, the navigation aid on the dash vibrating so hard Teela almost couldn't follow the blinking dot indicating her location.

"Teela?" she heard Andra's voice call over the engine. She must've been on watch. "Teela, what are you—"

Now or never. Teela kicked the gas, and the bike shot skyward. The wind whipped at Teela's hair, tearing it out of its plait, and the roar of the engine drowned out Andra's shouting behind her. Branches were whipping at her face as she tore through the canopy, snapping and scattering off the nose of the sled.

Teela clung to the handlebars, throwing her weight into them until the bike evened out. She wasn't sure how high she could take the Sky Sled, and she'd rather not find out. The dot on the console blinked as she moved, tracking her progress. South. She needed to go south.

An idea occurred to her suddenly—she could follow the riverbed. She knew it intersected with the waterways surrounding the palace, and the canopy would be lighter there. Fewer trees to accidentally hit.

She guided the Sky Sled through the forest, circling the clearing until she found the dry, cracked bed where the river used to run. She pointed the nose of the sled south and hit the thrusters, jolting forward toward the capital.

Despite the navigation aid, Teela quickly lost track of how far she was from the camp. She kept waiting to spot the river beginning to flow again, but the streambed was dry all the way to the edge of the trees, which themselves had black rot creeping on their trunks, like a spreading stain. From this vantage point, it almost seemed as though the camp had formed a nexus from which the forest was sickening.

At last, Teela broke from the forest and guided the Sky Sled up into the foothills, hovering over the rocky crags until she crested the last peak and the ground suddenly opened ahead of her. She pulled up hard, staring out at the valley, the rivers and waterfalls still tumbling around the ruins of the city of Eternos as it blazed in the sun. Teela caught her breath. She could remember sitting on this same hillside with Adam, looking out at the palace, the sun catching the glass towers and reflecting it onto the river. The waterfall that separated the palace from Castle Grayskull always looked to her like mirrored glass, smooth and refracting rainbows. That was still the same—the waterfall, the hills flush with blooming wildflowers, the rocks that formed the crags the city sat upon.

But the palace was a skeleton of itself. The stained glass windows had been punched out and the gatehouse destroyed. The statues that had once loomed over the palace bailey had disappeared from the skyline, and Teela remembered watching one of those giant stone horses collapse into dust. Something about that—destruction just for the sake of it—seemed so cruel and needless. There were no more flags flying from the towers, and the once-bright colors all seemed dim and tarnished.

The last time she had seen this view was from the ground, when she and Duncan had been pulling themselves up the muddy bank of the moat, staring in horror at the city on fire. She remembered the way the ships had swooped through the clouds of smoke, indistinguishable from the storm swirling over Grayskull. The beams of light in the sky.

Now, smoke rose from the streets but in thin fingers, likely from the campfires of marauders and looters who still lived among the wreckage, picking off the corpses of the city. It all made Teela think of fruit left to rot on the vine. Anything that was not taken care of would wither. The sight of the city—her home—after all this time, so battered and depleted, made her eyes sting.

Teela blinked away her tears. She couldn't waste any more time on memories. She had to learn what she could and then get back to the camp. If there were answers about the Wellspring and the water to be had, Teela was sure they would be contained in the palace library.

Teela carefully landed the sled and left it on the banks of the waterfall separating Grayskull from the palace, to protect it from scavengers who would strip it for parts, before hiking up to the city gates. As she entered, she pulled Duncan's cloak over her head, covering her long red hair, and tied a scarf up over her face, hoping she might blend in with whatever lowlifes were roaming the city streets. Not that there were many people to blend in with: The gatehouse was unguarded, and she passed through it and into the streets without meeting anyone else. Every shop she passed was empty, windows smashed and contents looted. Some structures had been burned altogether, others overtaken by vagrants who had made their home amid the wreckage. They hissed at Teela as she passed, warning her away.

She followed the path from her memory over the cobbled streets, once pristine but now torn up, stones cracked and overturned or missing entirely in places. She could have closed her eyes and followed her memories straight to the gate, she had walked this path so many times with Adam. She could hear his voice in the back of her head, see his shadow on the bricks ahead of her. Was it at all possible he was still here, lost and forgotten among the ruins of his former city?

No. She shook the idea from her head, snuffing out the tiny flame of hope that had momentarily ignited. It was impossible, and she knew it.

But it was still good to see him, even if it was just in her head. His memory felt more present here. The whole experience of being back in the city felt like walking through a dream, everything familiar but at the same time not what she remembered at all.

At the gates of the palace, a band of Widgets were crouched around their campfires, rubbing their hands together as they argued over the price of a sachet of crystals spread around them. "Watch yourself," one of them called, and Teela stopped, hand straying to her sword.

The Widget who had called to her, a tiny old woman with no teeth, shook her cane at Teela. "No one goes in the palace, child."

"Why not?" Teela asked.

"Shadow Beasts," the woman whispered. "They've taken over."

A shiver ran up Teela's spine. She had forgotten about the Shadow Beasts—Evil-Lyn had mentioned them when she'd taken Teela to the palace all those weeks before. She would have to be careful to stay in the light.

"Best stay away," the woman advised, returning to her stewpot.

Teela looked up at the gates. "I don't know that I have a choice."

"Turn back," the woman said. "That's the choice."

Teela secured her cloak, then started to climb the locked gates. She heard the woman laugh. "Children never listen, do they?" she said to her comrades. Their laughter trailed behind Teela as she made her way up and over the gate.

TWENTY-SEVEN

Teela didn't expect the palace to feel so haunted.

When Evil-Lyn had brought her there, it hadn't felt so vast and empty, perhaps because it had been the two of them together, or perhaps because Teela had other things on her mind, her hair still wet from mountain snow and the sorceress still unambiguously her enemy, motivations unknown.

But now, as she stole through the halls of the empty palace, Teela felt herself jumping at every shadow—and not just because of the dangers she had been warned lurked there. The light and the dust and the palace hallways, like a play set where all her best memories had been staged, seemed to be conspiring together to conjure ghosts. Every time she reached an intersection, Teela felt like she could see figures out of the corner of her eye, only for them to vanish as soon as she fully turned her gaze upon them. Was it her memories of Adam or her younger self haunting the edges of her vision? Or, maybe, the ghosts of a future that might have been, had Skeletor and his men not attacked?

Without fully realizing she was heading there, Teela found herself in the apartments she had once shared with her father. Glass from the punched-out windows crunched under her feet as she crossed the room, staring around at her old home. She was sure that anything that had once been hers was gone, but to her surprise, when she opened one of the drawers built into the wall beside where her bed had once been, she found a square of ancient paper folded up and shoved into the corner. When she unfolded it, she found a drawing, one she couldn't remember doing but it was unmistakably hers. She must have been young when she did it—hardly old enough to write her name, the letters scratched out labeling each figure stiff and clumsy.

She had drawn herself, in what she assumed was meant to be the livery of the man-at-arms, and next to her was her father in his green uniform, breastplate a scribbled gray blob. He, too, was labeled, "DAD," and beside him, a faceless female figure with long red hair like Teela's and a white dress. "MOM," she had written underneath it. The woman had no features, but Teela had drawn her to look like an older version of herself. She assumed there must be some resemblance, since she didn't look much like Duncan. Her fiery hair had to have come from somewhere.

When she was young, she had tried several times to ask Duncan who her mother was, but he had always clammed up and told her to leave it alone. She had assumed he would tell her one day, but after the city fell to Skeletor, she hadn't wanted to burden her father further by pressing him. And there were other things to be worried about. She had Duncan. She had never needed anyone else.

But seeing this picture, realizing that if the world had turned out differently, she could have discovered who her mother was, have had the hard conversation with her father about whatever had happened to her—or happened between her and Duncan—that had caused her to leave them, suddenly made Teela feel hollowed out.

The onset of grief—in such an unexpected form—struck her so potently that she sat down on the floor, pulled off her hood and scarf, and took a deep breath. She wasn't crying, not exactly, but she wiped at her eyes with the back of her hand.

She didn't know her mother. She had no family other than Duncan, and he had raised her to be a warrior, as much a part of her identity as it always had been his.

Who was she, if not a warrior of Eternos? The singular purpose that her whole life revolved around—that the lives of everyone she knew revolved around—had been pulled from under them in a single night. Somehow it hadn't felt truly real until this moment, with the palace in ruins around her. A small part of her, she realized, had always thought she could come home. She had been so worried about Duncan lacking a purpose if his job as man-at-arms was taken away from him, but Teela realized it was she who was drifting without a fixed point to aim for. The question was not who her father would be if they left Eternos—it was who would Teela be? What star would she reorient her heading around now?

Was she foolish to stay in Eternia and think this wreckage around her could ever be what it had been? Was it just prolonging the inevitable? Was hope just a form of denial?

Outside the apartments, a shadow passed, and Teela's head shot up. The Shadow Beasts. She had been so caught up in her thoughts she had almost forgotten. Now she realized something was growling in the hallway, pacing in front of the door. She was sitting in sunlight, so they couldn't attack her here, but she knew they would be on her as soon as she left the apartments.

The library. She had to get to the library.

She remembered suddenly a passage behind the fireplace in her father's office—one of so many secret corridors in the palace. She and Adam had tried to map them all and had given up when the task had grown too overwhelming. But this one she remembered—they had emerged, to their total surprise and that of the others in the room, in her apartments, smack in the middle of a meeting Duncan was having with his generals, after climbing behind a portrait in the library.

Teela clambered to her feet, listening hard for any movement before she stole out of her old bedroom and down the hallway. There were no windows in the corridor, and she wasn't sure how sophisticated the Shadow Beasts were as hunters, but she didn't want to give them the chance to catch her scent and track her. She slipped into her father's office—the door now ripped from its hinges and the once magnificent oak desk smashed. She almost stopped—the urge to languish in memories and grief was strong. But then she heard a crash from the other side of the wall and knew she didn't have long.

Teela ran her fingers up and down along the side of the hearth, suddenly worried she had misremembered the location of the passageway, until she found the latch. She pulled, but the door didn't move. Perhaps it had become glued in place with neglect and dust. A shadow darted down the hallway, and Teela threw her entire weight into the hearth. The door gave abruptly, and Teela tumbled forward into the passageway. She heard the hiss of the door closing behind her, and a moment later, she was plunged into complete darkness.

Teela put a hand on the wall, stepping carefully as she eased her way down the corridor. She remembered there were stairs but wasn't sure where until she nearly fell down them face-first. The walls were thick with cobwebs, and she pulled the scarf up over her mouth again just to keep the dust out. She felt for each new stair with the toe of her foot before stepping lightly, until finally reaching level ground. As she inched forward, the stones under her feet felt uneven, emphasized by age and neglect.

The passage was longer than Teela remembered, and she had a sudden, irrational fear that she was going to be trapped down here in the dark until she died, when through the darkness she made out a small square of gray light.

The door at the end of the passage was already propped open, and Teela peered around to make sure she was alone before she crept out, knife in hand.

The library had fared better than other places in the palace. She had half expected to find the books burned, ripped apart to fuel fires, but most had been left untouched. Perhaps the Shadow Beasts had overtaken the palace before these inner rooms could be reached by looters. A few of the shelves had tipped over, spilling books, but the signs at the ends of the rows defining each section were still in place. Teela reached up and dusted off one of the etched gold plates with her sleeve, revealing the name of the section.

"Sorcery & Witchcraft."

Not the best place to start. Teela wound her way through the aisle, brushing dust off section signs until she found the one labeled "Eternia." She remembered spending time here when she was young, studying for geography tests, learning the anthropology of their planet and the species who inhabited it. It had never been her strongest subject in school—for all she knew, they might have learned about the Wellspring, and she had slept through the answers she needed now.

Teela followed the shelves, searching until she found the book she remembered. She couldn't believe it was still here, the book she and Adam had spent hours poring over, lying on the floor together. *The Atlas of Cursed and Enchanted Places.*

Teela slid down until she was sitting on the floor, then flipped open the book to the table of contents, running her finger down the list. She couldn't remember reading about it before—she and Adam had mostly been interested in famous battle sites and the sort of dark magical places that sucked your face off, or the swamp where stepping on the wrong stone would get you turned into a frog.

But there it was—"The Whispering Valley."

Teela flipped to the chapter. The pages stuck together with age, and she had to peel them apart carefully so they didn't rip. She scanned the chapter on the Whispering Valley.

The Whispering Valley is guarded both by the unicorn itself, along with the Sylani people who have dedicated their lives to its protection. Protective wards make the valley impossible to access by magic and limit the use of spells within the valley itself. There are several places within the valley where magic is cut off entirely, including the Unicorn Caverns (see page 135), the Lake of Sorrows (see page 140), and the Wellspring of Eternia (see page 142).

Teela flipped to page 142 and discovered a drawing of the peak line of the Mystic Mountains, the Whispering Valley at their base and, marked along the jagged line, a small dot labeled "The Wellspring of Eternia." Two insets led from the dot—the first a drawing of a slowly narrowing cave labeled "the path to the Wellspring," a line at its entrance demarcated as "beginning of the magical ward." The second inset was a drawing of the well, and the ancient stones that surrounded it in an arch.

In the illustration, the largest of the stones was carved with an inscription, too small to read but translated in the caption, "Drink Not, Lest the Wasting Begin."

The wasting? What did that mean? They'd all been consuming it for weeks in some way and nothing had happened. She flipped back to the section header and began to read from the beginning.

The Wellspring of Eternia

The waters of the Wellspring are classified by magical naturalists under wishing magic (see appendix 5-E), as their powers are channeled through intention of the bearer. Opportunities for experimentation have been limited, so the full extent of these magical abilities remains unknown.

The natural world is tied to the waters of the Wellspring of Eternia. The waters can be taken from the spring in only one of three enchanted vials made of unicorn horn, though in the history of Eternia, no one has ever taken a draught from the Wellspring, for fear of the wasting curse warned against on the stones that guard the entranceway. Though what exactly "the wasting" means is unknown, it is believed by scholars that a proportionate sacrifice will be required in exchange for any use of the water drained from the Wellspring, and that any magical benefits will result in proportionate losses in the immediate vicinity of where the Wellspring water was used.

Though the source of the carved warning is unknown, it is believed that an ancient pilgrim learned the hard way and decided to leave a message for others in his final moments. The rough-hewn letters suggest it was done in haste and without proper tools, and the dating on the stone reveals it is a recent—

Teela stopped reading, her heart pounding. She felt suddenly hot, her skin itching all over. *Wasting.* What did that mean? Would she turn to dust at any moment, her muscles atrophying and withering like vines in the sun? Nothing had happened to their company. Nothing but good things. Surely the side effects, if they existed, weren't that slow acting. And Granamyr had given her the vial when she asked for a way to cure her camp; while she knew a dragon's bargain could not always be trusted, surely not even he would be so cruel as to present her with such a malicious trap.

And why would the water work as a cure, only to then waste them away?

She racked her brain, trying to think of other meanings of the word *wasting*—magical riddles like that always contained double meanings, didn't they? Armies laid waste to each other in battle. Waste could mean excess—maybe they had been granted with excess magic through the water, though then the warning didn't make sense. Was wasting always a bad thing? She was trying desperately to spin this in her head, like the magic might bow to her linguistic gymnastics if she could only find a solution. Waste of time. Waste of space. Wasted water when the Karikoni had broken the jug they had been fighting over, water that wouldn't have been wasted had the river still been flowing . . .

Teela suddenly understood with the force of a blow. She almost staggered.

"Any magical benefits will resort in proportionate losses in the immediate vicinity of where the Wellspring water was used." The natural world was tied to the Wellspring, and it was now wasting away around them in the Evergreen Forest. The crumbling trees, the wyverns falling from the sky. The water, dried up.

The warriors weren't wasting away from the use of the Wellspring water—Eternia itself was.

Because she, Teela, had given the water to the comrades to heal the sick; she'd given the water to the earth so plants would grow; she'd given it to her own father, so he wouldn't die of his injuries.

Teela was killing the planet.

Something moved in the library behind her, and Teela sprang to her feet.

The library was dim, but there was enough light from the high windows that she had thought she would be protected from the Shadow Beasts. She held her breath, waiting, wondering if it was just her imagination. Then she heard it again—a noise too small and stealthy to be a beast of that size.

Teela tore the page about the Whispering Valley from the atlas and tucked it into her tunic.

Somewhere in the recesses of the shelves, she heard a stack of books fall. A floorboard creaked. A faint stream of breath against the back of her neck.

Teela jumped, accidentally slamming the book in her lap. A cloud of dust bloomed up from its pages, and she clapped a hand over her mouth, trying to suppress a cough. Whatever it was that was creeping up on her seemed to be everywhere—behind and in front of her, far away, close by. She couldn't track it. She felt toyed with.

Teela pulled her knife from her boot, dropping into a defensive crouch and waiting. She couldn't judge which way the threat was coming from, and she felt exposed no matter which direction she looked. She thought she heard footsteps approaching, fast and light like running on tiptoes, but they stopped at the end of the row of books.

But there was nothing there.

She waited for a long, silent moment. She felt like she was vibrating with anticipation. Finally, she edged to the end of the row and peered around it, her knife held in front of her.

But there was nothing there. Had she imagined it?

"Well, well," said a familiar voice behind her. "Fancy meeting you here."

And the world went black.

TWENTY-EIGHT

When Teela came to, it took a moment for her to recognize where she was.

The banners that had hung colorful and thick over the walls had become tattered and faded, the once-shining columns dull and cracked. The floor had been torn up, like an earthquake had split the stones. Sun tumbled through the glass cupola high above, highlighting the dust motes floating thickly through the air.

The palace Throne Room.

Someone had dropped her at the base of the dais the throne was erected upon, as if she were a citizen come to petition the king for a favor. Except that her wrists were bound behind her and her ankles tied. She struggled, though she knew it was pointless. She could feel the thrum of magic against her skin. The bindings were enchanted—there was no way for her to break them or wiggle free.

Her head was throbbing, and she could feel dried blood matted in her hair. She recalled the library, the book, learning of the wasting, hiding from the Shadow Beast that wasn't a Shadow Beast, stepping into the aisle with her dagger held in front of her. Then the voice . . .

Teela raised her head.

Evil-Lyn was lounging on the palace throne, her legs kicked up over the arm and her head thrown back. She had braided her long white hair into elaborate plaits that cascaded over her shoulders in multiple woven strands, intertwined with an ebony circlet that looked like it was fashioned from charred branches. "I look good here, don't I?" she asked, as if she and Teela had been talking for some time. "It's like it was made for me." Teela blinked up at her, trying to clear the stars from her vision. She wished she were hallucinating but knew she wasn't.

Evil-Lyn tipped her head back over the arm of the throne. Her braids nearly brushed the floor as she arched her back, preening. "Oh, but I was born to be painted. You don't know if any of the court painters survived, do you? Never mind, I'll find my own. There's a master painter on Equinos who does the most amazing hunting scenes. Mostly horse based, obviously, but the way he paints blood! It's not worth struggling," she said, and Teela realized that she had been subconsciously pushing against her restraints, trying to separate her hands. "You can't break them, darling, they're magic. Remember magic, that thing I have that you don't?" Evil-Lyn sat forward, elbows on her knees, and grinned at Teela. Her smile was wolfish, and Teela could easily imagine her teeth studded with blood. "Or rather, that thing you don't have without the help of a vial of magic water?"

"Let me go," Teela said through gritted teeth.

"Oh, well. Since you asked so nicely." Evil-Lyn flicked her fingers, and Teela thought for one deluded moment she was about to be freed. Instead, the restraints sparked, sending a jolt of electricity through her.

"I thought we were allies," Teela gasped out when the current had subsided. She could taste blood in the back of her throat. "You wanted our help to overthrow Skeletor!"

"No, darling, though it's hilarious you believed that. What could I possibly want with your little half-starved band of nobodies?" Evil-Lyn leaned back, fingers caressing the arms of the throne. "I'm the most powerful sorceress in Eternia, with or without you. I don't need backup, particularly not from the remnants of the king's pets. No, you weren't my ally, precious. You were my test."

"Your . . ." Teela blinked hard. She wanted to wake up—surely this was all a dream. "What do you mean?"

"Well, see, I've always wanted to make use of this most special water from the Wellspring. But the inscription gave me pause—I wasn't certain whether the wasting would happen to whoever used it, or maybe the ones who it was used on, or who ate the magic fruit it created. And I sure as hell wasn't going to test that on myself. No, there's far too much relying on this"—she motioned toward herself—"to risk something like that. Imagine making myself queen just to waste away within the hour? Tragic *and* ironic."

"You would have let me die?" Teela asked, a spark of hurt inexplicably flaring. *You're so stupid. How could you have thought she actually cared about you?*

"Oh, absolutely," Evil-Lyn said at once. "You and everyone you love. And don't mistake me." Evil-Lyn smiled again. "I still will."

"But what—what about the water?" Teela asked. "What do you need it for?"

"Well, I'm going to poison Skeletor, obviously. Wishing magic, darling, is all about intention. And I intend to kill him. You know what they say, if you're tired of waiting around for your megalomaniac leader to find the Sword of Power, you've got to do it yourself."

"But you're a sorceress," Teela said. "Why do you need another source of magic to kill him?"

"Magic just isn't what it used to be, what with the Sword lost and the Sorceress disappearing from Grayskull. And Skeletor, the feckless blowhard, is rather familiar with all my methods of spelling, so he's put some limits on what I'm able to do when I'm at Snake Mountain. Not because he doesn't trust me, obviously, but because he *cares*." She rolled her eyes. "I needed a new method. Something he wouldn't be able to see coming. And I just had to make sure that, if I did kill him, the cost to me wouldn't also be death. Or wasting away, whatever you want to call it."

"It's not you who would have wasted," Teela said. She felt almost lightheaded with rage. She could feel herself straining against the bonds again, though she knew it was fruitless. "It's the planet. Eternia is dying because I've been using the water!"

Evil-Lyn blinked. "So what's your point?"

"We—you—have slowly been killing Eternia this entire time."

"Not all of it," Evil-Lyn said with a shrug. "Just some of it. Who cares about the crab-men or the forest? So it turns to ash. So what? I don't want a forest; I want a palace." She threw her arms outward. "Maybe I'll keep this one, or maybe I'll level it and build some luxury condos. Still deciding."

"If you use the water to kill Skeletor," Teela said, "it won't just be the forest or the seas that die. It might be the whole planet. The atlas said it's proportionate. I would think killing comes at a higher cost than making fruit grow."

"Oh, look, she read one page of a book and now she knows everything!" Evil-Lyn said it as if she were addressing a Throne Room full of admirers, all laughing along with her, then turned back to Teela. "You really are your father's daughter."

"You're going to destroy the kingdom you want to rule!" Teela shouted.

Evil-Lyn shrugged. "No more than you already did."

"I didn't know it was happening," Teela snarled. "You do. If you keep using the water, you're complicit."

"Don't care." Evil-Lyn climbed down from the dais and stood over Teela, who had to crane her neck to see Evil-Lyn's face. The sun through the skylight dome backlit her like she was a saint painted onto a chapel fresco. "Now, I was going to do this when I knocked you out, but where's the fun in that?"

She reached out and hooked one finger at Teela's throat. Teela flinched, but all Evil-Lyn did was loop her finger around the chain and drag the bottle out from under Teela's tunic. She tugged hard enough that Teela's neck snapped forward and the chain broke. Evil-Lyn caught the vial, then tucked it into her robes. "Thank you. You saved me the trouble of bargaining with that dragon to find this. I don't think he would have accepted such a meager offering from me." Evil-Lyn held up the vial, the blue shadow from the glass falling in a square on her face. Teela watched as her triumphant expression faded, replaced for a moment by confusion. Evil-Lyn held the bottle against her ear and shook it, then popped the stopper from the bottle and tipped it sideways.

"You used it."

It wasn't a question, but Teela still somehow felt like it was a trick one. "I . . . yes?"

"You used *all of it*?" Evil-Lyn's voice rose, and Teela flinched.

"We needed it," she said. "That's why it was given to me—so I could use it to help my company!"

Evil-Lyn let out a sudden cry of frustration, and the stones beneath her feet rippled like the surface of a pond when a rock was thrown in. Teela felt the breeze lift her hair. "You stupid little twit," Evil-Lyn hissed at her. "I should have known."

"What are you talking about? You told me to use it!"

"This makes everything so much more complicated." She dropped the chain over her neck, jaw flexing. "You've put me days behind schedule—I was going to kill him tonight! You know, you've got no one to blame but yourself if Skeletor decides he has time to smoke you out of the Evergreen Forest while I'm on my way back to the Wellspring to refill this."

"You've been to the Wellspring?" Teela asked.

"Yes, and I intend to go again. This time with this vial, since last time I didn't know I needed it. Don't think I didn't try to draw the water without it. That didn't go well for any of us." She grimaced, and Teela saw for the first time the small chink in her armor, that vulnerable crease in her forehead that betrayed the sorceress's real emotions. The smallest crack where the light could get through.

"Why?" Teela asked carefully. Evil-Lyn wasn't stupid enough to monologue her evil plan to a captive, but she was vain, and she was hungry for credit. Teela had realized that over the course of their brief—and, apparently, false—friendship. The more information she was able to get out of Evil-Lyn about the Wellspring, the more she'd have to hopefully use against her. "What happened when you tried to take the water without the vial?"

"The Wellspring tried to take it back," Evil-Lyn said. "It flooded over and then—well, you know." She swept her hands through the air, wiggling her fingers. "*Whoosh.*"

"The rain," Teela said. "The rain that ruined our camp and made everyone sick—that was because of you."

Evil-Lyn inclined her head. "I'd say I'm sorry but . . . I'm really not. Though if it makes you feel better, it got some of Skeletor's men, too. Cut a path straight from the Wellspring through the forest—it had gotten much less intense by the time it leached out, and I think it petered out shortly after. But it caught a troop of our scouts on the Blood River, and they didn't survive. See? Look at the sacrifices I've made."

Teela's heart stuttered. "I trusted you."

"Sweetheart." Evil-Lyn bent down and took Teela's face in her hands, squeezing her cheeks like she was a child. "Did you think we were actually friends? That's so . . . tragic." She sighed, then kissed Teela on the top of her head before pushing her backward onto the moldering carpet. Evil-Lyn turned, climbing back up the dais as she called backward over her shoulder, "Anyway, must dash. I've got a dictator to overthrow and a throne to seize."

"What?!" Teela struggled to push herself back to her knees with her arms and legs bound. "You're going to leave me here?"

"I wasn't sure, but then I found out you used all the water and that made up my mind."

"No, wait! Please!"

"You're right, that's so cruel of me," Evil-Lyn said with no hint she was going to do anything about it. She raised her hand, palm facing up, and suddenly the sunlight flooding through the glass dome overhead began to dim. Teela looked up, realizing Evil-Lyn was using magic to close the metal panels built around it, blotting out the sun and casting the Throne Room into darkness.

And darkness meant Shadow Beasts.

Teela pulled helplessly at her bonds, the magic sizzling against her skin. Evil-Lyn lowered her hand, only a sliver of light falling on the floor between them like a blade. "All right, you pulled at my heartstrings," she said, and waved. Teela's bonds vanished, and she toppled onto her side as she was freed. She heard the final turn of the crank, and the room was thrown into total darkness.

"Good luck, darling," Evil-Lyn's voice floated around her, and Teela swore she felt the breath on the back of her neck once more. "I'm rooting for you."

TWENTY-NINE

Teela staggered to her feet. Evil-Lyn had taken her sword, and, she realized, as she groped in her boot, her knife, too. She was unarmed. The Throne Room was dark enough that she could see only a few feet in front of her. She started to run for the door, but a shadow suddenly filled the doorway, twice Teela's size, and she skidded to a halt. She changed course, running instead for one of the side entrances, but it, too, was suddenly filled by a massive hulking figure, more darkness than substance.

The Shadow Beasts had found her.

Another beast was suddenly behind her, and she could smell the blood and flesh matted into his skin. Three pairs of eyes glowed red through the darkness, closing in on her, snarling and snapping their teeth, with what sounded like heavy clubs making a smacking sound against their palms. One of them slammed a club into the ground, and the stone cracked beneath it, sending up a spray of gravel.

Teela had no weapons. No way to fight these creatures.

Think, she told herself, trying to calm her breathing and get her heartbeat under control. Duncan would tell her to assess the situation and determine what resources were at her disposal—every fight was different, and not all weapons were always equally valuable.

The Shadow Beasts could not survive in sunlight, she reminded herself, and she looked up to the skylight, the panels now firmly closed. It was probably over a hundred feet overhead. But if she could get even one panel open, she might stand a chance.

Evil-Lyn had done it with magic, but Teela could use strength and cunning. And she knew the Throne Room better than any of these beasts. She had grown up here.

One of the Shadow Beasts roared. Teela barely managed to dodge as another swung a club at her, the *whoosh* of the club whistling through the air her only warning in the darkness. The stones under her feet cracked when the club collided with the floor, and she was thrown onto her back. One of the Shadow Beasts let out a low rumble, which Teela thought might be the equivalent of a laugh.

Still on all fours, Teela scrambled up to the dais. The dais was built against the Throne Room's back wall, so the beasts could only come at her from the front if she faced off against them there. It was a small comfort, but she'd take anything she could get.

She needed a weapon. Even if she could wrestle a club from one of the Shadow Beasts, she knew she wouldn't be able to lift it. But the throne that sat atop the dais was decorated with large iron spikes and golden swirls of metal scrollwork. Teela felt her way to the dais and grabbed on to the throne, trying to shake one of the spikes free, but the metal was too strong.

Teela climbed up onto the seat of the throne and faced off against the Shadow Beasts, staring them down in their red eyes. The one in the lead bared his teeth, then swung his club sideways at her. Teela jumped off the throne, the height giving her enough space that she cleared the club's arc so that instead it smashed into the back of the throne, splintering the iron.

Teela crashed hard to the floor, trying to roll out from the circle of the three Shadow Beasts around her. One of them managed to grab her by the foot, dragging her backward across the dais. She could feel the skin peeling off her arms as the ragged stones that made up the Throne Room's floor tore against it. A Shadow Beast lifted Teela into the air by her feet, one massive hand wrapped around her boots. The creature swung her toward his face—hot, meaty breath lifting her hair—but Teela whipped off her cloak and tossed it over the creature's face, obscuring his vision. The Shadow Beast swung at her, missing, and instead thrust one giant hand through the back of King Randor's throne. Teela heard several of the long iron bars finally wrench free and skitter across the floor, landing outside the circle of apes.

The second Shadow Beast tried to grab Teela, but the one still holding her swung her away, roaring territorially. Teela felt her spine crack from the unnatural movement. She pulled herself up, grabbing her own knees and fiddling with the straps on her boots until they came free. She slid out of her boots and dropped to the floor, leaving the Shadow Beast yanking the cloth from his eyes to discover he was left with nothing but her shoes. He flung them at the wall as Teela scrambled across the floor toward the broken iron bars, her fingers closing in around two of them.

She dove into the narrow gap between the throne and the wall, too small for the apes to reach her. One of the Shadow Beasts wedged a hand there, trying to grab her, and she jammed one of the iron bars into the soft skin between his fingers. He yowled, reeling backward. She used the distraction to slip free, and, tucking the two iron bars into her belt, climbed up onto the overturned throne and threw herself toward the wall, where she grabbed on to the bottom of one of the banners.

She braced herself as she heard a ripping sound, but somehow the banner held her weight. She wrapped the fabric around her foot as she had been taught to climb a rope in cadet training and, using it as a hoist, started to haul herself upward toward the panels on the ceiling.

She was halfway up the banner when she heard it ripping again and felt herself slipping down the wall. She twisted, looking back over her shoulder to see one of the Shadow Beasts had grabbed the banner and was clawing at it, trying to pull it down.

Teela whipped one of the iron bars from her belt and jammed it hard into the wall, catching the bar into the grooves between the stones. The banner fell around her, and she hung from the bar, legs dangling in empty air. She could feel the metal vibrating in her hands. She wasn't sure how long it would hold her.

One of the Shadow Beasts swiped at her, but even he wasn't tall enough to reach her. He swung his club and it smashed into the wall, just missing Teela. A shower of pebbles and dust exploded into the air.

She tested the strength of the bar—it was jammed into a crack in the wall hard enough that it held when she swung her feet up and stood on it. She was still too far away to reach the skylight, and as she searched the wall for any handholds she could use to climb higher, one of the Shadow Beasts leaped onto another banner nearby, clawing its way up after her. The ape's banner began to rip, but he was climbing fast enough that it looked to Teela as though he might reach the top before it tore. Teela pulled the second iron bar from her belt and swung at the banner the beast was climbing, slamming the bar into the rope holding the banner in place. The sharp end frayed the rope but didn't sever it. She whacked it again, then again, but the Shadow Beast was reaching for her, grabbing the bar she was standing on. It couldn't hold both their weight, and Teela felt it bending, slipping out from where she had jammed it into the wall.

She looked around wildly, searching for an escape. There was another banner hanging on the opposite side of the alcove the throne was positioned in. It looked too far to jump, but she had to try.

She threw herself into the air, just as the iron bar she was standing on broke free from the stones, sending the Shadow Beast crashing to the floor.

Teela had jumped harder than she thought, for she hit the wall, managing to catch the bar the banner hung from before she fell. She heard a crack and felt her ribs break at impact, driving the breath from her lungs. She almost lost her hold as pain ricocheted through her.

She swung her legs up so that she was standing on the bar just as she'd done with the iron spike, the banner fluttering beneath her. She began to swing it back and forth and jumped, aiming for the balcony that ran along the top of the dome, just as a door there blasted open and another Shadow Beast careened out. As Teela jumped, he grabbed her by the waist, snatching her out of the air and holding her over the rail of the balcony, one massive hand wrapped around her.

Teela wiggled, struggling to get free. She swung the iron bar, but it fell short of her target. The Shadow Beast roared, his breath blowing her hair back off her face. She thought he was going to drop her, but instead, the creature whirled around, slamming her into the wall of the tower. Her vision blurred, and she struggled not to black out.

The Shadow Beast threw Teela over his shoulder, but she managed to twist up and around enough to jam the iron bar into his eye. The Shadow Beast reeled backward, roaring in pain. His foot missed the balcony ledge, and Teela felt herself beginning to fall, the creature's hand still wrapped around her. She scrambled, barely managing to grab the railing as the Shadow Beast tumbled over the edge of the balcony. She felt her shoulders wrench in their sockets as the ape's weight hit her, but then his arms relaxed, and he fell, leaving Teela hanging off the balcony. She managed to pull herself up and back onto the edge of the balcony, and she rolled onto her back, gasping. She was still at least twenty feet from the skylight.

Teela's back ached, and she felt like her ribs were pressing down on her lungs. It was hard to breathe. She couldn't imagine standing up, let alone fighting again. This was what it felt like, she realized—to be defeated. The same way she had never really believed the city had fallen until she saw the smoking wreckage again, she hadn't really known what it meant to feel like things were really over until she was right in it.

Maybe it was all over. Maybe that was all right. When she thought of going back to the camp—of telling them all what she had done and who she had trusted, and how it had come back around to bite her in the butt—she wanted to lie there and let the Shadow Beasts take her. Maybe it would be better for everyone—she'd already screwed it all up. She'd made everything worse, no matter how noble her intentions had been.

You gotta get up.

Teela turned her head. Someone was lying beside her—Adam. She knew she was hallucinating, but that didn't make the happiness she felt at seeing his face any less real.

Teela didn't move. Each hard-won breath sounded like a page tearing from the spine of a book.

Come on, she heard Adam say. *You don't give up this easy.*

"I don't want to go back," she said.

I know, Adam replied. *But who would you be if you stayed?*

Teela looked at him. It almost felt as if he were here with her. Like if she had reached out, her hand would have met his cheek and stayed there.

"I'm glad you're here," she said.

Adam smiled. *Don't give up.*

Okay, then.

Teela heaved herself sideways, rolling onto the balcony. It took so much effort, she couldn't imagine standing up. She pushed herself up onto all fours and swore she felt someone—maybe her imaginary Adam—pulling her upward. She staggered to her feet, clutching the balcony rail to stay upright.

The door to the balcony banged open again, and Teela turned as the last Shadow Beast charged onto the walkway, roaring at her. His eyes flared like embers, and he grabbed a piece of the iron railing, yanking it from the stone and hurling it at Teela. She dodged, nearly collapsing again.

Teela looked up at the skylight. It was too far away to jump. But now that she was closer, she noticed the skylight had two large handles jutting down, probably so someone standing on the balcony could catch it with a crook to open and close it. She couldn't remember if she'd ever seen it used. Why couldn't she remember?

A plan began to form in Teela's mind. She looked at the Shadow Beast, then snatched the hooked piece of railing at her feet. She forced herself to stand still as the Shadow Beast bore down on her, raising his club to squash her.

She jumped back at the last second, and the Shadow Beast's club smashed into the ground. Teela jumped onto the end of the club, bracing herself against one of the metal spikes buried there. She had one chance to get this right. One chance or she'd die.

But at least she'd die fighting.

The Shadow Beast swung his club, and Teela let the momentum carry her upward, into the empty air between the balcony and the ceiling. She stretched as far as she could and felt the metal hook catch one of the handles of the skylight. Her arm wrenched, legs dangling over the empty air.

She swung her body as hard as she could, and the panel of the skylight slid open. Sunlight poured into the Throne Room, and the remaining Shadow Beast on the balcony reared backward, screaming when the light touched his skin.

Teela swung herself up, her foot catching on the edge of the skylight so that she was able to push herself up onto the roof. She hauled herself out, then collapsed on the tiles, gasping for breath.

She had made it out. The sun on her face felt like a warm bath, and she laughed without knowing why.

Teela slid down the slope of the roof, her bare feet gripping the tiles and controlling her fall. She jumped from the ledge of the Throne

Room to a nearby eave, injuries already beginning to throb now that her adrenaline was coming down, and paused to look out over the city. Eternos was a dark, smoky skeleton of what it had once been, and beyond it, she could see all the way across the water, past the craggy towers of Castle Grayskull, to the mountains. She remembered hiking those mountains with Adam, remembered that, as they paused on the curving path, out of breath and flushed with exertion, looking out over the city, she had said to him, "Just think. One day this will all be yours, Your Majesty."

To which he had replied, "It's yours, too. Eternia belongs to all of us."

Teela felt a fierce swell of possessiveness in her chest. This land was hers. This country was hers. This whole planet was hers. She was its defender. Its protector. Of every person in every corner, of every leaf on every tree.

She would not let Eternia die.

THIRTY

It took Teela almost twice as long to get back to the camp as it had taken her to get to Eternos. When she finally dragged herself back to where she had left the Sky Sled, constantly stopping to catch her breath, she was relieved to find it untouched. The ride itself was bumpy in a way that hadn't plagued her on the journey there, but with her broken ribs was absolute agony. She swore she could feel her bones throbbing against her lungs as the frame of the bike rattled under her. She stopped when the pain got too much, afraid to sleep, but so exhausted she dropped off every time she sat down on the trail, waking up hours later, disoriented and panicked.

When she finally made it back into the clearing where the refugee camp was assembled, Malcolm was on watch. He shouted when he saw her, calling for help even as he ran to meet her. "Teela! Where have you been? Andra said she saw you take . . ." He broke off when she toppled off the Sky Sled, her legs so wobbly she had to cling to the sled to stay upright. "You're hurt!"

"I'm all right," she said, though she knew the words were contradicted by her ragged breath and the mess on her shirt, the black of the Shadow Beasts' blood mingling with her own.

Malcolm looped an arm around her, holding her up, and she hissed in pain as he jostled her. "Sigrid! Duncan!" He called out.

Ahead of them, on the gangplank of the *Helios*, Teela saw Duncan appear. He dropped the tools he was carrying as he sprinted toward her. Teela's face felt hot and tight, and she let out a small sob without meaning to. "Dad."

Malcolm let go of her, and she stumbled forward into Duncan's arms. She realized, as she pressed her face into his shoulder and inhaled the familiar scent of him, that there had been a moment in the Throne Room battling the Shadow Beasts when she had thought she'd never see him again. It had felt like a more real possibility than it had when he had been sick after the rain. Then, she had been so sure she could find something. She had trusted her own wits. In the Throne Room, she truly hadn't known whether she would survive. It had felt so out of her control.

"Teela." Duncan lifted her into his arms, carrying her up the gangplank of the *Helios*. Teela caught a glimpse of Locke standing in the door to the cockpit, face pale, and a moment later, Sigrid came running up, Malcolm on her heels.

This, she thought, as Duncan laid her down on her pallet on the observation deck, was her home. These were her people. Her family. Teela felt her eyes closing as she relaxed for the first time in what felt like ages.

She would always be a warrior of Eternos, so long as she had people to fight for.

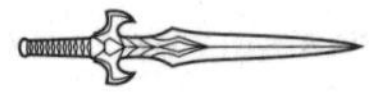

When Teela woke hours later, the dark sky had changed to the warm amber of dawn. Teela sat up slowly, her ribs still aching, but she remembered vaguely that at some point Sigrid had given her something for the pain, and it had helped. She was wearing a clean shirt, and the wounds on her hands and legs had been bandaged.

For a moment, she thought she had dreamed it—she *hoped* she had dreamed it. The palace and the Shadow Beasts and Evil-Lyn taking the vial. Teela reached up and touched the spot on her collarbone where she had been carrying the vial for weeks now, but it wasn't there. Dread curdled in her stomach, chased by regret. The weight of the decisions she'd made—the choice to ally herself with Evil-Lyn and fall for her trap—crashed over her head like a wave. How stupid it seemed now in hindsight. Stupid and desperate, and now she'd have to face the consequences.

The *Helios* observation deck was quiet, but she could hear activity on the deck below. She climbed down the ladder to the bridge and found Duncan in the cockpit. His face broke into a smile when he saw her. "You're awake. Come, sit down." She sank into the pilot's chair beside him as he took the copilot's seat. "How are you feeling?"

"I'm okay," Teela said.

"What happened, Teela? Why would you just run off somewhere without telling anyone or taking someone with you?" Duncan's voice was more concerned than angry.

Teela briefly closed her eyes, already exhausted at the thought of everything she'd need to tell him. "I went to the palace."

"You went to Eternos?" Duncan's brow furrowed. "Why?"

This was it. The moment she was going to have to tell her father everything. The secret of her meetings with Evil-Lyn and the Wellspring water had gotten too big for her, and now that she knew the truth of what she had done, she couldn't carry it alone any longer. She needed help. She needed advice. She needed someone to tell her she wasn't a bad person because she had placed her trust in the wrong person.

"Teela," Duncan said quietly.

Teela swallowed hard. "I have to tell you something." She looked up at him. His face was serious, and when he didn't say anything, she swallowed, then continued. "I made a mistake. I made an alliance I shouldn't have."

A crease appeared between Duncan's eyebrows. "An alliance?"

Teela took a deep breath. "With Evil-Lyn."

Teela braced herself for Duncan's anger. His disappointment. *Something.* Some reaction proportionate to the mistake she had made.

Duncan's eyebrows rose, but he stayed silent. Teela wished he would speak, just so she wouldn't have to anymore.

She swallowed hard. Her throat was feeling thick. "I'm sorry," she said, and her voice came out very small. "I should have told you."

"No," Duncan said, "there should never have been anything to tell, because you should never have made such an alliance to begin with."

"I know," Teela said, smarting under his tone. She had hoped—foolishly, she now realized—that he would be understanding. But no, she reminded herself, her father was a general, through and through. In this moment, she was his soldier, and she had made a mistake. It was his job to set her straight, and her job to take it on the chin. "I know that now."

"What was the nature of this . . . alliance?" Duncan asked.

The story came tumbling out of her, every detail, like a dam broken inside her: the water from Granamyr, the run-in with Evil-Lyn at Darksmoke, the antidote, the runes, discovering there was so much more that could be done with the magical water, and Evil-Lyn offering to teach her. The library atlas and the wasting sickness, the way the planet was dying because of her.

"I didn't know there was a consequence tied to using it," Teela said. "I thought I'd found a way to help the camp." When Duncan still looked disappointed, Teela added, "If I'd known, I would never have used it." Though she was sure they both heard the emptiness of the words. She would do anything for her father. She just wasn't sure if that was a strength or a weakness. Love was a chink in the armor; reason always bowed to it.

"But you did know," Duncan said, and Teela started to protest when he clarified, "You knew that Evil-Lyn could not be trusted, and that anything she could teach you would come with consequences and constraints. Surely, you knew that anything she offered you would have strings attached."

"She seemed . . . different," Teela said, then explained when Duncan raised an eyebrow. "Different from what I thought she was. Different from the rest of Skeletor's men. And I thought—" she drew in a quick breath, wincing at the answering flash of pain in her ribs "—she understood what it was like to be alone."

"You're not alone," Duncan said, but Teela shook her head.

"Sometimes I feel like I am. I feel like I'm the only one who cares if we stay here. The only one who wants to protect our home or cares about the life we had before."

"That's not true—" Duncan began, but Teela pushed on.

"I know things will never be the same, but Eternia is still important. It's still worth defending. And I thought she understood that. She made me think we weren't on different sides. We had a common enemy. And a common goal."

A pause. Teela felt foolish and vulnerable, voicing these feelings that had prompted her to place her trust in a villain. She had been so desperate for an ally, so alone in the camp among the other warriors who seemed to think survival was a state of being, not a temporary state until they returned to claim what was theirs. Who couldn't seem to see beyond the end of the day. But now, in hindsight, she could see all the holes in the story Evil-Lyn had fed her. They had been there all along. Teela had just been too lonely and desperate, too eager to be the hero and save the camp so everyone would stay, to look too closely.

"You," Duncan finally said quietly, "have shouldered so much responsibility."

"Everyone has to do what they can," Teela said.

"But they don't have to do it alone. You're not alone, Teela. You never have been. But you have to learn to trust other people. The right people," Duncan added. "The people who have shown you through their words and actions that they are worthy of your trust. No one in this camp is against you. Whether or not you agree with them, you need to learn to treat their ideas with the same respect you want them to treat yours."

"Are you saying I should listen to Locke and pretend to be totally fine with leaving?"

"No." Duncan shook his head. "But I'm saying that you do not have to look for allies in someone like Evil-Lyn. This camp is full of people who want the same thing as you."

Teela stared down at her hands, feeling small and foolish. In Duncan's even voice and sharp gaze, she couldn't imagine how she had ever thought it was a good idea to trust Evil-Lyn. She wished she could go back in time and step in between herself and the sorceress and scold herself, *You know better than this!* Because she had, but she had done it anyway. She had been so stupid, so naive, so—

Then Duncan reached out, took her hand in his, and squeezed it. "Thank you for telling me," he said. "Admitting we have made a mistake is often the hardest part of making them right."

Teela nodded, her heart feeling just a little less heavy.

"I only wish you had told me sooner," Duncan said.

"I couldn't tell you," Teela said. "Because you're . . ." She rubbed a hand over her cheek. "It's like you're not really here, sometimes. I was afraid that if we left Eternia, you'd have nothing left, and I . . ." she wiped at her eyes. "I couldn't stand the thought of losing you."

"As long as you are here with me," Duncan said, "I have something to fight for. Teela, you do not have to do this on your own. None of us do. It's why we are still all here together. We are stronger as a group."

"But have you given up on Eternia?" Teela asked.

Duncan leaned backward against the control panel of the ship with a heavy sigh. "It is hard," he said after a moment, "to know that I had one purpose in the court of the king, and I failed to uphold it when the time came. And that I have failed to make it right since."

"But you didn't fail," Teela said quietly. "You did what you could. We were outnumbered. Ambushed. It was an impossible situation."

"I could have done more," Duncan said, "or else I should have died there. The honorable death of a warrior of Eternos."

"I'm glad you didn't," Teela said. "I don't know what I would have done without you."

"I'll admit, at times I've lost sight of the path forward. Sometimes the shadow of that night overwhelms me, and it feels impossible to see through the darkness of it. But, Teela, I promise you, I have not given up. Not on Eternos. Not on the king and queen and Adam. Not on you. Never on you. I am so proud of the leadership you've taken on."

"You have no reason to be proud of me," Teela said miserably. "I picked the wrong ally and did damage to our planet. I had no idea what I was doing."

"None of us do. None of us can know the consequences of our actions. We can anticipate but never truly predict them. Life is random. The terrible secret of existence is that the universe is unfeeling and does not care for us. It is why we must care for each other."

Teela nodded. "So what do I do now?" she said. "If Evil-Lyn takes the water from the Wellspring, Eternia might die."

"I don't know that there's anything you can do."

"I can go after her. I can stop her."

"The Wellspring is almost impossible to reach. It's days of hard travel. And you don't know what awaits you when you reach the Whispering Valley. There might be more dangers we don't know of."

"But that gives us time," Teela said. "I know Evil-Lyn can't get there by magic, and that puts us on equal footing. She doesn't have the advantage over us. And if she's been there before, I can follow her. She knows how to access it."

Duncan ran a hand over his chin. "Teela . . ."

"I can reach the Wellspring, I know it. If she can, so can I."

"And then what? You fight her? She's a sorceress. She is powerful."

"So am I."

"My darling, delusional child," Duncan said with a laugh. "One of the truest signs of a warrior is knowing when it is time to admit defeat."

"We are not defeated," Teela corrected him. "A warrior will fight until the end. They will fight with their face in the dirt and blood in their eyes, because they would rather die for a cause than surrender." She knew the words felt pointed after what Duncan had said about wishing he had died in the service of the king and queen, but she didn't retreat from it.

Duncan's eyes darkened. "You cannot go to the Wellspring, Teela."

"I will not let our home die."

"I forbid it."

Teela almost laughed. "You forbid it? As my general?"

"And as your father," Duncan said firmly.

"Suddenly you're interested in being my father?" She saw Duncan's eyes widen and knew she was being cruel, but she was angry. "To say nothing of general. You have not been either of those things since Eternos fell."

"Teela."

"You cannot decide to step up again only when it suits you."

"I am trying to protect you."

"And I am trying to protect our home!"

"You are my home, Teela!" Duncan grabbed her by the shoulders. His eyes were sparking with emotion. "I cannot lose you." Teela felt her own eyes welling, and when Duncan opened his arms, she fell into them, pressing her face into his chest and taking a deep breath. He smelled like himself, still, like leather polish and rain.

"I have to make this right," Teela said quietly, her face against her father. "Please. You have to give me a chance to make this right."

"Do you remember," Duncan said quietly, "when you were young, and you and Adam convinced yourselves there was a ghost in the high tower?"

"There was," Teela muttered, and Duncan's chest rumbled as he laughed quietly.

"You set out wards and made salt barriers and stayed up all night, scaring yourselves silly waiting to see that ghost, but there was nothing there. It was only the two of you. Haunting yourselves. We will shake the ghosts of our past, Teela. Someday, if you'll give me time. And patience. I will stop haunting myself someday."

Teela nodded, but knew she'd never be free of her own ghosts. She didn't want to be. Better to have Adam in her mind than lose him altogether. She would be the ghost of Eternos, if that's what it took, refusing to leave or move on until she was sure that everything was the way it was meant to be.

THIRTY-ONE

Sigrid did what she could for Teela's injuries, though their supplies were limited. Despite knowing the consequences, Teela found herself wishing she had a drop of the Wellspring water left, that magical cure-all that could ease the pain in her ribs and heal the gash in her head from where Evil-Lyn had struck her.

She couldn't stop thinking about Evil-Lyn, no doubt on her way to the Wellspring already, the vial Teela had been wearing for so many weeks now nestled against the sorceress's chest. As Teela lay in the observation deck of the *Helios*, she pulled out the page she had ripped from the atlas in the library and studied it. She reread the words, blotted with blood but still legible, over and over until her eyes blurred.

Teela heard a creaking sound as someone climbed onto the ladder leading up to the deck. She expected her father, or perhaps Sigrid checking in on her. But instead, Locke's head appeared over the edge. "Hey."

"I can leave," Teela said quickly. "If you need to work here."

"No." Locke shook her head. "I was looking for you, actually." Locke pulled herself the rest of the way up the ladder and onto the observation deck. "Your dad told me," she said with no prelude. "About Evil-Lyn."

Teela pulled her knees up to her chest. "Have you come to gloat about how stupid I am?"

"Of course not," Locke said. "I came to see if you were okay."

Teela rested her chin on her arms and laughed wetly. "Not really, no."

Locke sat cross-legged across from Teela. Her knuckles were cracked and scraped, the creases lined black with grease from the ship.

"So does everyone know?" Teela said, more loudly than she meant to. "About my stupid alliance with the evilest woman in Eternia?"

"Word is getting around," Locke said. "Duncan told me because he wanted me to check on you. See if you were okay. Which . . ." She tipped her head. "Asked and answered."

Teela buried her face against her arms with a moan. "I'm going to have to tell everyone."

"Yeah," Locke said. "That's going to suck."

Teela laughed despite herself. "I thought you were supposed to be checking to see if I was okay. Not making things worse."

"It's going to suck," Locke pressed on, as though Teela hadn't spoken, "to have to tell everyone, because it always sucks to have to admit you did something wrong. But it's going to be okay because everyone here cares about you. And loves you. And will forgive you. I mean, we'd still all be dead without you."

"So now the planet's going to die instead," Teela muttered.

"Yeah, Duncan mentioned that, too."

When Locke fell silent, Teela looked up. Locke was biting her thumbnail, staring at the floor between them. Teela almost spoke, just to end the painful stretch of silence, but Locke spoke again before she could.

"Everyone will understand," she said. "We've all made compromises and sacrifices and bargains. We've all trusted people we regret. I know I have. And . . ." She cleared her throat, then looked up at Teela. "I'm sorry I've been hard on you."

Teela shrugged. "I deserved it. Clearly, I didn't know what I was doing."

Locke pursed her lips, and Teela found herself wishing Locke would say something in disagreement. Instead, she said, "I know we've had our differences, but I hope that we can at least understand each other. I don't want to leave Eternia either, Teela. I only want to do what's best for our company."

"But what about the ship?" Teela asked. "Why are you working so hard to get off the planet if you claim not to want to?"

"Because I want us to survive," Locke said. "Eternia is not just a place—it is its warriors and its people. It's us. I want to protect the world that exists within this camp. If there was any other way, I would take it, but I don't see how we stay here and survive with Skeletor in charge."

"But if we leave, who will fight him?" Teela countered. "It might be a risk, but someone has to fight for goodness and truth and righteousness and all those other things that sound cheesy as I'm saying it aloud."

"I don't disagree with you," Locke said carefully. "But I don't know if it should be us who stay to fight. We're just dooming ourselves to lose if we start a fight we aren't prepared for."

"Then who will?" Teela challenged her. "The planet needs a defender. Eternia is its people, but what are we without Eternia? Warriors don't give up. They don't leave or back down from a fight just because the odds are stacked against them. If we leave, who will we be?"

Locke fell silent. She rested her chin on her fists, elbows on her knees.

Teela was exhausted. Her head throbbed and she wanted to sleep. She couldn't remember the last time she had slept long and deep, from sundown to dawn, as she used to when she was a child.

"And I have to do something about it," Teela continued. "I made this mess—I hurt the planet."

"You didn't know—" Locke said, but Teela interrupted her.

"That doesn't matter. That doesn't absolve me. I'm going to stop Evil-Lyn from getting to the Wellspring. Even if we end up leaving Eternia, I won't let her destroy our planet."

"You," Locke said, "would have made a great man-at-arms."

Teela felt her face go red, though she wasn't sure if it was in pleasure at the compliment or shame.

"You still might," Locke said before Teela could answer. "When all this is over. When we can go home. Back to Eternos. I'll be proud to fight with you then, Teela. I'm proud to fight with you now." She reached out and put a hand on Teela's knee and squeezed. "So. What's our plan?"

"I don't really have one yet," Teela confessed, then realized what Locke had said. "*Our* plan?"

"Well, I'm not going to let you go alone. Think of all the trouble you got up to last time we let you wander off on your own to save the world." Locke grinned. "And the time before that, too, come to think of it."

"You don't have to," Teela said.

"I know," Locke said. "But I want to."

Teela nodded.

"So," Locke said, "what do you know about the Wellspring?"

Teela handed her the page torn from the book, and as Locke read it quickly, she explained her idea. "The Wellspring has wards against it—magic can't breach it. Evil-Lyn has been there before, so she'll know how to access it, but magic won't be able to help her. Even if it gets her some of the way there, she'll still need to get to the Wellspring itself without magic. Plus, she's operating in secret. She can't trust any of Skeletor's men, so she'll be doing this alone. She won't have reinforcements."

"Do you think we can head her off before she gets to the Whispering Valley?" Locke asked. "Try to track her? Did she give you any way to contact her or know where she is?"

Teela shook her head. "I guess we could wait near the entrance to the valley and see if she appears or comes out."

"That's leaving a lot up to chance." Locke pursed her lips. "Can she use magic once she's in the valley?"

"I don't think so," Teela said. "That's part of the protection wards."

"Then that's where we should face her," Locke said. "Somewhere she doesn't have the upper hand. You know she won't give it up without a fight, but if she has magic and we don't, she'll always have the upper hand. We wait for her to enter the valley, then accost her and take the vial. Once we have it, we destroy it."

"How do *we* get to the valley?" Teela asked.

"We can take the Sky Sled."

"Will it fit the both of us?" Teela asked.

Locke's forehead creased. "I might be able to repurpose some parts of the main ship to make a bigger base we could both fit on. Or a close approximation of one. I can't say it will last long, but it should get us to the valley, even if we have to walk back."

"But that means taking apart the *Helios,*" Teela said. "If something happens to the parts, you might not be able to put it back together. You'd be undoing all the hard work you put in to fix it."

"Well, then we'd better make sure nothing happens to it." Locke pushed herself to her feet and threw out a hand to pull Teela up after her. When Teela was on her feet, Locke punched her arm lightly and added, "I'm not done arguing with you yet."

THIRTY-TWO

Duncan didn't like their plan. Malcolm didn't like their plan. Sigrid didn't like their plan, though her concerns were more tied to the fact that Teela was still healing from her injuries.

But something had to be done to stop Evil-Lyn. And they didn't have time to waste. Evil-Lyn might already be on her way to the Wellspring. For all Teela knew, she might have gone there and back already and was in the process of using it to poison Skeletor. They might already be too late.

But they had to try.

Locke tried to fit the Sky Sled with several different bases stripped from the *Helios*, but none were light enough for the small engine to support them, even before Teela and Locke climbed on.

"We need something lighter," Locke said.

"Wood?" Teela suggested. "We could carve something from a felled tree."

"It won't be fire resistant," Locke said. "It needs to be light and able to withstand heat."

"What about the Karikoni shell?" Teela suggested, remembering the gift that the captured leader, Pinchent, had given her. "He said it was light—they use them as boats. And shields, so it's got to be tough."

Locke nodded thoughtfully. "Might as well try it."

Teela retrieved the shell and helped Locke connect the engine to it. When she switched on the power, the sled lifted like it weighed nothing, shifting and moving through the sky as Locke twisted the steering mechanism.

There wasn't room or weight to spare for much in the way of an armory on the Sky Sled, but they both had their swords and Teela a set of knives lent her by Andra, since Evil-Lyn had taken hers at the palace. Locke had Duncan's weapon strapped across her back beside her sword, the ammo clips on her belt.

Duncan stood beside Teela, both of them watching as Locke made the last checks to the sled before their departure. The early-morning dew coated the branches of the trees around the clearing, coating the world in silver. "I was going to give you a gift," he said. "My pin with the sign of Eternos on it."

"Oh . . ." Teela started, realizing she had never told her father she had taken it with her to Darksmoke.

He turned to her, the corners of his lips turned up. "But I hear it now belongs to a dragon."

"Well, you weren't exactly able to offer it up," Teela said.

Duncan grinned. "I was mostly interested in the symbolism. A way to show you we are all with you. To remind you what you're fighting for."

"I don't need a reminder," Teela said quietly. "I couldn't forget."

Duncan reached out and wrapped her in his arms. His embrace was fierce and familiar, and when his grip tightened around her, she wanted to stay there forever. Safe and warm and protected. She wanted him to always be here, this barrier between her and the world, keeping her safe from her own choices and their consequences.

But that was no way to live.

Locke called, "Teela. I'm ready if you are."

Duncan loosened his grip. "Be careful," he said, so quietly she almost didn't hear him. She looked over her shoulder at Locke, waiting for her, one hand on the handles she had rigged to the front of the shell for steering. Behind it, they had fitted the pilot's seat from the *Helios* cockpit. Locke would stand in the front and pilot, while Teela sat behind her.

"Ready?" Locke prompted.

Teela turned back to Duncan. "Locke told me," she said, "that on Geolon, they don't say goodbye. They say, *Until the circle closes.* Because it means you'll see the other person again. The circle always comes back around."

Duncan nodded, first to Locke, then to Teela. "Until the circle closes," he said, and pressed his hand to his heart.

Locke did the same, head bowed.

"Take care of each other," Duncan said. "Come home."

Teela climbed up onto the seat behind Locke. Locke kicked the engine to life, and the sled vibrated under them. Teela stared down at Duncan as the sled rose into the air, soaring toward the treetops and away from their camp and the clearing. He stayed, face to the sky, watching them go, until they were out of sight.

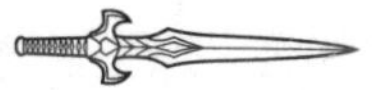

Teela lost track of how long they were in the air. Her whole body was so tense she could feel the ache in her still-healing ribs. She was braced for the sled to fall from the sky—somehow it still seemed impossible they were airborne. Locke had installed the navigation system from the escape pod between the handlebars, and as she steered, Teela stared over her shoulder, following their progress on the panel lit up on the dashboard. The small dot representing their sled drew closer and closer to the edge of the map. When the triangles of peaks appeared on the map, Teela looked up, face to the wind, and saw the Mystic Mountains ahead of them, their jagged tops like broken teeth breaking through the clouds.

Their climb through the mountains was treacherous, but Locke was a good pilot. Even with a ship that barely followed her commands, and an engine in danger of falling out entirely, she led them through the peaks and crags with a deft hand until finally they crested a ledge and the Whispering Valley opened before them.

The valley was a wide expanse of green nestled between the peaks, overgrown with thick trees that were in stark contrast to the anemic, charred trees that were currently populating the forest. Their roots burst from the ground, pushing their fingers through the grass and forming twisted bridges that Teela was sure were higher than she was tall. The wind that had been whipping at their hair the whole journey seemed to die suddenly, and the air smelled of rain and new greenery. Teela felt her heart kick against her rib cage. Somehow, even as they were building the sled and preparing to leave, she had never believed they'd actually make it here. She felt as if she were standing on the edge of a cliff, toes hanging off, leaning toward free fall.

"So," Locke shouted over the engine, "where to now?"

Teela pulled the page ripped from the atlas out of her pocket and turned it until the compass sketched beneath it lined up with the sun. It was an illustration more than a map, but there was a star drawn along the peak line, leading to the inset illustration of the passage leading to the Wellspring. "There should be a fissure," she said, turning the map until the shapes of the valley walls mirrored the inked outlines. "That way." She pointed ahead, where the valley twisted out of sight between the peaks. It was hard to tell if it was actually narrowing there or if it was simply an optical illusion, perspective forced by the mountains.

Locke pulled back on the handlebars, and the sled glided down from the edge of the vista, skimming the treetops.

As they crossed the valley, the rock walls around them began to narrow, the ground climbing up to meet them. It felt like the whole valley was narrowing around them, turning cavernous and enclosed. The trees vanished, and the grass dwindled until it was just bare, tumbled rock below them.

Locke pulled up suddenly as the valley walls slowly tapered around them. Teela was beginning to worry she'd directed them down the wrong path, when Locke pointed below. "Look there!"

Teela squinted ahead. The sun was almost blotted out by the narrowing walls overhead, and it was getting hard to see. Then, she spotted it, too. A ship had been abandoned on the floor of the valley. The leaves and debris that had been piled on top of the ship in an attempt to camouflage it had blown asunder just enough that the dragonfly-like wings jutting from the sides were visible.

"That's a Fright Fighter," Teela observed.

"Straight from Snake Mountain, I'd bet," Locke said.

Teela felt a shiver go through her. Evil-Lyn was here. The idea suddenly made her dizzy with fear, far greater than the first time when she had faced the sorceress across the ice bridge in Darksmoke. Evil-Lyn knew her now. And Teela knew what she was capable of.

"Looks like the wings were too wide for her to get any closer," Locke said. "She must be on foot. Do you think the cave is ahead?"

Teela looked around at the walls curving around them. "I think this is the cave," she said. "The whole valley runs into it."

Locke looked around, too. "On we go, then."

Locke and Teela continued on the sled as the passage around them narrowed farther. Locke had to slow them down, navigating carefully to keep the sled from wrecking against the craggy sides of the tunnel. Sparks flew from the rock whenever the Karikoni shell base of the sled scraped the stone. Locke winced every time.

"I don't know how much farther we can go," she called to Teela over her shoulder. "I can hardly see, and I'm worried I'm going to hit something."

She was right, Teela realized. The sun was far at their backs now, though the change had been so gradual she had hardly noticed it. "Brace yourself," Locke said. "I'm bringing us down." The sled began to sink, their descent interrupted when they struck the edge of a rock formation. The shell tipped, and Teela gripped the edges of her seat.

Locke settled their sled on the loose gravel, and they climbed down. Teela's legs were stiff after sitting for so long, her ribs still aching, and she adjusted her sword on her hip. She shivered. With the engine off and no longer blowing hot exhaust around them, the air in the cave was wet and cool. Teela could smell mud and the rot of water on stone.

"Good thing we didn't keep going," Locke said, pointing ahead, and as Teela's eyes adjusted, she saw that the tunnel narrowed ahead of them to a tiny point of light far in the distance. Locke unhooked a small light from her belt, which she had rescued from the tool kit she found on the *Helios*, and held it up to illuminate the rock walls ahead of them. The beam reached only a few feet in front of them, and with the long, narrowing passage behind, Teela felt a small surge of fear. They were so deep in these mountains it felt like there was nothing ahead and nothing behind. Like they could walk forever and never get anywhere.

"Ready?" Locke asked, and Teela squared her shoulders.

"As I'll ever be."

They had to walk single file, Teela in front and Locke behind her, and the tunnel soon narrowed so much that they both had to crouch, then crawl on hands and knees. Teela's sword dug into her side, scraping the roof of the tunnel when she hooked it to her back, so she ended up taking it off her belt and hooking it to her boot, dragging it behind her. Behind her, she could hear Locke's breath thickening.

"Teela," she called as the tunnel narrowed further, and Teela felt the scrape of wet rock against her back. "Are you sure this is right?"

"Not at all," Teela said, but she could see that small point of light ahead of them. She'd thought it would get bigger as they grew closer, but instead it stayed small, like they weren't moving at all. It was the way that it stayed so unchangingly the same that made her sure it was magic, not just the end of a slowly narrowing tunnel. She was sure she could see sky through it.

Teela pushed forward, braced for her head to strike a stone—the tunnel looked too narrow for them to fit any farther—but somehow she kept going. She could feel the stone pushing in all around her like she was being buried alive, and she had to force herself to keep her breaths even and slow to stop herself from panicking.

"Teela," Locke said again, her voice pitched with the same fear Teela felt tightening in her own chest, but Teela didn't stop.

"We're almost there," she called back to Locke.

"How do you know?"

"I don't!" Teela called, but somehow she was certain. She could feel it thrumming in her blood. She reached out a hand, stretching as far as she could, and she felt a breeze. She felt the sun.

And, suddenly, she tumbled out of the narrowing tunnel and into the open air.

THIRTY-THREE

Teela collapsed, gasping, onto her back on a patch of green grass, soft and perfumed as the finest carpets in the Royal Palace at Eternos. A moment later, Locke tumbled seemingly out of the solid wall behind her, falling directly onto Teela and knocking the breath out of her.

Locke rolled off Teela, her chest heaving, and they lay side by side for a moment before Locke laughed. "Wow," she said. "I thought you were insane."

Teela sat up, looking around at the glen they had fallen into. The rock walls soared above them on all sides, so high that if there was a top, they couldn't see it. Water dripped down the walls in clear rivulets, striping the rocks with mineral deposits. The glen was flush with bright green ferns, a heavy down of thick grass and moss. Willow branches dipped low, creating intermittent curtains across the path ahead like the curtains of a stage. A thin mist hung over everything, shifting and shimmering.

Teela climbed to her feet, using her sword for support, then threw out a hand to help Locke up. "Come on."

They started forward side by side, both with their hands on the hilts of their swords. The willow branches were so thick it was hard to see where they were going in places, and Teela kept expecting to run directly into one of the canyon walls. She was braced, too, for Evil-Lyn to appear suddenly in front of them. Knowing the sorceress couldn't use her magic here was a small comfort—but she was a formidable warrior, even without magical assistance, and Teela wasn't sure if they were about to be ambushed or be the ones doing the ambushing.

They emerged from the thick tangle of willows into a wide clearing, still surrounded by the soaring stone canyon walls. Teela was damp all over, her hair sticking to her face from the mist.

Locke grabbed her arm, halting her progress. "There it is."

Teela turned, and there was the Wellspring, just as it had looked in the illustration in the atlas. A small waterfall poured from a source unseen—maybe the air, maybe the stone walls of the canyon, so perfect and beautiful it looked like it had been built to imitate nature in a palace garden. The water was a bright clear blue like a transparent summer sky, and it burbled quietly over the stones.

Teela looked around. Other than the soft sound of the water, the clearing was silent. And deserted. "There's no one here," Teela said.

"Maybe she already came and left," Locke said.

"Without her ship?" Teela asked, referencing the vehicle they'd seen in the valley tunnel.

"Maybe she wrecked it and left it there."

Teela shook her head. "I think we'd know if she's been here and taken the water. I think this place would feel different." She took a step forward, the moss spongy and soft beneath her feet. She felt hypnotized by the falling water, drunk on the feeling of the soft mist against her skin. She couldn't think straight.

Then she heard a *thump* behind her and turned.

Locke was standing rigidly still, as though she had heard something. Then Teela noticed her eyes were glazed, like she wasn't seeing what was in front of her.

"Locke?" Teela said, just as Locke slumped forward onto her knees, a dagger sticking out of her back. *My daggers*, Teela realized with horror, the ones Evil-Lyn had taken from her at the palace. "Locke!" Teela leaped toward her, just as Teela's other dagger sunk into the soft earth where she had been standing moments before. She looked around wildly, but there was no one there. She grabbed Locke under the arms and dragged her backward into the shelter of the willow branches, though it occurred to her that might be where the knives were being thrown from. It was impossible to tell in that thick curtain.

Locke was gasping for breath, blood seeping through the back of her tunic around the hilt of Teela's dagger as Teela laid her on her side. She wanted to pull the dagger out, but she knew better. "It's okay," Teela said, though it wasn't. She didn't know what else to say.

"Teela . . ." Locke struggled to speak. "She's behind . . ."

Teela whipped around, hand on her sword hilt, but there was no one there, just the rippling willow branches.

Teela turned, just as another blade sailed through the air inches from their heads, slicing off the willow branches sheltering them. Teela bit back a scream of frustration.

Locke's hand tightened on Teela's arm. "Go."

"I'll come back for you," Teela said, her voice breaking.

"I know," Locke said, her voice a whisper.

Teela drew her sword, staggering to her feet. She pushed forward into the willow branches, parting them with her blade held in front of her.

"Are you too scared to face me," she called, "now that you can't use your magic?"

Silence. Only the sound of the willow branches rustling against each other. Teela strained, trying to hear anyone moving or even the babbling of the Wellspring, something to help orient herself besides the pounding of her own heart.

Something moved behind her, and she spun, dropping into a crouch. Another knife hit the tree behind her, so close to her face that it severed a chunk of her hair. She rolled into the shade of the tree, pressing herself against the trunk. She knew which direction the knife had come from now.

She could feel her shoulders heaving, and she tried to breathe as quietly as possible. She unhooked an ammo clip from her belt and tossed it ahead of her as far as she could. A pause, then another knife flew from the trees in front of her in the direction of the clip. Teela crawled forward in the direction of where the knife had flown from, then tossed another clip. This time, when the knife flew, she knew exactly where it had come from.

Teela eased herself to her feet, creeping forward as silently as she could, though it was hard to sneak through the curtain of willow branches that rippled every time she moved. She could see it now, the shadow ahead through the trees.

She saw a flash of white hair.

Evil-Lyn had one hand on the trunk of the nearest tree, her head tipped. It was strange, Teela realized, to see the sorceress in a moment of complete vulnerability. No one was watching her. Teela could see in her posture, her face, the way she reached for another knife at her waist, that without magic, Evil-Lyn wasn't sure how to fight.

Teela raised her sword, but it disrupted the branches between them. Evil-Lyn turned, just as Teela swung her blade. Evil-Lyn threw up her knife, and the blades connected with a clang.

When Evil-Lyn saw Teela, she laughed, the sound ringing out so loudly that it almost knocked Teela off-balance. "Well," Evil-Lyn said. "And here I thought nothing could surprise me."

Teela didn't bother to answer, just swung at her again, and Evil-Lyn drew her own sword. This time Teela's swing struck the steel with such force it sent vibrations through her arms. Teela swung again, and Evil-Lyn dodged. The tip of Teela's blade caught the shirt of the sorceress's dress, tearing open the neck. The vial swung out from under her shirt, and Teela could see it was still empty.

Teela swung again, and Evil-Lyn ducked. Teela's blade lodged in the trunk of the tree.

"I really thought you wouldn't make it out of the palace," Evil-Lyn said. "Perhaps I underestimated you. Or perhaps you just got lucky. I suppose there's only one way to find out which one it is."

Teela unwedged her blade from the willow tree, but Evil-Lyn danced out of the range of her next swing, disappearing into the thick willow branches. Teela lunged forward, blade in front of her, but Evil-Lyn wasn't there. She swung at the branches, combing through them.

"Teela!" She could hear someone calling her name—not Evil-Lyn. Locke? Adam? She thought for a wild moment she could see him, a rippling flash through the branches, the same way she had seen him at the palace. "Teela!"

She ducked around the trunk of the tree, sword held in front of her. Something moved behind her, and she turned, just as Evil-Lyn lunged at her. Evil-Lyn's knife went through Teela's shoulder, pinning her to the tree. She screamed in pain, and her sword fell from her hand. Evil-Lyn tipped her head. "Well, that answers that. Just . . ." She twisted the knife, and Teela screamed in pain. "Dumb . . . luck."

Teela struggled, trying to kick or strike or do anything to knock the sorceress off her feet. "This," Evil-Lyn said, "is an even more embarrassing death than you would have died in the palace. How sad. Do you want me to tell your father the truth of your sorry end, or should I lie?"

Suddenly, the chain around Evil-Lyn's neck snapped and the vial fell. Evil-Lyn grabbed for it, but Teela realized it hadn't fallen—the chain had been snapped by Locke, who was standing behind the sorceress. She had pulled Evil-Lyn's knife from her back and had used it to hook the chain, pulling the vial from around the sorceress's throat. Evil-Lyn spun, but Teela kicked, her foot connecting with Evil-Lyn's legs, sweeping them out from under her. Evil-Lyn hit the ground hard, striking her head. Teela locked eyes with Locke. She nodded, and Locke smashed the vial into the tree trunk.

It didn't break.

Locke stared down at the vial in her hand, like she was trying to make sense of it. She tried slashing it with her knife next, but the blade bounced off. Locke looked up at Teela, and Teela saw her own sickening realization mirrored in Locke's face.

The vial couldn't be destroyed.

Teela yanked the knife out of her shoulder, blood soaking through the fabric of her tunic, then threw out a hand to Locke. Teela threw Locke's arm over one shoulder, helping her as they stumbled forward into the trees. Teela felt the pull in her injured shoulder, but she kept going.

"What do we do?" Locke's voice was ragged, heavy breaths punching through each word. "If we can't . . . destroy it. She'll take it from us . . . or find it . . ."

Teela's feet slipped on the wet moss, and she caught herself against a tree. Locke winced in pain, and Teela thought of the tunnel ahead of them, the long, dark scramble it would take for them to get out of here. The pain in her shoulder seemed to pulse at just the thought of it, claustrophobia clawing at her chest when she imagined herself stuck in that narrow cavern, crawling forward forever as the walls closed in around her.

Which was when the idea suddenly occurred to her.

They couldn't destroy the vial.

But they could close off the source.

"We have to collapse the tunnel," Teela said. "We have to close off any access to the well. The vial isn't worth anything if she can't fill it."

Her foot caught a tree root, and she stumbled again, this time falling all the way to her knees. Locke slumped beside her, bracing herself against the soft earth.

"Teela," she said, panting, "just leave me here. I'm slowing you down."

"No."

"It's too late."

Teela felt tears stinging her eyes. She looked back toward the glen, where she could hear the water flowing. Just one drop would heal Locke. One last time—she'd only use the vial one last time. What was one more drop? Teela pried the vial from Locke's hands and tipped it, hoping somehow there would be one last drop. One final last dreg she had missed.

Locke seemed to read her mind, and she slapped at Teela's hand. "Don't you dare."

"I have to save you!"

"You can't," Locke said, sounding so exhausted and, more terrifying to Teela, resigned. "Sometimes you can't."

Teela clenched her jaw. She knew it was wrong—she knew she shouldn't. No matter how heroic her intentions. She'd had good intentions before, and it had made no difference. The planet had still suffered. Others had still suffered.

"I'm going to get you out of here," Teela said, shoving the vial down the front of her tunic. The chain was broken, but it wedged snugly between her bandolier and her skin. "We're going to get back to the forest. I promise."

She dragged Locke forward, struggling through the trees. She was disoriented and starting to feel lightheaded as blood continued to leak from the wound in her shoulder. Her muscles strained as she supported Locke, and she kept thinking she could hear Evil-Lyn behind them, closing in.

Finally, they broke from the branches of the willows and tumbled onto the soft, mossy ground. Ahead of them was the cliff face, but Teela had no idea how they were going to find the way they had come in. The point of light she had seen in the tunnel was behind them, and she didn't know how she'd find it again. She struggled to her feet, leaving Locke on the ground, and raised her sword. She hacked at the rock. The blade bounced off, and Teela screamed in frustration, trying to find that tiny space they had come through.

"Please!" she shouted, not sure who she was imploring. She sheathed her sword and began to claw at the wall like it might turn into putty that could be peeled away. "Please, please, let us out! We're going to help you! We're going to save this place! Please!"

Her fingers suddenly found a crag, and she caught it, pulling hard. It was like a curtain pulled back, flooding the valley with a burst of that damp, stony air. "Come on!" she shouted, throwing out a hand to Locke and pulling her to her feet. Together, they stumbled through the fissure and into the tunnel.

Teela lost her grip on the rock, and suddenly they were back in darkness, in the narrow tunnel, the stone pressing in on them from all sides. The darkness was so all-encompassing that Teela felt trapped. She didn't know which way was forward or up or down. She could feel Locke's body pressed against hers. Her skin was cold.

Teela felt her hand fasten around Locke's arm, and she dragged her forward, crawling on her belly. Her forearms were scraped raw by the stone, but finally the tunnel began to open up around them, until Teela was able to pull Locke onto her shoulders and back, then crawl forward. She clapped a hand over the vial, making sure it was still there.

She could barely make out the lines of the sled ahead of her, wedged where they had left it in between the walls of the cave. Teela wondered suddenly if it could be used like a stopper on a bottle to barricade the entrance to the well. If they could use it to trap Evil-Lyn in the valley and keep anyone else who might use the well waters out. If they couldn't destroy the vial, they would take it back to Darksmoke. They would cast it back into the dragon's lair. They would throw it in the sea, or into the belly of a volcano, or something—anything. But even if it was found again, the Wellspring would be protected.

"We're almost there," Teela said—both to Locke and to herself. She'd get Locke to the end of the tunnel—to safety—then she'd see what she could do to rig the sled to crash into the tunnel and collapse the entrance. How she would manage that without physically being on the sled when it crashed, she wasn't sure. And how they'd get back to the Evergreen Forest, both of them injured and bleeding . . .

She'd figure it out. She'd find a way. There had to be a way.

Teela squeezed over the top of the sled, then reached back to pull Locke up after her. But suddenly, as if her foot had caught on something, Locke's body stopped, and she cried out in pain. "Teela!" She grabbed Teela, locking her hands around Teela's wrists, so hard her nails dug into Teela's skin. For a moment, Teela couldn't figure out what was happening, or what Locke was caught on.

Then she saw Evil-Lyn behind Locke, her hands around Locke's feet, pulling her backward into the tunnel. Her white hair was dyed red with blood, and her eyes glinted manically through the darkness. She yanked hard, and Locke's grip on Teela's hands slipped. Evil-Lyn dragged Locke off the sled and back down the tunnel.

"Let her go!" Teela shouted, scrambling to the opposite side of the sled, hoping to lure Evil-Lyn away from Locke. The tunnel here was too narrow for a fight—she wasn't even sure she could properly unsheathe her sword. But if she could get Evil-Lyn away from Locke—away from the Wellspring—she could face her.

Teela grabbed the vial from under her shirt and thrust it into the air, though she wasn't sure if the sorceress could see it through the darkness. "Hey, she doesn't have it! I do! It's me! Come fight me, you coward!"

Evil-Lyn appeared suddenly on the other side of the sled, and Teela scrambled backward, turning and running back down the tunnel path in hopes of Evil-Lyn following. Behind her, she heard the scrape of metal on rock as Evil-Lyn dragged herself over the sled, then her boots crunching against the ground as she raced after Teela.

Teela hadn't gotten far when Evil-Lyn leaped forward, catching Teela around the waist and knocking her off her feet. Teela hit the ground hard, knocking her chin into the stone and biting her lip. Blood flooded her mouth.

Evil-Lyn flipped her over, slamming Teela into the ground with an arm pressed to her throat as she dug her fingers into Teela's palm, trying to get her to drop the vial. Teela kicked and swung, but Evil-Lyn pushed her knee hard into Teela's shoulder, right over the stab wound.

Teela's scream of pain was drowned out by the sudden roar of an engine. Evil-Lyn stopped attacking Teela and turned. Teela raised her head as behind them the tunnel was lit by a sudden flare of light—the glow of the sled engine igniting. The roar of the engine sounded twice as loud as it echoed off the walls of the tunnel.

Locke had dragged herself onto the sled, her face lit by the glow of the navigation panel between the handlebars. Her eyes blazed as she looked forward, and for a moment, her gaze met Teela's. She saluted, and Teela realized what Locke was about to do the moment before she did it.

"No!"

Teela wasn't sure if it was her or Evil-Lyn who shouted as Locke hit the thrusters on the sled. The sled rose from the ground, hovering for a moment, before Locke hit the thrusters into reverse, and the sled careened backward, down the narrowing tunnel, and slammed into the wall, where it exploded.

THIRTY-FOUR

L*ocke.*

Her tough-as-nails, beautiful, loyal comrade and friend.

A wave of grief suffused Teela, but suddenly she was hit with a wave of heat and debris that billowed back down the tunnel toward her from the sled explosion. The tunnel rumbled, and Teela felt the soft patter of stone falling on her skin, first small pieces of gravel, then larger ones. The ceiling of the cave was beginning to collapse around them from the force of the explosion, closing off the entrance to the Wellspring and taking Teela and Evil-Lyn with it.

Evil-Lyn had been thrown backward off Teela by the blast, and she staggered upright. She and Teela stared at each other for a moment.

Then, Evil-Lyn turned and began to run toward the tunnel entrance.

Debris from the ship was scattered across the ground, and Teela was shocked to spot the crab warrior's shell, smoldering and blackened but still in one piece. She grabbed it and threw it over her shoulders, trying to shield herself from the blast as she followed Evil-Lyn.

As Teela ran, a boulder bounced against her legs, knocking them out from under her. Before she could get back on her feet, another heavy stone broke from the wall and onto her leg, pinning her against the wall. Teela struggled, trying in vain to free herself, but she was wedged firmly. She screamed in frustration, trying to dig the shell into the ground and use it to lever her forward, but she couldn't get enough purchase.

Ahead of her, Teela saw Evil-Lyn stop and look back over her shoulder. Teela wasn't sure what had caught the sorceress's attention, then realized it must have been her scream. She was probably checking to see if Teela was dead, or if she needed to be ready to fight when—if—they both emerged from the mouth of the tunnel.

But Evil-Lyn didn't move. Teela could see her in silhouette, backlit by the pale sliver of light ahead of them. The sky felt so close. Teela dug her hands into the earth until she felt her fingernails break, trying in vain to pull herself free from under the rock.

Then she felt someone grab her hand.

She raised her head, and Evil-Lyn was in front of her, one hand fastened around Teela's wrist, pulling. Teela felt her leg shift under the boulder pinning her against the wall. She screamed with exertion, and Evil-Lyn pulled harder.

Teela felt like the bones in her ankle were bending. Another chunk of stone cascaded down on top of her. Evil-Lyn dropped her arm suddenly, and Teela thought the sorceress must have come to her senses and realized what she was doing. But then she climbed past Teela, back toward where her leg was trapped under the rock. She pulled a knife from her belt, and for a moment, Teela had a horrible thought that Evil-Lyn was about to try to chop off her leg to free her. Either that or finish her off at last. Instead, Evil-Lyn dug the blade in between Teela's leg and her knee-high boot, splitting the leather all the way to Teela's ankle. She sheathed her dagger, then grabbed Teela's hands again and pulled. Teela felt her foot slide from the torn boot and out from under the rock, and suddenly she flew forward into Evil-Lyn, free of the boulder. They both tumbled backward, rolling down the slope of the cave, the steep incline on the way up now a steep decline. Something hard dug into Teela's back, and she realized she was lying on the Karikoni shell. The slick coral was sliding easily along the slope, like a sled in snow, hurtling toward the cave mouth with Teela on top of it. She felt Evil-Lyn jump onto the shell beside her.

The shell flew down the slope, faster than the boulders and dust and rocks collapsing overhead. Teela could see the entrance to the cave coming closer and closer, daylight pouring through. Several rocks struck the back of her head, and she felt one tear skin. A boulder bigger than she was bounced past, slamming into the wall with such force it started another landslide.

Suddenly, overhead, there was light. The narrowing walls of the valley were opening, the slope evening out. The shell began to slow, and Teela rolled off it, out of the landslide's path and up onto the patchy grass of the hillside, Evil-Lyn following her. A torrent of boulders rolled from the entrance before, finally, there was only an all-consuming, sudden silence.

Teela coughed hard, clearing her lungs of the dust, then raised her head. The entrance to the cave was blocked by a thick stopper of boulders where it hadn't collapsed entirely. The Wellspring was blocked. She reached up to grab the vial, only to discover that it was gone. It must have fallen off somewhere in the tunnel.

Beside her, Evil-Lyn rolled over, groaning. Her face was gray with dust, and with her white hair stained with blood, she looked like a ghostly apparition in a story. A bloody spot on her forehead was dripping into her eyes, and she wiped it away with the back of her hand.

"Don't," Evil-Lyn said, her breathing ragged, "say I never did anything for you."

Then she staggered to her feet and began to limp away.

"Hey!" Teela shouted at her retreating back. "Come back!"

"Why?" Evil-Lyn shouted. A patch of loose gravel collapsed under her, and she fell to her knees, but she was back on her feet so quickly that, for a moment, Teela thought she had only imagined it. "So you can shout at me and tell me I should feel bad? It won't do any good, because I don't, so let's save us both time and energy."

Teela *did* want to scream at her. She wanted to tackle her back to the ground and slam her fists into Evil-Lyn until . . . until what? Until she felt better? Like punching enough could expel all the pain and frustration and anger from her?

"You didn't have to help me back there," Teela shouted after the sorceress's retreating form.

Evil-Lyn stopped. She didn't turn back, and in silhouette against the sun, Teela could see her shoulders rising and falling as she struggled to catch her breath. "Believe me, I know." Finally, she turned back to Teela, pushing her hair out of her face as she flashed her one of her stiletto smiles. "It never would have worked between us, darling. You still have a soul." Was it Teela's imagination, or did Evil-Lyn hesitate for a moment, her throat bobbing as she swallowed hard? Then she said, her voice halting, "Don't . . . don't lose it."

Teela didn't say anything. Evil-Lyn picked up a stone off the ground, and it glowed the same bioluminescent blue as the ones in the forest that had guided Teela to the Skytree. Her magic was working again—they must have passed the invisible line that cut magic off from the Wellspring. "We'll see each other again, I'm sure," Evil-Lyn said.

The sorceress threw the stone to Teela, who caught it automatically. The blue flashed white, the light filling Teela's eyes and blotting out everything else for a moment before the world came back into focus, thick pine branches bowing over her head and the sounds of the Whispering Valley replaced by the familiar sounds of the refugee camp.

She was back in the Evergreen Forest.

She was home.

EPILOGUE

The grass around the small graveyard off the camp had been burned by the rain, leaving only bare mud, but in between the roots of the trees, the buds of small pink flowers were beginning to sprout. Since there was no body, Teela and Duncan carved Locke's name on the trunk of a tree, beside the names of the others who had died in the raid on Snake Mountain.

This time, when everyone looked to Duncan to speak, Duncan looked to Teela.

Teela swallowed. Her throat felt dry as she adjusted her aching shoulder in its sling.

"Locke," Teela started, then cleared her throat, "Locke and I didn't always get along."

Duncan glanced at her out of the corner of his eye, and Teela tried not to regret starting a eulogy with a negative.

"But the thing we always had in common," Teela continued, "was that we loved our home. We loved Eternia, and the people in it. She died protecting us. Protecting the planet." She looked down at the row of graves. "They all did. We can't let them down. We have to make sure their sacrifices were worth it. Not because we win, but because we fight."

At her side, Teela felt Duncan put a hand on her good shoulder, squeezing encouragingly.

Teela looked out at the members of her company, their faces turned to her in expectation. She thought of Adam, who always knew what to say, and wished he was here with her. Maybe he was, she thought, in her memory. He walked beside her every day. So did the lost people of Eternos; so did King Randor and Queen Marlena. And now, so did Locke. Everyone who had known and loved her into this moment was beside her.

She fought for them—and for herself—because she carried them all with her. An army inside her heart.

Overhead, she saw the silhouette of a wyvern against the sun, rising from the treetops before diving back down between the branches. The world was coming back to life.

"We fight in their name and in their honor," Teela said, and all around her, the company members raised their swords. "We fight for our home. We fight for Eternia."